Kentucky Summers 2

Treehawk

Kentucky Summers 2: Treehawk
Copyright 2020 by Tim Callahan. All rights reserved.

Cover design by Tim Callahan & Cārucandra Klupp
Cover Photography by Tim Callahan

Published in the United States of America by Kindle Direct
ISBN: 9798652730468
1. Southern Fiction / Young Adult, Adult

Kentucky Summers 2

Book 5

Treehawk

By

Tim Callahan

Books

By

Tim Callahan

Kentucky Summers Series 1:

1. The Cave, the Cabin & the Tattoo Man
2. Coty & the Wolf Pack
3. Dark Days in Morgan County
4. Above Devil's Creek
5. Timmy & Susie & the Bootleggers' Revenge
6. Kentucky Snow & the Crow
7. Red River, Junior & the Witch
8. Forever the Pack

Kentucky Summers Series 2:
1. Muddied Waters
2. We Saw Something
3. The Indian Summer of '64
4. The Sound of Tears
5. Treehawk
6. Roadkill in Blaze
7. Tick
8. A Broken Wing

Children's Illustrated Book
1. Catching Crawdads

Others:
Sleepy Valley
Come Home, Joe
Nashville Sounds
Leah's Path

This book is dedicated

In memory of:

My friend & editor

Peggy C. Cramer

12/5/46 – 5/16/20

Contents

Chapter 1

Something is in the Lake

Sweat was already soaking my shirt as I walked toward the lake. The morning heat had woken me early. I couldn't take lying under the sheet that covered me in bed another second. I had thrown the sheet off, which didn't seem to help at all, and then decided to end the misery by getting up.

James Ernest must have spent the night at the Washington farm, because he was missing from the bottom bunk. I was going to really miss him this fall when he leaves for college. He graduated at the top of his class last Friday and had been accepted at Berea College.

Berea College seemed to be the perfect fit for James Ernest. The College was the first interracial and coeducational college in the South. Despite physical, financial, and legal risk, Berea College continued in its mission to educate students of all races. The motto "God has made of one blood all peoples of the earth" had inspired many over the years. The college was a work-study program, which meant you worked while going there instead of paying an admission fee. Neither James Ernest nor our family had money for tuition.

Students learned many crafts while there along with their usual studies. It was the perfect fit for him.

He was excited about entering college, but I was going to be lost without him. I depended on him for so much. But we still had three months before he would leave and I wanted to make the most of it.

The sun was just now adding some light to the darkened sky. Mom, Dad and Janie were still asleep when I had left through the front door. I knew it was too hot for fishermen to come to the lake. For the past two days it had been pretty much void of fishermen. The temperatures had reached the mid-nineties each day.

I was heading to the swimming hole behind the lake for a cooling dip before the day began. It would have been nice to have Rock with me for the early morning swim. Rock had been my girlfriend for the last nine months after Susie and I had broken up.

I was walking over the last rise in the path before getting to the slanted rock when I noticed something in the middle of the back bay. It was still nearly dark in the bay with all the trees closing around me. I stopped on the rise and tried studying the object to see what it was floating in the water.

It looked like a body. Maybe it was a large sack or something. I hurried down the path and climbed onto the slanted rock to where I could get a closer look.

I was then fifteen feet from what I knew was a dead body!

I was stunned and scared at the same time. I looked around me to see if anyone else was nearby. I was hoping I was alone. I then realized I needed to get to the store to tell Dad, Sheriff Hagar Cane, about the dead guy in the lake.

I jumped from the rock and ran around the path as sweat dripped from my body. As I ran I wondered who the person was floating in the lake. Was it someone I knew? Was it someone I cared about? Or was it a stranger? Of course I still cared even if it was a stranger, just not as much.

Coty heard me running and came out of his doghouse to greet me. I ran past him and jumped onto the back porch and into the kitchen.

"Mom! Dad!" I yelled out. I knocked hard on their door.

They opened up the door to their bedroom dressed in their robes.

"What in tarnation are you shouting about?" Mom cried out.

Janie walked into the room rubbing at her eyes.

"There's a dead body floating in the lake!" I yelled out. I wasn't sure why I was yelling. They were standing right in front of me.

"Are you sure?" Dad asked calmly. Apparently he had more experience with dead bodies than I did.

"Yes," I said, finally calming a little.

"I'll get dressed and we'll go see." He turned to go back into the bedroom.

"I want to go see the dead body," Janie said. She started toward her bedroom to change.

"You most certainly will not, young lady."

I don't know if I would have called her a lady since she wanted to check out a floating dead guy.

"Aw, Mom, I never get to do anything fun," Janie whined. I think that proved my point.

Hagar had quickly dressed. Mom was dialing the phone. I knew she was probably calling Papaw.

After confirming that I was right – it was a dead person floating in the lake – Dad left to call for help. He asked me to stay and watch the body. I wasn't sure what I was watching for. He

9

definitely wasn't going anywhere unless a big catfish grabbed one of his fingers and took off with him. There was nothing I could do about that.

It was light enough by then to tell it was a man's face on the dead body. He was floating face up, which was creepy. He didn't look familiar. I couldn't help but wonder how he had died. Was he killed and thrown in the lake? Had he stumbled into the lake and drowned? Was he a paying fisherman?

As two of the deputies pulled the body from the lake I saw the answer to my first question. An arrow was sticking out of the man's back.

Chapter 2

Thank you, Mom

The body was being loaded into the ambulance. Hagar pushed open the screen door and came out of the store carrying an arrow. It looked like one of mine that Cat had given me.

Men had gathered on the porch to watch the spectacle. Mud and Louis had stopped by on their way to the quarry. Papaw and Clayton were there.

I heard Mud ask the crowd, "Anyone recognize the poor guy?"

They all shook their heads.

Sheriff Cane walked over to the body, which was lying face down on a stretcher on the ground while the men unloaded the ambulance's gurney. He held the arrow that was in his hand next to the arrow which was still embedded in the dead man.

"Is it a match?" Louis Lewis asked.

"Can't comment, Louis," Dad said.

I knew what it meant if the two arrows matched. It meant Catahecassa would be the main suspect in the murder.

Henry Washington drove by and stopped when he saw the commotion. The body had been loaded into the ambulance by then. After being told about the body, Henry asked, "Why is Hagar carrying around an Arrow?"

Clayton answered, "He was comparing the arrow Cat made for Timmy with the arrow protruding from the dead man's back."

"There's no way Cat killed that man," Henry said as Sheriff Cane began to climb the steps.

Henry had become close to Catahecassa, most everyone called him Cat or Cata. Cat was a Shawnee Indian who lived just up the road from us in a Hobbit House he had built under an overhanging cliff. The two men had bonded.

"No one is jumping to conclusions," Sheriff Cane said.

"How long has the man been dead?" Mud asked.

"I'll have to wait for the coroner's report," Hagar said. "But it doesn't look like it's been long."

Hagar started to go inside, but then stopped and asked, "Timmy, how many arrows do you have?"

"Six," I answered. Cat had crafted and given me a bow and six arrows for my birthday last year. I was thrilled with the present. He had also sold many bow and arrow sets over the last year to folks who ordered them.

"Why are there only five in your room?" he asked.

I said, after hesitating in thought, "I don't know."

Everyone looked at me with questioning eyes. I quickly tried to remember if I had lost one while target shooting, or had I gone hunting with James Ernest and lost one.

I figured my dad now had two suspects in the killing.

I was really sweating now, not just from the weather.

"Where did the guy come from?"

"He had to have walked here. There's no car or truck here without a driver."

"You think he was killed and fell into the lake."

"Maybe he was killed somewhere else and dumped in the lake to make it look like Cat or Timmy killed him."

"Maybe one of them did kill the guy."

12

"I'm standing right here, guys," I said. The men were discussing every angle of the killing. It wouldn't take long before they'd have someone convicted and hung if it was up to them.

"Maybe you men have some type of work to do somewhere else. Leave the policing to real police," I told them.

Mud looked at his watch and said, "We'd better go. We're late." Mud and Louis hurried off.

"I guess I'm late, also," Henry said.

Papaw decided to stay at the store for a while, and Clayton went home to watch his corn and tobacco grow.

Dad was in the living room telling Mom he was going to the office and start filling out the report. As he walked through the store he said, "The pay lake is closed for fishing until we can search for clues, and try to remember where that missing arrow went."

"Yes, sir," I said.

Hagar left, and Papaw and I stood in the store. He was leaning against the counter as I paced around the room looking for something to do.

"You really think he suspects me of the murder?"

Papaw said, "Of course not. I think he wants to know how the killer might have gotten one of your arrows."

"But Cat has sold a lot of bows and arrows in the last year," I said.

"Yes, he has. I guess the killer could be almost anyone," Papaw said.

"Can you watch the store? I need to go see Cat," I said.

"I can stay for a few hours," Papaw told me.

I left through the screen door. Coty caught sight of me and followed. We walked up the road in the morning heat. Coty's tongue hung out the side of his mouth after only a short distance. I couldn't imagine having a fur coat on in this warmth.

We cut across the field and as I neared his home and saw him up on the balcony of his treehouse. He noticed me, and I waved. He waved back. We finally arrived and I climbed the steps to the house in the trees. Coty flopped on a rock under a tree to soak up the coolness.

I sat and took a deep breathe.

"It's cooler up here in the trees," Cat said.

"I don't believe it's cool anywhere on this earth," I moaned.

"What's new?" Cat asked.

I took a moment to answer as I took a few deep breaths.

"You and I are the main suspects in a murder investigation," I said.

"Is this a game?"

"Nope."

"What are you talking about?"

I spent the next five minutes, starting from the time I first saw the body, telling him about the morning thus far. Cat didn't say anything. He sat there whittling on a stick that I knew he was making into an arrow.

"Are you suddenly down an arrow?" I asked, pointing to the arrow, with a grin.

"Blue Wren ordered a bow and arrow set. This is for him."

"Who is Blue Wren?" I asked.

"He's a friend from my old tribe," Cat explained.

"Any ideas?" I asked after watching him for a couple of minutes.

"No idea as to who killed who, if that's what you're asking," he said. "I didn't kill anyone. If that's what you want to know."

"I never thought you did. Plus, I know I didn't do it."

"So, who did?" Cat said.

"We usually blame Purty for everything that happens, and we're usually right," I said.

"Then we have another suspect," Cat said. We both laughed.

When I got back to the store I saw Rock sitting in the porch swing with Uncle Morton. Two police cruisers were in the parking lot. I walked up the porch steps and Uncle Morton said, "Keep walking, Timmy. I'm trying to steal your girlfriend."

"Why would she want an old coot like you?"

"Because I'm charming and handsome and I have more money than you," he said.

"Any one has more money than me," I said.

"She must like you for your other qualities then," Uncle Morton said.

"I'm still looking for them," Rock said.

"Ouch," I said.

I took a seat in one of the rocking chairs. Coty was lying between us on the wooden porch. The screen door opened and Homer walked out, followed by Papaw.

"Are they up at the lake looking for clues?" I asked, pointing to the police cars.

"Two deputies," Papaw said.

Homer stopped and asked, "Did Cata confess to the murder?"

"Not yet. We decided to blame Purty for the killing," I told him.

"I wonder if he could hit the broad side of a barn with an arrow," Papaw said.

"He's really good with a slingshot, and it's kind of the same thing," I said.

15

"Then you might be on to something," Homer said and laughed.

Years earlier, two men who had kidnapped Susie and I were chasing us through a creek trying to kill us. Purty began pelting them with rocks from his slingshot. He helped save us that night.

"Uncle Morton told me about you finding the body in the lake. That's terrible," Rock said. "Cat is a suspect?"

"Cat and Timmy, both," Homer said.

"You're a suspect! Why?" Rock asked, sounding alarmed.

"The arrow sticking from the man's back matched the ones Cat makes. One of the arrows Cat gave me is missing from my room," I explained.

"Uncle Morton, I might take you up on your offer," Rock said, teasingly.

"Anytime, girlfriend," he said.

Homer turned to leave, but stopped when Rock asked, "How are Shauna and Sally?"

"They're doing very well. I can tell you they are very happy to be out of school for the summer."

"Every kid is," I said.

"Shauna's been a big help around the farm and she's taking care of her Bantam chickens. I think she's going to enter one of them in the Morgan County fair."

Shauna's mother was sent to prison for child endangerment. Her stepdad was sentenced to eight years in prison for raping her. Homer and Ruby took the girls into their home as foster kids. They went to Shauna's old house to gather up her chickens once they were settled.

Homer left, and Papaw took a seat in the other rocking chair. I glanced over at Rock. She looked very pretty today. Her dark hair flowed onto her shoulders and the left side of her face was

16

partially hidden with the hair. She was wearing short cutoff jeans and a sleeveless, checkered red top.

After a few minutes of conversation Papaw asked, "Are you watching the store now?"

"Yes," I said.

"I guess Morton and I are going to mosey up to the farm where it's a little cooler."

"Okay."

Papaw's farm sat on the top of the hill a mile from the store. Eight large oak trees stood fifty feet from the side porch. There was always a breeze through the trees.

They left, and Rock asked, "Is it okay if I watch the store with you today?"

"That would be great," I said.

I moved over to the spot Morton vacated. She scooted as close as she could to me and we kissed.

The two deputies walked around the side of the store and climbed the steps.

"Did you find anything?" I asked.

"Can't answer that," Deputy Clouse said.

"You're a suspect, remember," Deputy Stutts reminded me.

"You may have found my footprints up there," I said.

"There were dozens of foot prints around the lake in the loose soil," Deputy Clouse. "We need some rain."

The deputies went inside and got soft drinks. I followed them inside and took their money. I then went back out to the porch when they left. "You can open the lake now."

I didn't think anyone would be fishing today anyway due to the heat.

"It's too bad we don't have time to go back to the swimming hole," Rock said. Last fall Rock and I had gone skinny dipping twice - two of the best days of my life. We did leave on our underwear; although Rock hadn't worn a bra. We hadn't been swimming since. But I had thought of those swims every day.

I smiled and suggested, "Maybe later this evening or tonight in the moonlight."

She and I both nodded our heads in agreement. It sounded like a great idea. The moon was almost full last night and there wasn't a cloud in the sky. It would be a great way to cool off and having Rock with me would make it even better.

Two fishermen arrived. I was wrong. We followed them into the store. They grabbed two cold pops from the cooler and asked for nightcrawlers and chicken livers. Rock left to get the bait. She had learned where everything was from helping me before. The men paid and left. Before the door could close, Tucky and Purty walked in.

"What are you two love birds doing?" Purty asked.

"Trying to stay cool," I said.

"Impossible," Tucky said. "That's like trying to find mud in the parking lot."

"Anything new?" Purty asked.

Rock told him, "You're being blamed for the murder at the lake."

"What?" they both exclaimed.

I explained to them about the body and who the two suspects were. "Cat and I decided to blame you since you're usually the one who does things."

"The guy really had an arrow sticking out of his back?" Tucky asked.

"Yeah," I answered.

"Was the arrow going in or coming out of his back?" Purty asked.

18

"What?" Rock questioned.

"How could an arrow be coming out of his back?" I asked.

"He could have been shot at close range and the force of the shot went all the way through," Purty explained.

"I don't think that could happen," I said.

"I bet it could," Purty argued.

"How are you guys going to prove who's right?" Rock asked.

"Let's shoot Purty with an arrow at close range and see," Tucky suggested.

"Good friend, real good friend," Purty said.

"Have you seen Shauna lately?" Rock asked Purty, to change the subject.

"No. We were going up there next," Purty said. Purty liked Shauna, and for some reason, Shauna seemed to like Purty. Purty was now driving Randy's pickup truck since Randy was away in the service. Their dad had bought the truck for both of them. It was now Purty's pride and joy. He washed it so much the rust was falling off, leaving holes in the fenders. But the pickup ran great.

"We were thinking about going swimming since it's so hot," Tucky told us.

"We're going this evening. Let's make it a party," Rock suggested.

No-No-No. Why did she do that? I was looking forward to the two of us having time alone and maybe skinny dipping again. I guess that wasn't happening.

"That sounds like fun. I'll ask Shauna. You guys can call the others. Let's say around eight tonight," Purty said, as he ran with the idea.

19

Purty went to the cooler and grabbed two Nehi-grape drinks and told me to put it on his dad's tab. He handed one to Tucky and they left.

Rock could tell I wasn't happy about her invites and said, "We have all summer to skinny dip," and then she kissed me. It did make me feel better.

Mom walked into the store. She came from the kitchen where she was canning beans.

"Oh. Hello, Rock. Did I hear something about swimming?" she asked.

"We're planning a swimming party later this evening since it's so hot today," I said.

"That sounds refreshing. Rock, you can wear one of my swimming suits if you would like. I have one that might fit you."

"Okay."

Last summer, Dad had caught Rock and me skinny dipping and Rock explained that her family couldn't afford swimming suits for eight kids and that they always skinny dipped. The next thing I knew Mom went shopping for swimming suits. I knew she had picked one out especially for Rock. Thank you so much, Mom!

Sheriff Cane

*T*hat evening I went to find Cata. I knew I had to question him about the dead body. When I walked up to his house under the cliff I saw him standing next to a tree skinning a squirrel.

Before I had a chance to say something, Cat said, "Good evening, Sheriff."

"Call me Hagar, please."

"I figured this was a business call rather than a social visit."

"It is, unfortunately."

20

"I knew you would need to talk to me about the body in the lake," Cata said.

He plunged the knife into a stump and left the skinned body of the grey squirrel hanging by a nail on the tree.

"I know the answer before I ask it. Do you have anyone to vouch for your where-abouts last night till dawn?" I knew Cat lived alone and stayed solitary unless he had visitors.

"I was here alone all night," Cat answered.

"Did you happen to go to the pay lake during the night?"

"No. I never left my land."

"Did you kill a man last night?"

"No."

"Can you explain how one of your arrows was found in the dead man's back?" I asked.

"I've built a few bow and arrows sets since I've moved here, as you know. Once they leave here I have no idea where they end up. I'm not the only Indian that makes these arrows. Most of the men in my tribe craft the same type of arrow. The art has been passed down from generations."

"But you are the only one making them here in this area. Do you know if you are missing any arrows?"

"I wouldn't know. I have quite a few. I usually make quite a few at a time and keep them for the bows I make. I may have between thirty to forty on hand at any time. I've never kept track of the number."

"Did you know Tim is missing one of the arrows you gave him?"

"Yes. He told me earlier today."

"Can you give me a list of the folks you've sold or given arrows to since you've been here?"

"I can do that, Hagar. Do you have a pen and paper?"

I reached into my shirt pocket and pulled out a pad and a pen and handed them to him. It only took him a couple of minutes to write the list of customers.

"Add Timmy to the list," Cat told me.

"Is there anyone on the list that would stand out as a person I should consider?"

"None that jumps out at me."

I looked over the list and recognized most of the names.

"Who is Harper Cisco?" I asked.

"That was an order I received by mail. I didn't know the man. He sent a check paying in advance."

"Do you recall where he was from?"

"It was a post office box in Lexington if I remember correctly," Cat told me.

"I'd have to look around to see if I saved it."

"Let me know if you find it," I told him.

I got up to leave. "Have a nice evening. This is a great place to beat the heat."

"It is. Take care. Have a good night," Cat said.

I left and went back to the store. Cat was a hard person to read. I had grown fond of him over the past year. I knew he was capable of shooting a person with his bow. But was he capable of murder? I thought he was capable of killing, but I had no idea about murder.

Chapter 3
Kentucky Rain

*R*ock and I had watched the store all day. Sneaking kisses when no customers were in the store. Rock made a call to Susie telling her about the swim party, she said she would call Rhonda, Raven and Sadie, who would tell Francis. That took care of the Bear Troop.

I knew Raven would tell Junior and James Ernest. So that took care of the Wolf Pack; one call – easy peasy.

Dad came home around six-thirty that evening. He told us the dead man was William Foot. He had lived in Crockett which was located at the eastern side of Morgan County, around twenty miles or so from here. I wondered how he ended up with an arrow in his back in our lake.

Dad said Mr. Foot was twenty-six, lived alone, and was unemployed. He told us that one of his deputies recognized the man. He then told us he was going to light up the charcoal in the grill and cook hamburgers for supper. Mom had made potato salad. Rock stayed with us to eat. I wondered what roadkill her parents were grilling that evening.

I had heard people say 'You are what you eat'. Did that mean I was dating roadkill?

Friends began arriving around seven-thirty. Clayton and Monie brought Susie, Rhonda and the twins. Janie was happy to have someone to play with. The Washington family arrived. Homer and Ruby came with Shauna and Sally. Purty drove everyone else to the store. By eight everyone was ready to head out for the swimming hole.

The younger kids were in the backyard playing games. The adults were socializing in the store. Purty told the adults he would drop everyone off after the party was over. I wasn't sure that made the parents feel any better.

As soon as we made it to the swimming hole we began shedding our shirts and pants. The girls all wore bathing suits. The boys wore either swimming trunks or cut-offs. Rock looked very pretty in the blue and white suit Mom had bought her. Sadie, Susie and Rhonda wore two piece suits.

Shauna and Purty hung out together most of the evening. The water felt so refreshing after the hot humid day. I saw Susie watching Rock and me several times. After an hour of playing in the water, Purty brought up the dead body I had found in the lake that morning.

It was news to a lot of my friends. James Ernest looked more surprised than anyone. I had to tell everyone about the body, the arrow, and how Cat and I were the main suspects.

"The sheriff can't really think either of you would have done it," Raven said.

"I don't know. I guess he has to follow the clues," I said.

We discussed the murder for the next thirty minutes. We then did chicken fights. After Rock and I got knocked out of the game Rock said, "Susie and Rhonda haven't had a chance to play. Susie why don't you pair up with Timmy and Rhonda can pair up with Tucky."

I looked at Rock to see if she was serious.

"That's okay. I don't need to play," Susie said.

"Don't be silly. Jump up on Timmy's shoulders and have fun," Rock said. I looked at Susie and said, "Okay with me if you want to." Susie swam over to where I was and I sank into the water and she climbed onto my shoulders. I rose with my hands on her legs holding her on. It felt so strange to have my hands touching her legs. It felt so wrong. Rhonda was on top of Tucky's shoulders and we began battling. I was only half into it and we lost quickly as Susie fell off. I knew that Susie wasn't into it either. No team had a chance against James Ernest and Raven.

The evening was tremendous fun. We knew it had to be around midnight when we finally climbed from the water. We began the walk back to the store. The moon was so bright in the sky we had no trouble walking on the path.

"We'll have to do this again, soon," Purty said.

"That was so much fun. I've never done anything like that," Shauna said. It was nice seeing Shauna have fun after all she had been through.

James Ernest and I waved as Purty pulled out of the lot. The bed of his truck was filled with passengers. I was hoping the bed didn't collapse from the rust.

Susie

I couldn't believe Rock told me to pair up with Timmy for the chicken fights. What was she thinking? I hesitated, but didn't want to be the party pooper, so I did. When he placed his hands on my legs it felt nice. I had missed Timmy ever since I broke up with him. He seemed so happy with Rock I knew I would probably never win him back.

I told myself that it was okay. At times it could be exhausting being his girlfriend. He was always involved in some sort of

25

drama. I spent half my time worrying over him, if I wasn't worried about myself, like when we were kidnapped together.

But, I would take on all that worry to have him back as my boyfriend.

Friday, June 4

*T*hunder woke me up before daylight. Lightning flashes lit up the bedroom. I could tell the storm was coming from the west and would be pelting us soon. No sooner than I thought it, the rain began falling onto the tin roof making a racket that I loved. I stayed there on my bed with one leg out from under the sheet listening to the sound of the hard rain. I was hoping maybe a mist would drift through the window screen.

"I love a storm here in Kentucky," I said, hoping James Ernest was awake.

"What's different about Kentucky?" he asked.

"In Ohio, we didn't have a tin roof. Sometimes you wouldn't even know it was raining until you looked outside. Here, you know, even if it's only a sprinkle."

"There is something soothing about it," he said.

I thought about the 'soothing' rain for a moment. Soothing was not a word I would have used. I then asked, "Who killed William Foot?"

"Gee, let me reach into my brain and pull it out," James Ernest said.

I figured that was sarcasm. "I was just thinking out loud. Isn't it strange that a man from Crockett would be shot and killed with an arrow at our lake? Why?"

"We know he wasn't a fisherman. And they didn't find any evidence at the lake."

"Why was he even there? It would seem like he would have driven here from Crockett. But his car wasn't here," I said.

"It could be he was killed somewhere else and then dumped in the lake to make it look like Cat killed him."

"It seems like we would have heard a vehicle drive up to dump the body," I said.

"Unless they parked up the road and carried him to the lake."

"Maybe we could find blood on the road," I said, excited.

"Not with this rain. The water will wash the blood away."

So much for that excitement, I thought.

"How are we going to solve it?" I asked.

"We're not. Dad and his deputies will," James Ernest said.

"But I'm a suspect. I need to clear my name."

"You don't really think they believe you could have killed him, do you?"

"The evidence points more to me than anyone else," I said.

"Go back to sleep," James Ernest said as a lightning bolt struck near the store. I almost jumped out of the top bunk.

"How can I sleep knowing I might be in prison soon?"

"Goofball."

I was wide awake, and knew I wouldn't be able to go back to sleep as the rain pelted onto the roof. I slid off the top bunk and stumbled back onto James Ernest. He pushed me off and I landed on the floor. I slipped on my shorts and a tee-shirt and made my way to the front porch.

I took a seat in one of the rocking chairs and watched the rain pour down in buckets. When the sky lit up from the lightning I could see streams of water running across the gravel lot toward the creek.

As I sat there watching and listening to the rain I started to drift off until I heard the crunching of gravel. I looked up to see a

27

truck parked on the road to my left. It was still dark but I could see the shape of the pickup. I then heard someone half-way running down the path from the lake. It looked like he had a bad, or hurt leg by the way he ran. He was carrying a flashlight. He ran straight to the truck and jumped into the cab. Lightning flashed, and I could see the blue truck like it was daylight, but I couldn't see the runner or the driver's faces.

The pickup quickly headed down the road toward Wrigley. I thought of waking Dad. I wasn't sure what to do. I decided I should. I hurried inside and knocked on their bedroom door. Mom opened the door after a few seconds.

"What is it, Timmy?"

I quickly explained what I had seen. I saw James Ernest behind me as I told Mom and Dad.

"I'll be right there," Dad said.

James Ernest and I went out to the porch and I showed him where the truck had stopped. Sheriff Cane came out in his robe. I pointed to the spot where the runner met the truck.

"Did you get a look at the two men?" He had to shout to be heard over the pinging on the roof.

"No." I told him the pickup was a blue color.

"Let's go inside."

Mom was up making coffee. We sat around the table as I explained in better detail what I had seen.

"Why would someone be at the lake now?" I asked, even though I knew no one had an answer.

"It had to have something to do with the murder," James Ernest said. I had to agree. I had been thinking it all along.

"It could be. But I can't jump to conclusions," Dad said.

"He could have been covering up something, or looking for something he left behind," James Ernest offered.

28

"He could have thrown another body into the lake," I said.

"That's an awful thought," Mom said as she poured coffee for the three of them. I didn't drink coffee. I was drinking an RC Cola I had grabbed on the way to the table.

"You think the first body was placed in the lake?" Dad asked.

"Since no clues or blood was found around the lake it would make sense that Foot was killed somewhere else and then thrown in the lake," I explained.

"It could be they were trying to frame Cat or Timmy," James Ernest said.

Dad sat quiet as he thought about it. We all took a drink at the same time.

"It doesn't seem very smart to dispose of bodies behind the sheriff's house," Mom said after the silence.

"Most murderers aren't very smart," Dad said.

"But who would want to frame Cat, or especially Tim?" Mom questioned.

"I can't believe Cat has made any enemies. Tim has been involved in quite a few things people might want revenge for," Dad said.

"Perhaps the KKK," James Ernest said. "I'm sure they're not real happy with Cat."

When four members of the KKK had attempted to burn down the Washington's house and barn Cat had shot each of them with arrows, injuring all of them. All four were still in prison.

"You're right. But why kill William Foot? What was he to the KKK, if it was them? I'll have to find out if there's a connection," Dad said.

"Oh yeah, I remember something. The man ran with a limp," I told them.

When the rain finally let up and it got light enough we headed for the lake.

James Ernest, Dad and I walked up the lane to the dam. I expected to see another body floating in the water. None was to be seen.

"Let's walk around the lake," I said.

Coty heard us and came running. He began sniffing the ground. We started walking around the west side of the lake since it was the easiest side of the lake to walk. The east side was narrower and would be terribly slippery with the mud and rain.

"I'll go around the other side," James Ernest said. "Meet you at the stream."

There was no clue that we could see as we walked. There were no notes telling who had done it. We didn't see another body floating on the surface. As we came over the last rise before getting to the slanted rock I was filled with dread. I didn't want to look. I knew the body would be there in the shallows.

"Nothing," I heard Hagar say.

I looked up and over to the water. He was right. We saw James Ernest on the opposite path. We met at the point where the stream flowed into the lake. It looked more like a small creek with all the water pouring in from the hard rain.

"I didn't see anything," James Ernest reported.

"Why was he up here?" I wondered out loud.

"It doesn't mean he didn't dump another body. It could have sunk."

"I thought a dead body floated," I said.

"There are several factors," Dad explained.

"Like what?" I asked.

30

"It depends on how he died. It depends on how long he had been dead. Whether there is air in his lungs. If a body sinks it will then float when the body begins to rot."

"Great, so one day I could be fishing and a body could float up to join me," I said.

"Or if you're catfishing, you could hook it and drag it in," James Ernest said.

"That would be Uncle Morton's luck," I said, laughing.

The rain began to fall harder. We headed back home. James Ernest ran through the stream and walked with us.

The rain lasted all morning. Dad asked us to not say anything about our early morning visitor. We knew the men didn't realize I had seen them in the rain. It was dark and the porch light wasn't on. We had the element of surprise if they came back.

Dad said that he was going to close the lake for the weekend. Fishing wouldn't be very good due to all the rain anyway. The lake was muddy and it would take a couple of days to clear up. Once the rain stopped, I walked to the bridge in front of the store and looked down at the creek. Rushing brown water was high above its usual depth.

It was much too wet for farmers to work in their fields or gardens, so they gathered on the store's porch to talk about the rain and everything else that came to mind. Clayton, Homer, Robert and Uncle Morton were carrying on conversations. They also took turns bashing me and telling me how miserable I would be in prison.

I was glad when Cat rode up on his horse, Friend. He tied him to the railing and climbed the steps to his execution. "Perhaps the two of you were in on the caper together," Robert started.

"When was the last time a person was killed with an arrow in Morgan County?" Homer asked.

"Around 1825, I think," Clayton chimed in.

"That's when Indians used to roam these lands," Uncle Morton added.

"And now we have another Indian living in our midst, and another man is killed with an arrow. Coincidence?" Homer said, smiling.

"I'm glad you showed up. I was the killer before you got here," I said to Cat.

"Since they know about us, let's get our bows and get rid of our accusers," Cat teased.

"You won't see it coming," Cat told them.

"Especially, Uncle Morton," I teased.

The banter back and forth continued for the next hour or so.

Chapter 4
Red Chevy

Saturday, June 5

The rain from the day before was followed by a cooling front. The humidity was low and big white pillows of clouds speckled the blue sky. Temperatures were expected to stay in the seventies for the weekend.

Mom had asked James Ernest and me to stay around the store that morning. Janie had spent the night with Delma and Thelma. Mamaw and Papaw came down to the store at ten. Mom and Dad told us to get in the car because we were taking a trip.

"What do you mean, we're taking a trip? Where are we going?" I asked. I had so many questions. We never did that. We were always watching the store. "Do I need to pack?"

We were swept off. It was frustrating, but also the not knowing was exciting and fun. James Ernest and I sat in the back and guessed where we could be going.

The last big trip I had been on was after my dad had died five years earlier. I was sent back to Kentucky to stay with Mamaw and Papaw while Mom and Janie stayed with an aunt while Mom was trying to work and save money.

Hager drove up the hill and out the ridge following Route 711 to the end. He then turned left heading to Morehead. I wondered if we were going to Ohio to visit my Aunts and Uncles. But surely we would have packed overnight clothes if that was the case.

Twenty minutes later we were in Morehead. We rode down the main street and I saw all the shoppers walking from store to store. Saturday was the day when most folks did their shopping and the sidewalks were crowded. I thought Dad was trying to find a parking spot but he passed up so many I knew that wasn't what we were doing. At the end of the street he turned right and we headed toward either Flemingsburg or I-64. I-64 stretched from Louisville to Ashland and passed by Lexington. We could be going anywhere.

After turning, Hagar drove a couple of miles and slowed down. He pulled into a car dealership. What were we doing?

He parked and we exited the car. A salesman greeted us in the parking lot. "Good to see you again, Mr. Cane."

"This is my wife, Betty, and these are our sons, James Ernest and Tim."

"Well, this is a big day. Follow me this way."

I was beginning to figure out why we were there. James Ernest had turned sixteen this past spring and already had his driver's license. I was turning sixteen in a month and a half. They were buying both of us cars!

We walked around to the side of the showroom and stopped short of a red and white Chevrolet pickup with a matching red and white cap over the bed of the truck. The salesman turned to James Ernest and said, "I believe these belong to you." He handed a set of keys to him.

James Ernest's face turned into a huge smile. "Really!?" he said as he turned to face Mom and Dad. "It's all yours," Mom said. James Ernest threw his arms around Mom and then Dad.

"Thank you, so much!" he said as he moved closer to the truck.

I now figured we would walk on to the area where my pickup was. I looked around the lot searching for another used pickup washed and ready for me to take ownership of. I didn't see one.

I looked over and saw James Ernest sitting behind the steering wheel. I was happy for him, but not nearly as happy as he was. I knew I was being a little selfish at the moment, but I couldn't help it. Maybe I would get mine after I turned sixteen and had a license.

I ran to the passenger door and hopped into the cab with James Ernest.

"Isn't this great?" he said.

"Is this a brand new truck?"

"It is to me," he said through his stupid grin.

It was a 1962 Chevrolet C10 step side pickup. It was cool looking. The spare tire was mounted on the side just behind the driver's door. The body was red and the cab was white.

We rolled the windows down and Dad told James Ernest that he and Mom figured with the cap on it he would be able to carry his baskets to shows without them blowing out.

A few minutes later we walked into the showroom. James Ernest and Dad went with the salesman to sign the title of the truck. I walked around looking at the new trucks and cars. I got in one of the new pickups and sat behind the steering wheel imagining myself tooling down the road with Rock at my side. I couldn't wait.

Mom came over to where I was and she said, "You'll be driving soon."

"It won't be long." I then said, "It was really nice that you guys bought the truck for James Ernest."

"He'll need it for college. Maybe he'll make it home more often while he's there. I know you would like that," Mom said.

She was right. "I'm really going to miss him. I can't imagine not having him with us."

"Raven will surely miss him terribly also."

"I know," I said.

"Would you want a car or a pickup?"

"A pickup," I said quickly.

I didn't know any boy that would rather have a car. A guy could do so much with a pickup.

I looked over and saw James Ernest and Dad walking our way. I climbed out of the truck and met them.

"I guess you want to ride back with us instead of James Ernest," Dad said to me.

"I think you know better than that. But first, I think we should go out for lunch. Let's go get pizza," Mom said.

I know this is going to sound like a lie, but I had never eaten pizza before that day. In Ohio, we never got takeout food or went to restaurants. In Kentucky we lived so far out in the country it was the same. If we ever ate out it was usually at a local mom and pop restaurant.

We walked into the pizza joint and it was so different, almost magical. I had no idea what to order on the pizza. You could order a pizza with almost anything you wanted on it. I didn't even know what pepperoni was. Dad ended up ordering two large pizzas with what he thought we would like.

That day I fell in love with pizza and Italian food. James Ernest and I devoured the large pepperoni and sausage pizza and then started eating what was left of the other pepperoni, onions, and green pepper pizza.

After the meal was over, James Ernest and I hopped into the pickup and followed Mom and Dad back to Oak Hills. The stupid smile never left his face as he drove. He was a good driver. He shifted the gears as though he had done it for years.

"I can teach you to drive in this," he told me. I smiled.

When we got to the Washington farm lane, James Ernest put on his turn signal and he turned down the lane. He drove to the house.

I saw Raven looking out the front door. She turned her head and said something and then she and Junior came bursting through the door and jumped off the porch.

"Whose truck is this?" Raven asked.

James Ernest pointed to himself. She started jumping up and down and squealing.

"Take me for a ride!" she screamed. I hopped out of the truck and Raven hopped in next to James Ernest. Junior got in next.

"I'll wait here for you," I said. Samantha came out on the porch followed by Henry and Coal. James Ernest took off as we waved to them.

I walked up on the porch and told them, "Mom and Dad bought the truck for James Ernest for college."

"That's a nice pickup," Henry said. "Is that a '62?"

"It is," I said.

"That's a right handsome truck," Henry said.

James Ernest came back to pick me up. Then the four of us spent the next hour going to see Purty, Sadie and Francis and then Rock and Tucky. We drove around with five of us in the bed of the truck, under the canopy, while showing off the truck.

When we finally got back home Papaw and Mamaw came out of the store to see the truck.

"That's a good looking truck."

"That's prettier than a speckled pup," Mamaw said. Mamaw had always liked red. I took after her in that regard.

James Ernest and Raven had done the big Christmas art festival in Lexington again before this past Christmas and again they sold everything they took. John had also taken his pottery and it was his best show of the year. I was happy for them.

Pricilla gave birth to a new baby boy on May the eleventh. They needed the money badly. They named the baby, Elvis.

James Ernest had me start helping him and Raven make the baskets, teaching me his art. I found that I enjoyed it. He thought Raven needed help making the baskets once he was off to college. Raven was very good at weaving and creating the styles, but needed help cutting down trees and beating and striping off the wood so she could weave the baskets.

My only problem was finding time away from the store to learn and help. I wasn't sure how much time I would have. Junior was also being taught so that he could also help.

James Ernest

What would my life be without Betty and Timmy in my life? When Timmy and I met eight years ago I was living in the trailer on the hill above the store. Dad had left us. Mom was in a deep two year depression and seldom said anything. I didn't talk at all from age five to ten. What a family we were!

Dad returned when I was twelve, and then left with Mom, abandoning me. They later died that year in a wreck when their car slid off the icy road and over a mountain. Betty took me in their home even though they had little themselves. She treated me like a son. Timmy always felt like my brother, even more so now. When Sheriff Cane married Betty I wondered how things would change. But they didn't. Hagar was a good man and a great father figure.

I owe so much to the people I now call Mom and Dad. And for them now to buy me a vehicle for college, it was unbelievable. It was perfect. I had so much in my life to be grateful for. I still missed my Mom, but the hurt had slowly vanished with the love I received. I had the Washington's as a second family and their daughter, Raven, was the love of my life. I knew she would always be. God had truly watched over and blessed me through it all.

*A*s I was waiting on a customer inside the store I heard a vehicle roll in next to the gas pump. I finished giving a lady her change and then looked out the window. I followed her out of the store and down the steps to the pump. The man asked for three dollars of gas.

I didn't know the man driving, but I thought the dark blue pickup he was driving could have been the one I had seen pull away after the man had ran from the lake. Of course I hadn't really gotten a good look at the truck due to the darkness, but I did know the truck was blue, and this one was blue and dark.

I cleaned his front windshield without asking him if he wanted it cleaned. The window was so filthy I couldn't see why he would object. As I cleaned the driver's side of the window, I asked, "Hey, mister, I've never seen you before. Where are you from?"

"Just passing through."

That didn't answer my question. I had noticed his license plates had MaGoffin County on them.

"Where are you headin'?"

"South," was all he said.

There was nothing in the bed of his truck except for some old cans and a spare tire.

I looked up to see that the pump window was nearing three dollars. I ran around the truck and shut it off at twenty cents over.

I walked to his window and said, "I'm sorry sir, you got three dollars and twenty cents of gas."

"You should be paying more attention to what you're doing instead of askin' so many questions." He handed me three dollars.

There were a lot of rude people in the world. As I took the dollars in my hand I noticed what was leaning against the passenger seat – an Indian bow and a rifle.

As he pulled away I read his license number – three–two-six-Y-X-9.

I ran inside repeating 326YX9, 326YX9, 326YX9, 329YX6, to myself. I hurried behind the counter and wrote the license number down two-three-nine-X-Y-six. I was sure that was right. Maybe I had found the killer,

Two minutes later, Mud McCobb and Louis Lewis walked into the store. "I need a dozen nightcrawlers," Mud said.

"Me too," Louis followed.

I collected their money and gave them change.

"You gave me too much change back," Louis complained. "Not that I mind having change in my pocket."

"He did the same to me," Mud said. "You didn't charge me the lake fishing fee. Are you feeling okay?"

"The lake is closed," I announced.

"Why is the lake closed?" Louis asked, disappointedly.

"It's muddier than a pig's nose for one reason."

"What's the second reason?" Mud asked.

"Can't tell you that," I said.

"Then why did you sell us crawlers?" Louis asked.

"You asked for them," I answered.

"Where are we supposed to fish then?" Louis continued.

"You can fish in a mud puddle for all I care. You would catch just as many fish," I told him.

Mud began laughing. "He's telling the truth," Mud roared.

"I'd out fish you any day of the week," Louis argued with Mud.

"You won't out fish me today, because it looks like we ain't fishing at all." I gave them back their money they paid for the nightcrawlers. They left through the door yelling at one another, the best of friends.

When Dad got home I told him about the man in the dark pickup and the bow. I gave him the license plate number I had written down.

"I'll check it out tomorrow," he said.

Dad grilled out hotdogs for supper. Mom made baked beans. Rock walked into the store at the same time Clayton and the entire family pulled into the gravel lot.

Dad saw them and asked if he could put more dogs on the fire. Monie said, "We've already eaten supper. Sorry we're interrupting."

Mom said, "Its fine. Hagar got home late. Come on in."

"Rock, will you eat with us?"

"Okay, thank you," she answered

The twins ran off with Janie. Brenda went with Monie and Mom. Clayton followed Dad to the grill. I stood there with Rock and Susie. It was awkward.

Rock and Susie exchanged pleasantries. Rock asked her, "Are we going to have a Bear Troop meeting anytime soon?"

"We probably should," Susie said.

It reminded me of the Wolf Pack. We needed to plan something for the summer before James Ernest leaves for college.

"Is there anything the two clubs could do together?" Rock asked.

It was strange standing in the store with Susie and Rock. I didn't know what to do, or to say, or who to look at. I felt like a hen in a fox house. It was different when the three of us were with the gang, it was still odd, but this was as uncomfortable as it got.

I wondered why Susie had come with her parents. Did she want to talk to me? Or did her parents ask her to come. It was also strange that Brenda came too.

"I could talk to the Wolf Pack. We could always do another hike or wade one of the creeks" I said.

"We can drive now. We could take a trip," Rock said.

She was right, I thought.

"Where would we go?" Susie asked.

"We could go to the Smoky Mountains and camp," Rock said.

I had always wanted to go to the Smokies. I had seen pictures in magazines and saw shows on TV about the Smoky Mountains. But would our parents let us go off to Tennessee?

"Purty and James Ernest have their driver's license," I said.

"Rhonda got her license, but she doesn't have a car," Susie said.

"She could help drive though," Rock said.

"I'll probably have my license by the end of next month," I said.

"I guess we should have a meeting to talk about it," I said.

"When?" Susie asked.

"Let's have one tomorrow night at the cabin," I suggested.

"It's supposed to be hot tomorrow. What if we have a meeting at the swimming hole?" Rock said.

"That's a great idea," Susie agreed.

"Sounds good to me," I agreed also.

"We could talk to our parents now to see if they would let us go before we bring it up at the meeting," Susie said.

I wanted to talk to James Ernest before talking to my parents. I knew that they would be more on board if the idea came from him than me.

"Let's wait until after the meeting to see what everyone thinks. There's more strength in numbers," I suggested.

The girls finally agreed.

After eating, the three of us went for a walk around the lake. Rock held my hand as Susie led the way. I showed them again where I had found the floating body. The lake was still muddy. We decided to continue up the stream to the swimming hole to see if it was muddy since we planned on having the meeting there.

When we arrived we saw that the swimming hole wasn't that muddy and figured by the next evening it would be fine for swimming. While Susie was looking at the water Rock kissed me. Susie turned at that moment and saw us. I saw her and pulled away.

"It's okay. The two of you make a nice couple. It's okay if you kiss in front of me. I don't mind," Susie said.

We turned to head back to the store.

That night James Ernest and I were on the front porch enjoying the sound of the night birds. I heard coyotes in the distance.

"Susie, Rock and I planned a combined Wolf Pack and Bear Troop meeting for tomorrow evening at the swimming hole. Is that okay with you?"

"It sounds good to me. We need to plan something for the summer."

"We also came up with a thought on that."

"What is it?"

"Since you and Purty have trucks now and since this is your last summer before going off to college we thought about doing something big. We want to take a trip to the Smoky Mountains for a few days. We can camp and hike and swim. It would be great."

James Ernest smiled as he thought about it. "Do you really think all of our parents would let us go?"

"Remember when we gathered all the parents and you pitched the idea for the canoe trip down the Red River to them. We can do the same thing again," I explained.

"We could try, I guess."

"Give them your puppy dog eyes. They never say no to you."

"I love the idea, but I'm not sure my eyes are going to do much good with this," James Ernest said.

Chapter 5
You're u-g-l-y

Sunday, June 6

*T*hat morning before church Dad told me the license number of the dark blue pickup didn't pan out. He told us there was no such license number. I was sure I had written it down correctly. I figured it must have been a fake plate.

James Ernest was driving separately to church. I rode with him. We went to pick up Rock and Tucky. The four of us squeezed into the cab and we were off to church.

"Did Rock tell you about going to the Smoky Mountains?" I asked Tucky.

"Sounds like a plan to me. Dad said for us to have a good time," Tucky said. Their parents didn't really care about what their kids did. The only thing I had ever heard of them getting upset or mad about was when Monk and Chuck up and joined the army.

Purty's brother, Randy, had come home on leave last Christmas. He was here for two weeks before leaving for a marine base in Georgia. He believed he would end up in Vietnam before the end of the summer or fall. The Key family still had not heard a word from Monk and Chuck since they left for basic training.

I wasn't surprised that Rock and Tucky were told they could go on the excursion. Now we had to convince Mom and Dad. That would not be easy to do.

That evening each member of the Wolf Pack and Bear Troop met at the store around six-thirty. We headed for the swimming hole. It was a warm evening. The thermometer that hung on one of the porch posts read that it was still eighty-five degrees. It would be great relief to jump in the water.

As we neared the swimming hole Purty said, "Each of the Wolf Pack members has jumped from the cliff except for you, Junior. I think it's about time you did it."

I quickly thought to the day Daniel Sugarman, 'Sugarspoon', had jumped and shattered a bone when he hit his arm against the rocks on the side of the pool.

"It's not something a member has to do, Purty," I said.

"I know, but we all have done it," Purty urged.

As we came to the water hole I saw Junior glance up at the top of the cliff. We began striping down to our swimming suits and jumping in. I was the first one in and felt the cooling waters soak into my skin. I stayed under the water, not wanting to stick my head back up into the heat.

I wanted to swim into the underground cave where it would be even cooler, but I knew I couldn't do that. It was a secret I had kept to myself except for three other people – James Ernest, Susie and Papaw. When I finally came up out of the water and wiped the water from my eyes I looked up to see Junior above me on the edge of the cliff.

"Junior is going to jump!" I yelled out. Everyone swam to the edges of the water and watched as Junior readied himself. He backed away from the edge.

"He's not going to do it," Purty was saying as Junior leaped from the edge and soared through the air. He did a complete flip and then landed feet first in the center of the swimming hole. He rose to the top to great applause. Junior was a natural athlete.

We had been in the pool a couple of hours, as the evening was cooling off we began getting out and drying off. James Ernest said, "The main reason we all came tonight is to have our club meetings. Susie and I felt we should have a combined meeting to discuss an idea for an adventure we might want to do."

Most of us sat in a circle on a huge stone rock. "I believe we should start the meeting. The members of the Wolf Pack stood in a small circle and chanted, "Wolf Pack, Wolf Pack, Wolf Pack, Wolf Pack, Wolf Pack, Wolf Pack" and then we howled toward the sky. It was the same way we always started a meeting. As always, Coty howled with us.

In the distant hills we heard howling coming back at us. The Bear Troop didn't have a chant so we began the meeting.

"Before we give you our idea, does anyone else have an idea for a combined adventure?" Susie asked.

Purty raised his arm and said, "A canoe trip would be fun like the one we did down Red River."

"It would be fun for everyone except for the person in your canoe," Tucky said, remembering the last canoe trip when he and Purty turned over at least a hundred times.

"And that would probably be you, Shauna," Sadie said.

"I enjoyed our last overnight hike. We could maybe go for two nights," Francis suggested.

"I like the hiking idea," Shauna said and laughed.

"What is your idea?" Raven asked, looking at James Ernest and Susie.

"This was actually suggested by Rock. We liked the idea, but it might not be feasible," Susie said.

"Tell us, already," Junior said.

"She suggested we take a trip to the Smoky Mountains," James Ernest said. Everyone began talking at the same time. I had never seen all of us so excited at the same time.

"How would we do that?" Rhonda asked suddenly.

Everyone hushed to hear the plan. I decided to tell the plan. "James Ernest and Purty both drive and have pickups now. They could both drive, and we would camp for three of four nights, or maybe even a week. We could hike, swim, play in the streams, and see the animals. It would be great."

"Our problem is getting all our parents to agree to it," Susie said.

"If we gather all the parents together and let James Ernest explain the plan we would have a better chance," I told them.

"All of them are picking us up at nine tonight, aren't they?" Rhonda said.

"Whose parents aren't going to be there tonight?" Susie asked.

Rock said, "Ours, but they already said we could go."

Purty said, "I drove us, so our parents aren't, but we could call them and ask them to come down."

"Is there anyone that knows for sure they couldn't go?" James Ernest asked.

No one said anything until Sadie said, "I know we're going on vacation to visit relatives. So we couldn't go during that time."

"We can be flexible with the dates. We have all summer," I said.

"Who is in favor of going to the Smoky Mountains?" James Ernest yelled out. We all shouted and Coty howled.

We decided to head back to the store so Purty could call his parents and we could give our parents the plan.

The store and porch was filled with parents and families when we got to the store. We each told our parents that we wanted to have a quick meeting. Sadie called her parents instead of Purty. Mr. Tuttle reluctantly agreed to come.

Within ten minutes everyone was gathered on the front porch or standing in the lot listening.

I began first, "This is James Ernest's last summer before he leaves for college, and the Wolf Pack and Bear Troop want to do something special this summer for him. I'm going to let him tell you our plan."

"Oh, no. It has to be bad if they're having James Ernest explain it," Monie said.

The other parents laughed. They had figured out our tricks, I thought.

James Ernest began, "We want to take a trip to the Smoky Mountains." He just threw it out there. He ripped the Band-Aid right off. He didn't even try to slowly ease into it.

He continued before the parents could voice their displeasure, "Purty and I both have trucks and our license and we could drive. We'd be careful. We would plan on camping in one of the park's campgrounds. We could hike, and swim, and see the beautiful mountains. The trip wouldn't cost much money if we all shared the cost of the gas and food and camp fees."

"No," Mr. Tuttle said. "I'm sorry, but I'm not having three of my kids go off three hundred miles away with no adult supervision."

"I don't like the idea either," Rhonda's mother, Mary, said.

This was quickly getting away from us. I knew it was doomed. It had been a longshot at best anyway.

Dad raised his arms and got everyone's attention. He then shocked me when he said, "Betty and I never had a honeymoon. I've always wanted to see the Smokies. What if we went with them as chaperones? Would everyone agree then? I think the kids have proven to be trustworthy and good kids. I think they would have a great time. I'm actually envious."

"I would agree if you two went along," Mr. Tuttle said.

Soon, all the parents agreed. Mom had a big smile on her face.

Dad continued, "Now, I have to say this. I don't believe I want to spend my honeymoon in a tent, so Betty and I would stay in a motel just a few miles away, and only a phone call away. We would check on them every day and maybe do some hikes with them. We would enjoy that. I want to make sure you know we won't be with them twenty four hours a day. But, we aren't with them when they campout at the cabin. And there will be Park Rangers at the campground."

The parents still agreed. Mom then said, "Rock, Kenny, your parents aren't here."

"They already said we could go," Tucky said.

We then discussed dates and it was decided the first week of August would be best. It also gave us plenty of time to plan everything.

I was so happy that night when I went to bed. I couldn't believe Dad had stepped up and saved our trip. I had really looked forward to our canoe trip down the Red River, but this was way beyond that excitement. I had so much trouble going to sleep.

We talked about what the mountains might look like. We talked about all the animals we might see and the trails we would hike. I wanted to meet Yogi Bear. James Ernest tried telling me Yogi Bear wasn't real. James Ernest said he would go to library to see if they had information on the Smokies.

James Ernest and I talked about the trip for a long time that night before he finally fell asleep. I listened to the tree frogs until I went to sleep.

Monday, June 7

I had just opened the store when Purty and Tucky walked through the front door. We had decided to open the lake back up for fishing, but I knew they weren't there for fishing.

"We couldn't sleep so we decided to come see you and James Ernest to talk about the trip," Purty said. The joy on his face was hard to deny. Dad walked into the store.

"I wanted to see who was here so early," he said. Purty ran over to him and threw his arms around Dad. Dad tried to resist and push him away, but Purty was not letting go, so Dad finally gave up and hugged him back.

"Thank you. Thank you. Thank you," Purty said over and over.

"You're awfully happy this morning," Dad said.

"You don't understand. Mom and Dad decided to take their annual trip to my aunt's house the same week we're going to the Smokies," Purty explained.

"But you'll miss the trip to your aunt's house," Dad said.

"I know. Thank you. Thank you. The visit is the worst week of the year. My mom's sister talks more than Mom does. It starts the moment we get there and doesn't stop until we leave. They both talk at the same time and no one listens to either of them, including each other," Purty said. "You may have saved our lives. I think the main reason Randy joined the Marines was so he could get out of the yearly trip," Purty exaggerated.

"Glad I could help," Dad said as he pried Purty's arms off of him.

51

I couldn't imagine having two Loraine's in the same room. It was bad enough having one. I could understand his happiness.

Dad said, "I think I hear Betty calling." He quickly left to find her.

"I didn't hear anything," Purty said. Tucky and I laughed.

"I don't think he's used to having a seventeen year old boy hugging him. It was as awkward as a tit in the middle of your back," Tucky said. I just looked at him.

"What are you doing today?" Purty asked.

"I guess I'm watching the store," I said.

"We need to plan the trip," Purty said.

"We've got two months," I said.

"I know, it will be here before we know it. Is James Ernest in your bedroom?" Purty continued.

"I think so," I said.

The two of them headed for the bedroom. I knew James Ernest would be thrilled.

Then I heard, "Get off me, you knucklehead!"

Mud McCobb and Louis Lewis walked through the front door. They heard the arguing coming from the bedroom.

"What's going on in there?" Mud asked.

"Happiness," I answered.

"Doesn't sound like it," Louis said.

"On your way to work?" I asked.

"Yep, another week, another dollar," Mud said.

"Has the sheriff caught the killer yet?" Louis asked.

"Not yet."

"We might be back this evening to fish if you can guarantee we won't catch a body while we're fishing," Mud said.

"I can do one better. I can guarantee you won't catch a thing," I said. Louis started laughing.

"I haven't seen your stringer hauling out any fish," Mud told him.

"I release my catches," Louis argued.

"The only thing you release are the nightcrawlers," Mud said as he paid for his pint of milk and snack cake.

"Well – you're u-g-l-y," Louis countered.

"Instead of slapping you when you were born, the doctor slapped your Daddy,"

"You keep my daddy out of this," Louis said as he handed me a dollar. I gave him his change and they followed each other out the door. What a pleasant morning it had become.

Purty and Tucky reentered the room and Purty said, "He was in a grumpy mood."

"Gee, I wonder why," I said.

"Purty is excited about spending a week with Shauna," Tucky said.

"She'll finally get to know the real you," I warned him.

"I hadn't thought of that," Purty said.

"She may run for the mountaintops," Tucky told him.

"I'll be on my best behavior," Purty said seriously.

"Yeah, that will work."

"I may buy a two man tent for me and her," Purty said.

"You fart one time in there and you will never see her again," Tucky said.

They stayed for another hour. They mainly pestered me for an hour. Dad left for work by going out the back door and around the house to avoid Purty. I guess he didn't need another hug. James Ernest left to go make baskets.

"How much money do you think we'll need for the trip?" Tucky asked James Ernest as he was walking through the store.

"I would think if everyone chipped in fifty or sixty dollars each it would cover everything," he answered.

"I've got the money we earned for cutting down the marijuana field," Tucky said.

"Me too," Purty said.

"What about Rock?" I asked.

"I don't know where she'll come up with the money. I know Dad won't give her a hundred bucks," Tucky said. "I don't have enough."

"I guess we didn't think about the cost. I'll figure out how much it will actually be. We'll come up with something," James Ernest said. He then left.

"We're heading out also. See you later, alligator," Purty said

"After while, crocodile," I returned.

"After noon, you big baboon," Tucky shouted as they were getting into Purty's pickup.

Mom heard them leave and came into the store. She came over and gave me a hug. "Smoky Mountains will be fun," she said.

"We were talking about whether or not everyone will be able to come up with the money to go. We hadn't thought about that."

Mom asked, "Who are you worried about?"

"Raven, Junior, and Rock mainly, I guess," I answered.

"Raven should have money from selling her baskets, shouldn't she?"

"I don't know. She gives most of what she makes to her family to help out."

"We can help out with Rock if we need to. We don't want anyone to be left behind," Mom assured me.

"Thanks, Mom, you're the best."

Chapter 6
Leave Her Alone

Wednesday, June 9

*J*ames Ernest came home last night with information on the trip. We spent the evening adding numbers and making plans for the trip. Camping was only six dollars a night per campsite. We decided with having twelve going we would need two sites together. Mom and Dad said it would be best to leave Sunday, August the first, after church. We would be there by evening.

We would be returning the next Saturday. That would mean we would be camping six nights. Camping would cost us $72. I figured how much the gas would cost us for the trip. We rounded up to make the gas cost us $120.

Mom said we could get lunchmeat and bread for sandwiches from the store at cost. We included snacks and hotdogs. It would take a lot to feed twelve teenagers. Dad said there was a carryout at the campsite and a grocery not far from the campground. We figured three dollars a day per person for food. It came out that it would only cost around $40.00 per person with no extras. But to be safe each of us should have $10 to $20 extra with them.

I woke up feeling better about the trip and everyone being able to go. I would pay for anyone who didn't have the money. I had almost four hundred dollars in the bank doing nothing. I would be happy to help my friends.

Mom went shopping with Miss Rebecca. Janie and Bobbie Lee went to stay and play with the twins, Delma and Thelma. I was glad I wasn't at the Perry farm.

I was left to tend the store by myself. I was sitting on the front porch and was happy to see Rock walking up the road. She gave me a big wave when she saw me looking at her. I couldn't wait for the smile to turn into a kiss.

As she got near the bridge a truck came up from Wrigley behind her. The driver and passenger slowed down when they got to her. I could see her waving them away but they looked like they weren't happy with her decision. The passenger door opened and the man started to get out.

I yelled, "Leave her alone."

The man turned and looked at me and then grabbed Rock by the arm. I jumped off the porch and ran toward the truck. I saw Rock kick the man in the shin. He grabbed both of her arms and she kneed him in the balls. He bent down and let go of her and she ran toward me.

She turned toward them and shouted, "You low-life scumbags." We were standing together at the side of the road as they slowly drove past us.

"You don't know what you're missing. Another time, b____!" the passenger yelled out the window.

I then noticed the color of the pickup. It was dark blue. I looked at the back license plate as they peeled away, but the dust rising from the road blocked me from seeing it. But I recognized the driver as the same man who had bought gas earlier in the week.

Rock put her head against my chest and cried. Her body was shaking terribly. I placed my arms around her and squeezed her to me to stop the shaking. It didn't work. We turned and walked toward the store. She was still crying and quivering. We made it to the porch and sat in the swing together.

"I'm so sorry that happened to you," I said.

Her crying finally subsided and she said, "I didn't think I was going to get away from them. It's no telling what they would be doing to me right now."

"Don't even think about that. You're safe. I need to go inside and call Dad."

"Okay."

When I got up Rock started to stand. "You should stay and rest," I said.

"You are not leaving me alone today," Rock said with a look that told me she meant it. We went inside, and I picked up the receiver from the wall phone and dialed the police station.

"Is Sheriff Cane there?" I asked his secretary.

"Hi, Timmy. Yes, he's here. Hold on," she said.

When he came on the line I quickly told him what had happened. He said he would be there soon.

We stood in the store, and she wrapped her arms around like she would never let me go. We were so fortunate the two men hadn't been five minutes earlier where she wouldn't have had an escape route. I knew deep down that those were the two men who had killed the man I had found in the lake. But how would I prove it?

It seemed as though there had been more crimes in the past couple of years than ever before. One night I heard Dad telling some of the men out on the porch that he believed drugs was the reason for most of the crimes. Marijuana and LSD was ruining people's lives. I had seen it first hand with the marijuana field we had found and a storage locker we had discovered that had LSD

57

inside. I heard Dad tell them that people were stealing in order to buy more drugs.

Cat walked into the front door. Rock released me when she heard the door open. She still looked shaken. Cat took one look at her and knew something was up.

"Is everything okay?" he asked.

"Two men tried to kidnap Rock over at the bridge," I explained.

"Oh, no."

At that moment I heard the cruiser pull into the lot. Dad ran into the store. He came over and hugged Rock and asked if she was okay.

Then he asked us to tell him what had happened. Rock gave her version and then I told him what I had seen.

"Did you happen to notice anything inside the pickup?" Dad asked her.

"No. I was just trying to get away."

"Can you describe the man who grabbed you?"

"He was around five foot eight. Not much taller than me. He had hair on his chin."

"Did he have a mustache to go with it?"

"No. He was balding though."

"How old would you say he was?"

"In his thirties, maybe. His eyes were sunk into his head. I think he looked older than he was," Rock told him.

"Like he was on drugs?" Dad asked.

"Yeah."

"Did you get a look at the driver?"

"No. I didn't see him at all."

I then said, "The driver was the same guy that had bought gas the other day."

"You're sure?"

"Yes," I said.

"I'm going to drive the ridge to look for them, but I doubt I'll have any luck. Are you staying here Rock, or do you want me to take you home?"

"I was going to spend the day with Timmy if that's okay," Rock said.

"That's fine. I don't want you walking home alone. Someone will take you home this evening. Okay?"

"Okay."

"I don't think they'll be back today," Dad said. "But be careful."

Dad left and Cat bought some bread and corn meal before leaving.

Rock and I decided to have a pop and snack cake. We went out to the porch and sat on the swing. She sat as close to me as she could. I didn't mind at all.

We spent the day waiting on customers and talking about the trip to the Smokies. I told her how much we figured the trip would cost. I assured her that if she didn't have the money I would cover it for her.

Dad called later and told me he hadn't found the men. He also wanted to make sure we were okay. Around two that afternoon, Mom and Miss Rebecca returned from their shopping trip. Mom was truly upset when she heard what had happened to Rock.

"I'm okay," Rock told her.

"I'd like for you to stay for supper," Mom said.

"I'd love to," Rock told her.

After Mud and Louis got off work they came into the store to pay for fishing. After standing in the store arguing about who was going to catch the most fish, they left to try and do it.

It was going to be a nice evening for fishing and the lake had cleared up from the rain so we had a number of fishermen. I took their money while Rock went to get the bait from the back porch fridge.

Rock enjoyed helping at the store. She had told me there wasn't much to do at home. She said she got teased a lot by her sisters for going to school and church. They called her a goody two shoes and a princess.

She also had told me that one of her older sisters, Sugar Cook, was dating a boy from Blaze. "I don't like the guy. He looks like trouble. His name is Hiram," she had told me.

I knew who he was instantly. He was the leader of the Boys from Blaze, the Wolf Pack's nemesis over the years. For years we had a feud with their gang, but had lately worked out our differences. We stayed out of their area and they stayed out of ours. I still knew they could be trouble.

The last dealings we had with Hiram was when he asked us to search for Foster Banks, a member of the boys from Blaze who had went missing two winters before. Hiram had graduated with James Ernest. I didn't really know what kind of guy he was now, so I kept my opinion to myself.

The lot quickly filled with customers and fishermen. Rock and I were kept busy with the store, the fishermen, and pumping gas. Mom had to come in to help.

Once the fishermen were through arriving, the store became normal again. When Dad got home from work he told us they didn't find the dark blue pickup. He said, "All of the deputies are aware of the truck and the description of the men and they are keeping an eye out for them."

After supper was over we were out on the porch as the sun began to sink. Mud and Louis came from the lake and went inside to get a soda. When they came back out they took seats on the porch edge.

"How was the fishing?" Dad asked them.

"It was good," Mud said.

"I beat him again," Louis said.

"He caught a two inch bluegill and counted it so he could beat me by one," Mud complained.

"A fish is a fish, is it not?" Louis said.

James Ernest said, "Isn't that Shakespeare?"

"He wouldn't know Shakespeare from a Snoopy comic," Mud said.

After the laughter died down Mud said, "There was a strange man at the lake this evening asking questions."

"Yeah, he was strange," Louis agreed.

Dad asked, "What did he want to know?"

"He started asking if we knew of any caves around the lake," Mud told us.

"Why did he want to know about caves?" Mom asked.

"What did you tell him?" Dad asked.

"I told him I had heard there was one," Mud said.

"Then what?" I asked.

"He wanted to know where it was," Louis said.

"I told him we had no idea where it was. I remember hearing about the cave Timmy had trapped the Tattoo man in, but I never knew exactly where it was," Mud said.

"Did you ask him why he wanted to know?" Dad asked.

"Louis did. But he told us he was a scientist and was looking for caves to examine. He didn't look like any scientist," Mud said.

"What did he look like?" I asked.

Louis answered, "He was skinny with shaggy brown hair and long sideburns. He acted as if he was better than us. He was a little on the creepy side."

He was describing the driver of the dark blue pickup that had stopped for gas the day I took down the license number. "That's the guy who drove the dark blue pickup," I said.

"Was it the same guy driving the truck today?" Dad asked.

"I think it was. I was paying so much attention to the guy who had grabbed Rock that I hadn't paid much attention to the driver until he yelled out the window as they sped off. I'm sure it's the same man," I assured him again.

We then told Mud and Louis about the attempted kidnapping.

"Why would they want to know about a cave in the area?" Mom asked. No one knew.

"He must have parked away from here and walked to the lake, because I've been watching for the pickup all day," Rock said.

"Me too," I said.

"It is strange," Dad said.

"It worries me," Mom said.

"I'd better get you home," Dad said to Rock.

"I can walk."

"No you will not," Mom told her.

"I'll drive her and Timmy can go with us," James Ernest said.

The three of us left. We dropped Rock off but not before she gave me a big kiss.

On the way back to the store James Ernest said, "You two are really getting serious,"

"I really like her," I said.

Chapter 7
Treehawk

*P*apaw and I were at the barber shop. I was letting my hair grow out longer. After all, it was 1965 and most of the boys were doing the same thing. Mom told me she at least wanted it trimmed. I was sitting in the barber chair, and "Razor" McGill was beginning to trim my hair.

Papaw was sitting in a chair waiting his turn. He and Razor began talking while my hair was being cut.

Razor asked, "What do you know about a man being killed in a cave near your store?"

"What? Where did you hear that?" Papaw asked.

"A customer asked me about it the other day," Razor told us.

"There was a man killed that we found in the lake," Papaw said.

"I heard about that. But this man specifically asked about a body being found in a cave."

"I think he was mistaken," Papaw told him.

Four winters earlier a few of us found a cave behind a waterfall. Inside the cave we found a chest and two skeletons of men who had been murdered. The question quickly reminded me of that time. I decided not to mention it for a couple of reasons, the main one being that it wasn't near the lake. The cave was on the property of Clayton's farm in the woods toward Devil's creek.

I wondered what in the world was going on. A man was at the lake on Wednesday asking about the location of a cave near the lake and now we hear that a man was inquiring about a dead man in a cave. The Tattoo man had died in a cave near the lake, but he wasn't found dead, he died when he fell from a rope while trying to kill me.

"What did the man look like?" I asked.

"He was a skinny man with bushy hair," Razor said. "He sat there asking the questions and then walked out without getting a haircut."

"Did he have long sideburns?" I asked.

"Yes. He did," Razor answered.

This was the same man that I had pumped gas for and had asked Mud and Louis about a cave and now had asked Razor. He was definitely trying to find a cave for some reason. I wondered what he was looking for. Had he heard about the Indian drawings in my secret cave? Was he looking for something hidden in a cave? I didn't have the foggiest idea.

Razor finished my haircut and Papaw took my place in the chair. "You don't even look like you got a haircut," Papaw said.

"He cut a hair," I said grinning.

"I wouldn't pay you a nickel for a haircut like that," Papaw complained to Razor.

"You're just a jealous old man with no hair. I think I might find one hair on your head to cut," Razor said and then laughed.

Papaw didn't think it was that funny.

"I'm going to run to the bank while he's cutting that hair," I told Papaw.

"It won't take long," Razor said and then laughed again, as Papaw frowned.

The bank was on the opposite side of the road and a half block down. I walked into the bank and saw Miss Rebecca at one of the teller windows. She had worked here full time and now only worked a couple of days a week. I waited until her window was open and walked up to her.

She looked up to see me and said, "Hi, Timmy. What brings you in today?"

"Hi, Miss Rebecca. Can you tell me how much money I have in my savings?"

She looked it up and then said, "You have four hundred and twenty two dollars and some change. Do you want to remove some of it today?"

"No. Not today. The Wolf Pack and Bear Troop are going to the Smoky Mountains in August, and I might need to get some of it then."

"Betty told me about the trip. It sounds like so much fun," Miss Rebecca told me.

"I don't know if all the members can afford it, so I'm thinking I might pay the way for the ones who can't," I said.

"That is so kind of you," she said.

"You might want to talk to Mr. Harney. At times groups do car washes in the parking lot to raise money. I'm quite sure he would let you guys have one to make money for the trip."

"That's a great idea," I said.

"Let me get him to come out and talk to you," she said.

She picked up the phone and called his office and I heard her tell him that I was there. She hung up, and thirty seconds later he was standing next to me. She explained what we were doing and

Mr. Harney said they would be happy to let us have a car wash. He said a Friday evening or a Saturday would be best.

I thanked him and told him we would decide on a date and let him know. As I turned to leave he said, "Hey, Timmy."

I turned around and walked back to him, "I have another way you guys could make some money. We're having an estate auction at the end of this month. We could use help setting up all the stuff and help with the auction like you did at the Robbins auction."

"That would be great. We could do that. Thanks, Mr. Harney."

"I'll call with the details," he said.

I was excited with the possibilities that we could work to raise the money for those that needed it for the trip. I knew that any of us would rather earn the money instead of taking charity. I left the bank and headed to the barber shop to see if Razor had found that hair to cut.

I saw Papaw standing outside the shop talking to a man on the sidewalk. As I walked up to them Papaw said, "Ah, here he is now. This is my grandson, Timmy. Timmy, this is Ralph Tree, better known as Treehawk."

I shook his hand. I knew right away that he was an Indian by his looks and his name. "He's here visiting friends, and Ralph is also looking for Cat, an old friend. I told him about Cat and his Hobbit House that he built."

We said our goodbyes and headed to the truck. Papaw wanted to stop at the General store to get something for the farm. I went inside to look at the fishing poles and sporting goods.

"Good morning, Martin, Timmy," Mr. Cobb greeted as we walked in.

We greeted him back and I took off for the back of the store. I heard Papaw ask him for fencing staples.

The fly rods caught my eye. I was looking at them when Papaw made his way to where I stood. I had always wanted to learn how to use a fly rod for the creeks around us. With us now taking a trip to the Smoky Mountains it would be great to take one on the trip.

"What are you looking at?" Papaw asked.

"The fly rods. I've always wanted to learn how to use one. Would you loan me the money to buy one? I'll pay you back. I've got plenty of money in the bank."

"They are fun. I've tried them before, but never owned one," Papaw said.

"I think it would be fun to use one in the Smoky Mountain streams," I told him.

Mr. Cobb made his way back to where we stood. "Thinking of fly fishing?" he asked.

"We might be," Papaw said.

"I am," I said.

"Which one would you recommend for two beginners?" Papaw asked him.

Mr. Cobb picked up one of them and said, "This is the one I would choose. The rod has a lot of action, and the reel is easy. It's not the cheapest, but it is the best one for the money. The price includes the rod, reel and line. If you twist my arm I might even throw in a few flies."

"I'll take two of them," Papaw said. My eyes got big when he said that. "We can learn together," Papaw said. "Then maybe James Ernest can borrow mine for the trip."

"Where are you going?" Mr. Cobb asked.

"The Wolf Pack is taking a trip to the Smoky Mountains in August," Papaw told him.

"Let's go pick out a few flies. I've got a couple made especially for fishing the streams in the Smokies," Mr. Cobb told us. He gave us four flies for the trip and Papaw bought four to use around here which Mr. Cobb said would be good for the smallmouth and bluegills.

We left the store and I asked, "Take me back to the bank and I'll get the money I owe you."

"Let's just say this is an early birthday gift." Papaw said and then rubbed the top of my head.

"Thank you. When you want to try them out?" I asked.

"I'll come down to the store this evening and we can go over to the creek and practice casting."

"That sounds like fun," I said.

We left town and headed home. When we got to Wrigley I asked Papaw if he would stop at the Key house for a minute. He turned onto Route 711 and two minutes later we were stopping at the house. I jumped out and ran to the door. Sugar Cook and Chero were sitting on the porch.

"Did you come to see us?" Chero asked, seductively.

"Is Rock here?" I asked them.

"She's no fun. You'd have more fun with me," Sugar Cook said as she smiled.

"Isn't Hiram your boyfriend?" I asked.

"I can have more than one," she said.

"Did Hiram agree to that?"

"He doesn't need to know."

"I did hear he had another girlfriend in Blaze," I lied.

"He'd better not have another lassie on his arm, that two-timing, no-good…"

68

Rock came to the screened door as Sugar was bad mouthing her guy.

"You doing anything?" I asked Rock.

"No."

"Want to come to the store and spend the rest of the day?"

"Sure."

"Bring your swimming suit," I told her.

She was back in thirty seconds and we ran to the truck. She slid in next to Papaw.

Two minutes later we were at the store. I waved goodbye as he left for the farm. James Ernest was watching the store for a change. I told him and Rock about the fly rods and about how we could make money for the trip. They both were excited about it.

"I didn't know what I was going to do about money for the trip. Kenny had told me he would give me money, but I hated for him to have to. He doesn't have much at all."

"I was going to pay your way," I told her.

"That's sweet, but I'd rather earn it if I can," Rock said.

"What about Raven and Junior?" I asked James Ernest.

"Raven has saved enough from the baskets and I think she has enough for Junior also."

"I knew she was helping her parents," I said.

"She does. But they wouldn't take all of her earnings. I think Henry is doing pretty well now at the quarry and with his crops," James Ernest said.

"When is the auction and car wash?" Rock asked.

"Mr. Harney said the auction was at the end of this month. He said for me to let him know when we want to do the car wash," I told them.

The three of us went out on the porch to sit. I told them about Treehawk.

"We should probably tell Cat about him," James Ernest said.

"You think so?" I said.

"Why don't you and Rock go tell him and I'll stay and watch the store till you get back," he said.

I looked at Rock and she nodded. I stood to leave and James Ernest threw me his keys and told me, "Take the truck. The road is too hot and dusty to be walking on."

"Really?"

"Yeah. You know how to drive."

I was excited to get behind the steering wheel. I started the truck and put it in reverse. I started to back up and the engine stopped. I started it again and my second try was better. I took off slowly up the road. Rock was sitting with her head out the window letting the wind blow her hair straight back. It was fun to drive.

I pulled into the field and drove the pickup as far as we could go. We walked the rest of the way. We didn't see Cat anywhere around his house. I tried the house first. I knocked on the opened door.

"Hello," Cat called out. "Come on in."

We walked into the Hobbit House. Being that it was built into an overhanging cliff the temperature inside was at least twenty degrees cooler than the ninety outside. It felt like it was air conditioned.

Cat was sitting inside carving on a bow that he was making.

"What brings you two for a visit?"

We found seats to sit and then I said, "I have some news we thought you should know."

I went ahead and told him about the barber shop and that a man was asking where Cat lived.

"Did you get a name?"

"Papaw said he called himself Treehawk."

"Ralph Tree," Cat quickly said.

"He told Papaw he was here visiting friends and looking for you."

"Treehawk is bad news."

I tensed when he said that. "What do you mean?" Rock asked.

"In our community he was always in trouble with our people and with the police. Always trying to make a quick and easy buck and that got him in trouble. We're not friends," Cat said.

"Why would he be here then?" I asked.

"That, my friend, is a good question," he said. "I will definitely be keeping an eye open for him. Did Martin tell him where I live?"

"I don't know. All Papaw told me was that he had told Treehawk about the Hobbit House, but he may have."

"It's good that you came and told me about him," Cat said.

"What should I do if he stops at the store asking for directions to where you live?" I asked.

"Go ahead and tell him. He'll find out from someone."

I told Cat that we needed to get back to the store to relieve James Ernest. We said our goodbyes and left.

Catahecassa

I wouldn't put anything past Treehawk. I knew if he was here in Morgan County then he was up to nothing good. I even considered that he could be behind the body they found in the lake. It could explain where the Shawnee arrow had come from.

But I couldn't think of a reason why he would be here other than revenge. I had testified against him the last time he went to prison. Tonight, I would be sleeping on the roof of the Hobbit House.

71

Chapter 8
Swish!

*T*he store was busy most of the afternoon and into the evening. Rock and I were worried that Treehawk would stop and ask for directions to Cat's house. It never happened.

James Ernest left to go to Raven's house. Mamaw and Papaw came to the store and had supper with us. Papaw and I took our fly rods to the creek for a little while for my first lesson of how to cast it. Rock and Coty came along.

It took me a few casts to get the hang of letting the line drift all the way back behind me before casting it forward again. I even caught a nice bluegill and it was fun watching the light rod bend with the fight. Afterwards, Rock and I decided to go to the swimming hole behind the lake.

I wore my swimming trunks and a tee-shirt. Rock wore her swimsuit with a pair of cut off jean shorts. She looked so good. When we got to the pool of water I took off my shirt and jumped in. I watched as Rock took off her jean shorts. She then surprised me by taking off her swimsuit. She dove into the pool and came up right in front of me. I was speechless as she kissed me.

We were there about an hour when we heard laughter. Before we knew it Purty and Shauna appeared on the path. Sadie and Tucky were right behind them.

They walked up to the edge and Purty said, "We came to see if you two wanted to do something with us."

"We are doing something," I said.

Purty looked over and saw Rock's swimming suit lying on a stone and said, "Are you guys skinny dipping? Oh, my gosh, you are, aren't you."

Rock moved behind me to hide her body. She put her arms around my neck and looked over my shoulder.

"We could join you guys," Purty said. I could have guessed what he was going to say.

"I'm game," Sadie said.

"I'm not going skinny dipping," Shauna said.

"What did you guys have in mind?" Rock asked.

"We were thinking about tipping over some cows," Tucky said.

"What?" I said.

Tucky explained, "Once it gets almost dark, we sneak up on a cow and push it from its side until it tips over."

"I don't think I'm going to be tipping over cows," I said.

"You haven't lived until you've tipped one," Purty said.

"You've done this before?" Rock asked.

"Tucky and I did it to one of our cows," Purty said.

"Monk told us how to do it," Tucky said.

I knew I definitely didn't want to do anything Monk suggested.

"The cow moos and then looks up at you with these big sad eyes full of surprise," Purty said.

There was supposed to be a three quarter moon tonight. "We could go park in a field somewhere and look up at the moon and listen to the radio. We could take a couple of old blankets."

"That sounds like more fun than tipping cows," Sadie said.

"Okay. Let's go," Purty suggested.

"You guys go on to the store and we'll catch up," I said.

"We won't look," Purty said.

Shauna grabbed him by the arm and said, "Come on, Todd. Give them some privacy."

They turned and left. Rock gave me a big kiss and we climbed out of the water and Rock got dressed. When we got back to the store Rock and I changed into our clothes and Mom found some old quilts we could use. We got drinks and snacks from the store. I found our cooler for the drinks, and then we took off.

Rock and I climbed into the back of the pickup while the other four squeezed into the cab. We decided to park in Papaws front yard. It was open and quiet and we would have a great view of the moon. We got there just before the moon began to rise. We spread three blankets on the ground and turned the radio to the top forty radio station.

Lightning bugs started to rise from the grass. The air was cooling. It was a perfect night to star gaze with your best girl. It was nice to see Purty with a girl that liked him. I was happy for him.

"Somebody turn that up. I love this song," Sadie said.

Tucky turned the volume up on the transistor radio. *What the World Needs Now* by Jackie De Shannon was playing. It was the perfect song for us; three couples snuggled up on the blankets.

'*What the world needs now is love sweet love.*
It's the only thing that there's just too little of.'

The girls sung along with most of the love songs that played. Finally a song that I liked came on. *Satisfaction* by The Rolling Stones played.

This was my introduction to really dating and parking with a girl. We kissed and hugged and watched all the stars and the moon and the fire flies in the sky. I couldn't have imagined a nicer evening. This was the first of many times we would do this.

"Think of the fun we're going to have in the Smokies," Sadie said. We all agreed. We talked about the trip. I told them about our chances to make money to help those that needed money for the trip. I told everyone about Treehawk.

Then The Beach Boys *Help Me, Rhonda* started playing. I worried that Purty might say something about Rhonda. I thought of them every time I heard the song. But much to his credit he didn't mention the song. He was so smitten by Shauna I didn't even think he noticed it.

I opened the cooler and passed out the drinks and snacks. The moon was big and bright and it seemed like it was speeding as it lifted from the horizon. It was nearly midnight when we gathered up the blankets to call it a night. My favorite song on the top twenty started to play, *Mr. Tambourine Man* by The Byrds.

First Purty dropped off Shauna at Homer and Ruby's farm and then he dropped me off at the store. Rock kissed me and said, "I'll probably see you tomorrow."

"Good," I said.

Saturday, June 12

A soft breeze was coming through my window when I woke up. I was tired from getting to bed so late, but I knew fishermen would start arriving at the store. James Ernest heard me stirring and asked, "Where were you at last night?"

I told him what the six of us had done. I wanted to tell him about all the other stuff that had happened and all that I had learned, but I had to pee.

I rushed out of the room to the bathroom. When I returned James Ernest was getting dressed. "What are you doing today?" I asked.

"I was planning to stay around here and help in the store," he said.

"Good."

I got dressed quickly and went to the front door, unlocked and opened it. The dawn was just breaking and I heard a rooster crow in the distance, I knew it came from the Tuttle farm.

Behind the counter we kept a broom and dustpan. I took the broom and began sweeping the floor. When the inside was finished I went out to sweep off the porch. It was a nice morning. I knew it would be a busy day. James Ernest appeared on the porch without me knowing he was there. It reminded me of the days when he didn't speak. He would appear and disappear as quickly as snapping a finger.

Coty came around the side of the house and jumped onto the porch. I knelt down and petted him. The first customer of the day pulled into the lot. Fred Wilson stepped out of his truck.

"It's a good morning to catch a big one," Fred greeted us.

"It is. You've beaten everyone to it," I said.

"I'll get my favorite spot in the shade," he told us.

"You want to enter the weekly fishing contest," I asked.

"What's that?" Fred asked.

Papaw had come up with the idea to generate more customers.

"You pay fifty cents extra and at the end of the week the person who has caught the longest fish will win all the prize money," I explained.

"Do I have to pay it every time I fish?"

"Just once a week," I told him. "It runs from Saturday to the end of Friday."

"Since I'm catching the big one this morning I guess I'll enter," Fred said.

76

We went inside and I took his money while James Ernest went to get his bait. The front door opened and in walked Mud and Louis. Sam Kendrick followed them and then Sam Johnson and Phillip Satch walked through the door. They each entered the contest.

Papaw's reasoning for the contest was that folks would come back more often for the chance to win the money. It looked like it might work.

Ten minutes later, a man and his wife walked in with their two young boys to fish. It was early to have so many fishermen.

Later that morning I went up to the lake to take orders and pick up any trash. Papaw had laid a tape measure beside the cash register. I took it with me to measure any big fish. Once I had made it to the dam I could hear men arguing about who was going to win the contest. It certainly had created a lot of excitement.

I walked around the lake asking if anyone had a fish they needed me to measure. Mud told me, "Louis has got one he needs measured."

"Very funny," Louis said.

Mud picked up a foot long stick that Louis had pulled out of the lake. I laughed and said, "I believe the rules state that the catch must have gills and a mouth."

"Well, this is about the best he's going to do," Mud said.

"Show him what you've caught," Louis said. "Oh yeah, you haven't caught anything." As they were harping at one another I saw Fred reeling in a big one.

"The money is mine," Fred yelled out.

At that moment his line went slack. He had lost the fish and the money he had already counted. The biggest fish I had measured was thirteen and a half inches until I got to the family. Their youngest son showed me a big bass he had caught. It had to be fourteen inches long. The problem was they hadn't entered the contest. But the boy had a smile on his face as if he had won.

When I returned to the store Papaw was there. He asked how the contest went over. I told him it seemed to be a hit. I showed him the list of the entries. Papaw had taken a notebook and dated the first page. We were to list each person who paid to get in the contest. That way we knew who and how many were entered and how much the prize money was up to.

We were constantly busy during the day. It may have been the busiest day at the store I had ever seen. Rock walked in around one that afternoon and started helping me. James Ernest was pumping gas and loading any feed bags customers bought.

Toward evening Treehawk walked onto the porch. Papaw and Uncle Morton were sitting on the rockers greeting customers. I watched Treehawk as they talked to him. I saw Papaw motioning how to find Cat's place.

Treehawk came on into the store and picked out a soft drink and bag of peanuts. "It's Timmy isn't it?" he said.

"Yes. This is my girlfriend, Rock."

"Rock, huh. We had a girl in our tribe we called Rock. But that was because she was as dumb as one. That's not the case with you, is it?" Treehawk asked.

I could tell that Rock was greatly offended. Especially when she said, "I would think that would be quite abusive of your tribe."

"Maybe so, but true, never the less," he said.

I saw Treehawk look down Rock's body and then he scanned down her legs. It gave me the creeps.

He paid the money he owed and then said, "I'll be back. Good day."

Rock walked behind the counter to join me and then she hugged me. "What a jerk," Rock said.

"I agree. No wonder Cat told us he was trouble."

By the end of the day the leader in the contest was Phillip Satch. He had caught a sixteen and a quarter inch catfish. Mud claimed he had one on that would have made Phillip's look small.

Louis said Mud had fallen asleep and had a dream.

The lake was still full of fishermen when Rock and I made a round at seven that evening. As we rounded the back end of the lake where the stream empties into the lake I heard a branch move and looked up the stream to see Treehawk walking along as though he was looking for something.

I didn't really want to subject Rock to him so I ignored seeing him and we continued around the lake. I couldn't help but wonder why he was back there. What was he looking for? Why had he come to this area?

I needed to go see Cat again.

When we got back to the store I told James Ernest what I had seen. I told him I wanted to go see Cat. We waited until a half hour before darkness would fall. I told Mom we were taking Rock home and then had something we needed to do.

After dropping Rock off I told James Ernest how Treehawk had leered at Rock's body. We hurried to Cat's place.

We found Cat sitting up on the balcony of his treehouse. "Come on up," Cat said upon seeing us.

"Kind of late to be visiting, isn't it? Something must be up," Cat said.

I began telling him about our encounter with Treehawk in the store.

"That sounds like him."

79

"I saw him walking around the lake and looking through the woods near the stream behind the lake" I said.

"He asked Martin where your place was," James Ernest said.

"It's only a matter of time before he shows up here. I've been keeping an eye out for him. I slept on the top of the house last night. I expected his visit. I didn't want to be ambushed in my sleep."

Swish!

An arrow flew past Cat's head and stuck in the side of the treehouse. We all dropped to the deck floor.

"He's here," Cat said. "Stay low and get inside. Quick!"

I crawled along the deck as fast as I could toward the doorway. I heard another arrow slam into the house behind me. I fell into the opening. James Ernest came in right behind me, followed by Cat. He moved catlike to his bow and arrows in the corner. He went to the doorway and snuck a look toward the shooter.

I could not believe I was in the middle of a fight between two Indians with arrows flying around us. I remembered playing cowboys and Indians in the woods pretending that bullets and arrows were flying all around. Here I was living it in real life. I was scared in the pretend battles as my imagination ran wild, but that was nothing compared to this fear. Treehawk was trying to kill us. Or at least he was trying to kill Cat.

It got dark quickly. I didn't even know how Treehawk could see us up in the trees. We never heard a third arrow. Cat told us to stay where we were. He left through the back window. I knew he was trying to chase Treehawk down.

We waited until he returned fifteen minutes later. "It's me," he called out as he climbed the ladder. We came out of the cover and watched him pull the arrows out of side of the treehouse.

80

"Take these to the sheriff and see if they match the one found in the body," Cat said. I chased him until I got to your truck. He had parked behind you and he was high-tailing it before I could get to him.

"I'll be at the store at daybreak to talk to Hagar about filing charges against Treehawk," Cat said.

"Did you get a good look at him?" I asked.

"Yes. He was driving the same truck he had when I left the tribe."

"Be careful tonight," James Ernest said.

"Thanks, boys," Cat said.

When we got back to the store we found Mom and Dad sitting in the porch swing. We told them what had just happened. I handed the two arrows to Dad. Mom kept saying, "Oh no," over and over.

"He asked us to tell you he would be here at daybreak," I said.

"This can't all be about a feud with Cat. How does the body you found in the lake play into it?" I thought he was thinking out loud, not really wanting an answer, which was good, because we didn't have an answer to it.

I told them about seeing Treehawk earlier at the lake.

"I wonder if he's connected to the two other men who have been sneaking around," Hagar said aloud.

We didn't have an answer to that one either.

I went inside to watch *Secret Agent* and *Gunsmoke*. Maybe I could make more sense of them. I grabbed an RC Cola and a bag of peanuts. I poured the peanuts into the bottle and then watched the shows with James Ernest and Janie. She got scared and went to bed fifteen minutes into *Gunsmoke* after saying, "I would have rather watched Bonanza with Little Joe." All of the females loved Little Joe.

Chapter 9
Big 'O' at UK

Sunday, June 13

Cat was on the porch when we woke up that morning. I opened the door and Cat came in. He retold the events of the previous evening to Dad.

"Do you know if he would have any other reason to be in this area besides getting revenge?" Dad asked.

"No."

"Would he know anyone else in the area?"

"I would doubt it, unless he brought others with him," Cat said.

"I hadn't thought of that. There are two other men hovering around that no one knows. It's hard to figure what they are up to," Dad told him.

Bobby Lee, the pastor's stepson, stood in front of the congregation ready to recite the day's verse. "Matthew eleven, verse 28," he began.

He hesitated, and then in the silence we all could hear Delma say, "He's going to mess it up big time."

"He's already forgot the verse," Thelma said.

Monie reached over and slapped the girls on their arms.

Bobby Lee looked at the twins with daggers shooting from his eyes. He mustered up the courage to continue, "Come unto me, all ye that labour and are heavy laden, and I will give you a **black eye**."

Pastor White jumped up from his chair and escorted his stepson to Miss Rebecca, his wife.

"Fortunately, the verse doesn't end with a fight. Jesus taught us to turn the other cheek, not to give others black eyes. Jesus said 'I will give you rest'. I think my son will have a lot of time to rest."

The congregation laughed.

James Ernest and Raven stood together on the platform and sung a hymn together. It was really good.

When James Ernest and I picked up Rock and Tucky for church we told them about Treehawk trying to kill Cat. Rock grabbed my arm and wouldn't let go. She still had hold of my arm. It was as though she was making sure nothing happened to me.

The service was over and we walked out to the parking lot. I saw Cat and Dad talking with Clayton and Henry Washington. Mom was talking with a few of the women. I heard Mom warning the women to not let their daughters walk the road alone. She was telling them about how the two men had tried to grab Rock.

I saw Mamaw talking to Ruby. I guided Rock toward them. I gave Mamaw a big hug. She even hugged Rock.

"I heard about the two men," Ruby said. "What is wrong with people? Are you okay, child?"

"I'm fine. It was scary at the time, but Timmy came to my rescue," Rock said.

"You be careful. We don't want anything happening to you," Mamaw told her.

"Thank you," Rock said.

We headed for James Ernest's truck. Raven was in the cab and Tucky was in the pickup bed.

"You could sit in the cab with Raven since you have on a dress," I suggested.

"It's okay. I want to stay with you. I jumped into the bed and helped her up. We sat behind the cab next to Tucky."

James Ernest took off and headed toward the Key house. Rock told me she might come to the store later in the day. James Ernest dropped them off at their house, and I jumped into the cab. We then went to the store. James Ernest changed clothes and he and Raven left for her house.

I went into the store to wait on any customers we might have. Mamaw and Papaw were coming down for Sunday dinner later. Papaw had a fence that needed to be repaired before they came. I was standing behind the counter when a woman walked into the store.

"Hello," I greeted her.

She nodded back. She scanned the store as though she was looking for something.

"Can I help you find something?" I asked.

She ignored my question and went to the cooler. She looked through the bottles and found what she wanted, a Coca Cola. She carried it to the counter and asked for a pack of Marlboros.

I turned to get the cigarettes off the back shelf. When I turned around she said, "Maybe you can help me find something."

"Yes Ma'am."

"I'm a professor from the University of Kentucky. You like UK basketball?"

84

"Of course I do. Who doesn't?"

"I could get you tickets to a game this coming season if you can help me," she said.

"Sure," I said, not believing anything she had said so far.

"I'm the head of the geo… geolo… geological department at the college and we're searching for artifacts and formations in Kentucky caves. We have heard there are a few caves in this area. Would you be able to tell me where any are?"

If this greasy haired woman was a professor at UK, I was a monkey's uncle, I thought. The woman looked like she had come from the coal camps in Harlan. But I decided to play along.

"Wow, I'd love tickets to a game. The coach, Oscar Robertson, is supposed to have a really good team this year."

"He sure is," she said. Any basketball fan or Kentucky professor would know that Adolph Rupp was the coach of UK basketball.

"Okay. The only cave I know of is along Devil's creek," I said.

"How do I get there?" she asked.

"You have to wade up this creek in front of the store. That's Devil's creek," I pointed out the door. About a half mile up the creek there's a big rock wall on the right. About seventy-five feet up the wall is a big opening. That's it."

She handed me a dollar and told me to keep the change. "Thanks so much for the info."

"How do I get the tickets?" I asked, as she started out the door.

"I'll have them sent to you."

"You want my name and address?" I asked, as she hurried through the door. She never answered.

I wasn't going to hold my breath.

The Wolf Pack had been trapped in the cave for three days a few years ago. We had seen everything there was to see in those caves. I knew there was nothing in them they were looking for. I looked out to see her driving away in a dark blue pickup, the dust blocking the view of the license plate again. I should have looked out earlier.

I wondered which of the men her prized boyfriend was. Was it the skinny balding guy who tried to snatch Rock or his partner with the long sideburns?

Dad had gone up to the farm to help Papaw with the fencing. I would wait until he got home to tell him about the woman. I was working on a plan in my head.

Raven

James Ernest was beating on a six foot log of white oak. He had stripped the bark and he was now loosening the rings of the log so he could pull strips from it. We then cut the strips in the desired size for the basket we were making. I watched him as he worked. He was so careful not to make a mistake.

I wondered how and why I got so fortunate to have him as my boyfriend. We've talked about marriage when he finishes college. I had no idea how I would exist without him. I dread the day he will leave for college. I would never ask him not to go. He has a dream of becoming a teacher, and the only way to make it come true is by going to college.

I knew he would be an excellent teacher. You can see it in his eyes. You can see it with his patience. He's always helping my brothers and sisters with their homework. He doesn't do the work for them, but he teaches them how they can do it themselves.

There is not a bad bone in his body. I worry about him due to some of the things he does. When he walks through the woods at

86

night, I worry. When he and Timmy get mixed up in solving trouble in the county, I worry. When he takes up for me at school, I worry.

I would do anything for the boy. I've given him my time. I've given him my love. I'd give him my life.

Some of the abuse I have at school I can ignore. Some of it makes me want to give up and quit. I know that my younger siblings are going through the same things. Junior seems to handle it better than anyone. He makes friends easily and stays out of harm's way the best he can.

I don't understand what makes white people hate us. And I don't mean all white people, just the ones who do. Even though we have been targeted many times here in Morgan County, I love the folks in our community.

My friends and family are great. Our church is great. I pray I never have to leave the community. I'd like to stay here like a baby bird in a nest and feel the protection that surrounds me.

James Ernest looks up from his work and smiles at me as I'm weaving an egg basket. I get up and walk over to him. I lean down and kiss him. His smile gets even wider.

*P*apaw and Dad arrived at the store around three that afternoon. Mom tells them dinner will be ready in fifteen minutes. The store was empty, so I have time to tell them about the woman and what she wanted. I did, and then added, "She was driving the dark blue pickup."

"I'm sure the men sent her in to get some info," Papaw said.

"What did you tell her?" Dad asked.

I explained what I had told her and why. I then went on to say, "I thought maybe it was a way to catch them. We could keep a lookout at the creek across from the cave. When they show up, we nab them."

I could see Dad thinking about my plan. He finally said, "There are a couple of problems with that. We have no idea when they might try to get in the cave, or even if they bought your story. Also, I don't have the manpower to keep a deputy staking the area twenty-four hours a day."

"They would pretty much only have to look for them in daylight hours. Who would wade the creek in the dark?" I said.

"Timmy is right about that," Papaw said.

"I would think they would start their trip between here and Cat's place. That would be the easiest access to the creek since they don't know the area. You guys could keep an eye out for them. I can tell Cat to watch for them," Dad said.

Mamaw called out that Sunday dinner was ready. I was hungry, and I could smell cherry dumplings on the stove for dessert.

That evening around seven, Rock came up out of the creek and crossed the road to the store. I was glad she wasn't taking a chance by walking the road. She looked very pretty as she walked toward me. She looked grown, like a young woman. She was barefoot and carrying a pair of flip flops. Her tanned wet legs were glistening in the sunlight.

She walked up the steps of the porch and sat beside me on the porch swing. She looked at me and grinned. She then kissed me, and we sat in silence looking at one another.

"Do you ever miss Susie? I mean as far as her being your girlfriend," she asked.

The question came so far out of the blue. I wasn't expecting it. I kept my eyes on hers as I studied to see if I might find a reason for the inquiry. She stared back at me as I thought.

"No," I finally said. "Not as a girlfriend. I do at times miss talking to her as a friend. I mean, we have been friends for ten years, and now I seldom talk to her unless we're in a group."

"I worry that you will go back to her when she wants you back," Rock said. She didn't say if, she said when, as though she knew one day Susie would want me back.

She continued, "I know everyone was shocked when you two broke up. I also know everyone expects the two of you to get back together like it's written in a book somewhere. The thing is, I don't want it to happen. I've fallen in love with you, Timmy. I wanted you to know how I felt in case you think about going back to her. I won't blame myself for not letting you know how I feel."

"I…"

"Don't say anything. I don't expect you to tell me you love me, and I don't expect you to make me promises. I want to live each day the best we can and see where that takes us," Rock said. She then kissed me again.

I wanted to tell her that I loved her too, but she stopped me. She was right, I couldn't make promises. I didn't know what would happen. I had promised Susie and look what had transpired.

I also knew we both were still young. I was going to be sixteen in July and she would turn sixteen in August. We were young, but not too young to make promises or to know what we wanted. Right now I wanted Rock as by girlfriend, not Susie.

Chapter 10
The Auction

Friday, June 25

We were to meet the auctioneer that morning at nine at the farm where the auction was taking place. The whole farm was up for sale. The lady that had lived there had died at the age of ninety-nine. We were in a small community called Cottle in Morgan County, which was southeast of West Liberty on State Route 7. James Ernest and Purty drove both the Wolf Pack and the Bear Troop to the site.

Mr. Harney was there, and he introduced us to the auctioneer, Mr. Emmet Pollard. We were to help go through the house and put things in piles. Some things were going to be thrown away. Other things were to be separated and numbered for the auction. The barn also had to be inventoried. Things that could be used, or be used for parts, were to be brought outside and placed in rows for the auction.

The guys headed for the barn and the girls to the house. There were also a couple of old sheds and a cellar we would need to go through. It was another hot day. We quickly worked up a sweat. An old tractor and pickup sat in the barn. We tried to get them started with no luck. James Ernest began tinkering with the tractor while the rest of us pulled out plows and tools and old antique looking things we weren't even sure what they had been used for. We had fun guessing their use.

We all took a break at lunch time. We gathered under a big maple tree in the side yard to eat.

"How are things going in the house?" I asked the girls.

Susie said, "I think it's sad going through a person's stuff after they've died. Things that meant so much to the person now put out for people to bid for. The items won't be nearly as important to the person who gets them."

"There was a pretty baby doll in her bedroom, and I wonder who it had belonged to," Francis said.

"That's all swell until you have to go through the ladies old underwear drawer. There were big white bloomers with holes in them. I don't think she would have had to pull them down to use the outhouse," Sadie said.

We all began laughing.

Tucky said, "Purty found a Playboy magazine in the barn loft. We didn't see him for an hour after he found it."

"It had a neat article in it," Purty said, as we laughed.

"What was the article about?" Shauna asked.

"It was about Marilyn Monroe," Purty said and smiled.

"I wonder who the magazine belonged to, her husband or maybe a son," Susie said.

Sadie said, "If the bloomers are a clue, I would guess her husband."

"We're all awful," Raven said.

It was time to get back to work. I went back to the barn. We still had things in the loft to carry down. Mr. Pollard began going through the stuff we had lined up. He had Tucky and Purty pull the things he thought were garbage from the lines.

"We need to see if the pickup will start. If it doesn't, then you need to push it out and wash it to get the dirt and grime off it," we were directed.

Mr. Pollard handed James Ernest the keys. We went inside to try and get it started. The pickup started right up even though it looked as if it hadn't been driven in years. It was a medium blue 1956 Chevrolet. The only way I could see the color was to rub a wet rag on it. Once we got it washed, it was really sharp.

We finally got done around five that evening and headed home. We had to be back by seven the next morning to bring the home goods outside and place them on tables for the auction. It would begin at ten.

I didn't see anything I was interested in bidding for.

We had kept our eyes open for the dark blue pickup all week with no luck. Cat was also keeping a close eye on things, especially since Treehawk had tried to kill him.

Rock came to the store with me after we had finished working at the auction site. After eating supper we decided to wade up Devil's creek to check on the cave. It was still warm and the creek water would feel nice. We entered the creek at the bridge in front of the store and began wading. I wore old shoes while Rock went barefoot.

We talked about the day we had spent and we laughed about the bloomers and Purty. We splashed each other and we kissed every so often. When we got parallel to where Cat lived I heard something in the trees. Cat stepped out onto the creek bank.

"Hello, Cat."

"Hi, Tim, Rock. I heard voices and wanted to make sure it wasn't Treehawk and his gang," Cat explained.

"We're heading up to the stone wall to check on things. It's a great evening to be in the water," I said.

"Be careful. Yell or howl if you need me," Cat said.

"Thanks," Rock said. He turned and disappeared into the trees.

We continued up the creek. Rock waded over closer to me and put her arms around me. She kissed me and when I opened my eyes I saw a head above the water. A water moccasin snake swam ten feet from us.

"Don't move," I warned.

She slowly turned her head and saw the snake swimming past her. The snake was also known as a cottonmouth. It was deadly venomous. I was ready to grab it by its tail and toss it if I had to. I watched it to make sure it didn't turn toward Rock. It seemed happy to leave us alone and continue on its way.

We stayed frozen in our spots until it was far downstream. I hadn't realized I had been holding my breath until I exhaled. We continued our trip up the creek. There were a lot of different water snakes around that weren't dangerous. Seldom had I ever seen a moccasin in the creeks.

Fifteen minutes later we were standing in the creek looking up at the cave opening in the hundred foot rock wall. There was no sign that the gang had been there. I thought I might see a rope hanging over the ledge reaching down to the cave. The Wolf Pack had built a rope ladder and tied it to a tree and then climbed down to get in the cave.

I thought that maybe they had come to see the opening and decided it wasn't what they were looking for. Perhaps I would get another visit from the lady professor. The thought of her being a professor made me laugh. If she was a professor I wasn't sure why James Ernest was going to college.

Rock and I turned and began the trek back to the store. When we got to where we could turn and follow the small stream to Cat's place, we did.

He opened the door to his hobbit house and stepped out to meet us. "Any luck?"

"No. We didn't see any sign of them," I answered.

"Can you visit for a while?"

"Sure," I said.

"Let's go up to the treehouse. It's cooler up in the trees," Cat told us.

We climbed the ladder to the treehouse deck and took a seat in the handmade chairs he had crafted.

"I was at the store earlier today and Betty told me you two were helping with an auction," Cat said.

"We were there most of the day," Rock answered.

"We have to be back tomorrow at seven," I added.

"I need a small dresser for my clothes," Cat said.

"I remember seeing one," Rock said. "It was nice."

"I don't have a lot of things, but I'm tired of them lying around the house."

"Can you, or someone, bid on it for me?" he asked.

"How much would you spend for one?" I asked.

"I'll give you fifteen dollars. See if you can get it for that." Cat reached into his pocket and handed me the money.

"What got you involved with the auction?" Cat asked.

"Some of us had helped out once before. I was at the bank a couple of weeks ago and mentioned to Mr. Harney that we were going to the Smokies and that we needed money for the trip. He suggested it. We're going to hold a car wash also," I explained.

The sun was beginning to set, so we said our goodbyes and headed back to the store. Once we were there Dad drove Rock home.

Saturday, June 26

*J*ames Ernest and I were up at the crack of dawn. Papaw was there to watch the store. I told him about the '56 Chevy pickup and how nice it was. James Ernest and I gobbled down some cereal and a snack cake. I grabbed an RC Cola and we were out the door. We had to pick up some of the gang while Purty was picking up the others.

We made it to the auction site a couple of minutes past seven. Purty still had not arrived. We quickly unloaded and began setting up tables in the yard and putting up the folding chairs the auctioneer had. We turned the front yard into the auction site.

It was seven-thirty, and Purty still hadn't arrived with the others. Raven, Junior, Rock, Tucky, James Ernest and I were there doing all the work. It became eight o'clock and Purty still wasn't there.

Purty was bringing Sadie, Francis, Susie, Shauna and Rhonda. We were carrying out the stuff from the house and placing it on the tables. A few early arrivals were beginning to sift through the goods to see what they wanted as we brought it out.

Mr. Pollard, the auctioneer, walked over to me and asked, "Weren't there more of you yesterday?"

"Yep, something must have happened. They should have been here an hour ago," I said.

"You need to make sure we get everything out here," he said. He seemed frustrated.

Eight-thirty came and went and Purty was still a no-show.

"My wife will show you guys what to hold up when the bidding starts," he said.

I knew from the last auction that we would need to hold up the item as it was being bid on so that everyone could see it. We would even walk around so people could get a closer look.

95

At ten minutes till nine Purty's truck pulled into the farm. I could tell by their faces the girls weren't happy. They began helping us carry out the last few things. The crowd was building as the starting time was nearing. The tables were crowded with folks looking through the stuff.

Men and boys were near the barn looking at all the tools and farm equipment.

"What happened?" I asked Purty.

"I got a late start and then I had a flat tire," Purty explained.

Sadie injected, "And guess what he doesn't know how to do?"

"He doesn't know how to change a tire," Rhonda said.

"He had to walk a half mile to find a phone and then call his dad to come help us," Sadie said.

"Well, all's well that ends well," I said, trying to defuse the situation.

Purty looked pretty deflated. The girls must have really raked him over the coals.

Papaw and Mamaw were at the auction with Homer and Ruby. Shauna's younger sister, Sally, was spending the day at the store with Janie.

I showed Papaw the dresser we needed to bid on for Cat. He said he would bid on it for me.

At ten o'clock the auctioneer welcomed everyone and told them how the auction would work. He then started the bidding for the first item. Sadie held up a pretty bowl and the bidding began. We formed a line and took turns holding up different things. For some reason it seemed the bidding was higher when the girls held up the pieces.

Mrs. Pollard soon decided that only the girls would hold up the pieces and that we guys would deliver the sold items and take care of other things. It took two hours to sell all the small items that were on the tables. Mamaw had bought a couple of aprons. Ruby had bought a serving bowl. Papaw bought a pocket watch that had a long chain.

We then started selling the furniture. The dresser finally came up for bidding. It started out at five dollars, and then six, and then seven. Papaw still hadn't bid as I watched him. It went to ten and the auctioneer said, "Going once. Going ... Do I hear eleven?"

Papaw then bid eleven. The lady he bid against looked upset. She gave Papaw the evil eye. She then bid twelve dollars. Papaw bid thirteen. She bid fourteen after thinking a bit. Papaw came right back bidding fifteen with no hesitation.

The woman was beside herself. She huffed and made quite a show before saying, "Fifteen and a half."

The auctioneer said, "Hadn't thought of that. Do I hear sixteen?"

I knew we had reached our limit. The woman would get the dresser. Papaw yelled out, "Seventeen dollars."

The old cow then flicked her hand at Papaw as if she was swatting a fly and gave up.

"Sold for seventeen dollars," Mr. Pollard announced.

Rock and I carried the dresser to James Ernest's pickup and placed it in the bed.

While they were selling the rest of the furniture I looked to see where Papaw was. I saw him and Homer checking out the Chevy pickup. James Ernest had slipped away and started the vehicle for them. Mr. Pollard announced that the vehicle was running now if anyone was interested in buying it. A few other men made their way over to it.

Papaw's truck was old, and I thought he was thinking of replacing it. Or he could have been just wasting time.

The furniture was sold and Mr. Pollard made his way over to the pickup and the tractor. He first sold the tractor. James Ernest was able to get the tractor started and it sold for seventy-five dollars.

Then they started the bidding for the pickup. The bidding started at a hundred dollars. Someone bid two hundred. The next bid was two-fifty. Papaw bid two-seventy five.

The bidding began going up by five dollar increments. A man had bid three-forty and then Papaw bid three-fifty. I was holding my breath as the other man looked at his wife for directions. He then bid three-fifty five and Papaw bid three-sixty five. The man looked at his wife and then gave up. Papaw had bought the pickup for three hundred and sixty-five dollars.

Papaw looked over at me, and I smiled. I was happy he had bought it.

The rest of the farm tools were sold, and the auction was over. We were busy helping folks load things into their cars and trucks. We were folding up chairs and tables and stacking them in the auctioneer's truck.

Mr. Harney came over to us as we were about to leave and said, "You guys did a great job. You earned your money. Mr. Pollard was very pleased with everything." He handed me an envelope with money in it.

"You're still doing the car wash at the bank in two weeks?" he asked.

"Yes," I answered.

Everyone thanked him for the money and he turned and left.

"How much did we make?" Purty asked.

We had all agreed that the money would go to pay for anyone who couldn't come up with money for the trip. I opened the envelope and counted out a hundred and fifty dollars. It seemed like a lot, but when we broke it down, the twelve of us had each worked for two days for $12.50 each.

"That doesn't seem like much," Purty complained.

"It's enough to pay for three or four of us who wouldn't have been able to go. I think we should be happy with that," James Ernest said.

"Plus, I think we all had a good time getting to hang out," I said.

"You girls will have to wear bikinis at the car wash. We could get a million cars," Purty said.

Shauna slapped him on the arm.

Chapter 11
Again

Monday, June 28

James Ernest spent the night at the Washington farm. Mom and Janie had gone shopping with Miss Rebecca. Dad left for work. I was watching the store by myself. Rock had told me she would come spend the day with me again. She had nothing at all to do at her house except getting teased by her sisters.

It was hotter than blue blazes this morning, and I knew it would get worse. I already had the floor fan in the doorway between the living room and the store. I had the backdoor and the front door open, trying to get air to circulate around the house. So far it was mostly blowing hot air from one spot to another.

A delivery was made around eight-thirty, and I began stocking the shelves with the can goods. I was expecting Rock at any time. I was surprised she hadn't gotten there by then. There were no fishermen thus far due to it being a Monday and the heat. I didn't expect any.

Suddenly, the front door flew open and in came the two men from the dark blue pickup. I didn't have time to do anything. I was standing across the room from the counter unable to get to where the shotgun was lying.

"Let's go," the man with the sideburns said.

"You need gas again?" I asked. He grabbed me by my collar and led me through the house and out the back door. Apparently he did not need gasoline. I knew I could out run them if I could get loose.

As though they knew my thoughts, the bald skinny guy pulled a gun from under his shirt and said, "Don't even think of trying to escape!" He placed the barrel against the side of my head.

"What do you want?"

We were walking toward the lake. It was a bad time for there not to be any fishermen at the lake. I wondered what Rock would do if she came to the store and no one was there.

"You are going to show us where the cave is, or we're the last people you'll ever see," sideburns said.

"I told your girlfriend where the cave was," I said.

"Yeah, we saw that. There's no way to get to it. You sent us on a wild goose chase, and I don't like goose."

"We know there's a cave somewhere near this lake. You are going to show us where it is," the man with the gun said.

"I don't know of another cave," I said.

The other man then said, "Shoot him and dump his body in the lake."

"Wait, wait, wait," I said.

"Did something jog your memory?" he said as he pecked me on the head with the gun. I was praying it wouldn't go off.

"There's a cavern back behind the lake, but there's nothing in it. It's more like a hole in the ground. Why do you want to see inside a cave?"

"You don't need to know. You need to lead us to it."

"You need a rope to get down in it," I said.

"What are you talking about? Why would we need a rope to get in a cave?"

"I told you. The opening is on the ground and there's a twenty foot drop down to the bottom," I explained.

"Do you have a rope?"

"We have one in the shed behind the store," I told him.

"Is it unlocked?"

I nodded.

"Give me the gun, and go get the rope." The man with the sideburns seemed to be the boss. The other bald man looked frustrated but did as he was told. He ran toward the store. He ran like a man with two bad knees. We stood on the west side of the lake and waited for the guy to get back. Hopefully, Rock wouldn't see him in the shed and confront him.

"What do you think is in the cave?" I asked.

He stared at me like I was stupid. I knew it was a stupid question. I wasn't sure if I was stupid myself.

"Where's your professor girlfriend?"

"What?"

"The girl I told about the other cave. She told me she would send me UK basketball tickets." I was just messing with him to see what he would say.

"Don't hold your breath."

"That's what I said."

We then saw the balding creep walking over the dam with a rope over his shoulder. When he arrived I was poked in the side with the gun and told to lead the way. I was tired of getting hit and poked with the gun. As we walked I was trying to come up with a plan.

We walked past the slanted rock and continued toward the swimming hole. I thought of diving into the water and disappearing into the Indian cave, but the man grabbed my arm and led me around the water.

We got to the spot where we had to climb the hill. Sideburns gave the gun back to his buddy and climbed first. I went second, followed by baldy. We made it to the top after the last guy struggled to make it up the hill.

We walked to the three large boulders. I was afraid they might kill me once I showed them the cave, so I said, "If this isn't the one, I just thought of another cave I could show you."

"Your memory seems to be improving by the minute."

I pointed to the hole and said, "This is it."

Rock

I knew Timmy would have the fans going in the house and I looked forward to sitting in front of the biggest one. I was sweating from every pore of my body. I opened the screen door to find an empty store. I took my spot and waited for him to return. I figured he was in the bathroom.

After ten minutes I went searching for him. I checked his bedroom and the bathroom. I yelled out his name. I checked the backyard. He wasn't there.

I knew he wouldn't go up to the lake and leave the store empty. There were no vehicles in the lot. I began to worry. I knew he was in some kind of trouble, but what could I do. I had no idea where he could be. I went to the front porch and yelled out his name. I then went to the back porch and did the same.

Did the two men return? Did Treehawk come into the store? I thought of going to get Cat. I could lock up the store and go, but I didn't have keys to get back inside. I went to the back door and locked it. I came to the front door and locked it. I then went to Timmy's bedroom and took the screen out of the window and climbed through. I closed the window to within a crack. I could always climb back inside.

I ran. I ran as fast as I could to Cat's place. The heat was suffocating me as my legs churned up the road. With each stride my worry deepened. I cut off the road and ran through the field. I was ready to collapse by the time I made it there. Cat saw me as I approached and ran to catch me as I fell to the ground.

He picked me up and hurried back to his place and quickly gave me a cup of water.

"What is wrong?"

"Timmy is missing. Something awful has happened. I just know it."

"Is no one at the store?"

I was trying to get my breath back. I was sucking air in. I managed to tell him, "I was supposed…to help him in the store today. Betty went shopping. I got there and he was gone. The store is empty. I think they took him."

"Let's go," Cat said. I didn't feel as though I could go anywhere. He ran to get his horse, Friend. He jumped on top of the horse and then pulled me up behind him.

"Hang on."

We were off in a flash. I had never been on a horse before and here I was riding for the first time bareback with a Shawnee Indian. We made it to the store in no time. Cat tied Friend up to the porch. The doors were still closed and locked. I explained how I had gotten out of the house and how we could get back in.

He jumped through the window and came around and unlocked the door.

"See if you can find the phone book," Cat said.

I looked behind the counter and it was on a lower shelf. Cat looked up Martin's number and dialed it.

"Hello, Corie," Cat greeted Timmy's mamaw.

"Would Timmy be there at the farm?"

He listened and then asked to speak to Martin. "Martin, Timmy is missing. I was hoping he was up there."

"Okay."

He hung up and said, "They are on their way."

"I didn't think of calling anyone. We don't have a phone, so I guess it didn't come to mind. That was so stupid of me."

By the time our conversation was over Martin drove up. They exited and hurried onto the porch.

"What has happened now? It is always something with that boy," Corie said, as she wrung her apron with her hands.

"This all seems to be about finding a certain cave. I'm guessing they took Timmy to force him to show them the cave," Cat said.

"I believe you're probably right," Martin said.

"Have you called Hagar?"

"No," both Cat and I said.

"Where would Timmy lead them?" Cat asked.

"I'll go phone the station," Corie said.

Martin answered Cat's question, "He may have taken them to the Tattoo Man cave up behind the lake."

"Do you know where it is?" Cat asked.

"I do."

"Let's go."

I followed the men off the porch. Martin stopped and said, "Rock, you need to stay here."

"I'm going," I said.

"You need to stay so you can tell Hagar where we've gone," Martin said.

I didn't like it at all. But I stayed and waited.

The creep with the sideburns looked down into the hole. He pulled a flashlight from his back pocket and pointed it down into the cave.

He told the other man to tie the rope off to the tree. He did as he was told. He then told me to go down first.

"Why do I need to go down? I'll stay up here," I said.

"How about you do what I tell you?" He tapped me on the head again with the gun, only a little harder. I was getting real tired of getting hit in the head.

I got down on my knees and then placed my legs over the edge and scooted down as I held the rope. I climbed down hand under hand to the bottom. He then sent the bald guy down. He didn't have the brains of a chicken with its head cut off. He slid down the rope and then yelled out, "Lordy, Lordy! My hands!"

He held his hands out in front of him and I could see, even in the dim light that his hands were skinned up from sliding down the rope. "Quit yelling, you fool!" the other man yelled. Why were crooks always so stupid?

Sideburns then made his way down the rope without cutting up his hands.

When he reached the bottom, his buddy said, "Look at my hands. They're chewed up."

"You dummy." He didn't show a lot of sympathy for the dummy.

"Where do you think it is?"

"We'll have to search." He then turned to me and asked, "Do you know any hiding spots in here?"

My first thought was the spiral shaped hole I had crawled through when I slid into the Indian cave. I knew they couldn't fit into the hole. I knew that I couldn't fit in the hole any longer. I was nine when I squeezed through it. I had been trapped in the cave, and the small hole had been my only chance of escaping.

I decided to tell them about the hole, knowing it wouldn't help them, but by showing them I was cooperating, and maybe they wouldn't kill me. I thought there was a good chance they might kill me if they found what they were looking for.

"Over there is a hole in the wall," I said, pointing to it. He shined the light on the hole and they hurried over. The man with the gun stuck his arm inside the hole with no luck.

"Do you know where this hole goes?" he asked me.

"No idea. I can't fit through it," I lied.

"There are small pockets all around the cave," I said.

He began shining the light all along the wall of the circular cave. Most of the small pockets went only a foot or so into the stone wall. He looked at the large rock in the center of the floor and said, "It could be under that rock."

His buddy looked at him with a befuddled look. "There's no way to move that thing." It was the smartest thing I'd heard him say. The stone was a rectangle shape that was close to six foot long and four foot wide and three foot high. It reminded me of a casket tomb. I wondered what it was that they thought could be under the stone.

After considering it, he continued his search along the wall. He finally came to the large hole that I had climbed into when I was searching for a way out. I knew it went a few feet and then turned, only to come to a dead end. I knew there was nothing inside it.

"If you told me what you were looking for maybe I could help," I offered.

He took his flashlight and tapped me on the head with it and said, "Stand over there and keep quiet." I backed away into the darkness against the wall.

The man began to crawl into the hole. He had the flashlight in his mouth and the gun tucked inside his belt.

Rock

The cruiser flew into the gravel lot and Timmy's stepdad quickly opened the door and ran to the porch.

Corie and I had been rocking and worrying while we waited for him to arrive. I told Sheriff Cane what had happened as quickly as possible.

"But no one is sure where he was taken?" the sheriff half-way asked, knowing the answer.

"Not for sure," I said.

"It was their best guess," Corie said.

"Do you know where this cave is?" Hagar asked me.

"Yes."

"You need to lead me then," he told me.

I was so happy to be doing something. Sitting on the porch was doing nothing but wasting time with worrying. I led the sheriff to the lake and around it. I was so worried about them not being at the cave. In that case where could they have taken him? I knew no one knew the answer to that question.

As the man with the long sideburns crawled into the hole, the other man had his head stuck in the hole, trying to ask him if he saw anything. Now was my time to get away. The gun was with the man inside the hole, so baldy couldn't shoot me, and I figured there was no way he could out-climb me with his hands in the shape they were in.

I quietly made my way to the rope. This was my second try to climb this rope. The first time I was skinny nine-year-old, ninety pound weakling. I wasn't that kid any longer. I grabbed hold of the rope and began climbing. I was half way up when the bald guy said something to me. I was no longer there to answer.

I found new energy and climbed faster hand-over-hand, my feet wrapped around the rope like they had taught us in gym class.

"Where are you?" I heard him ask.

I wasn't going to answer. He'd have a hard time knocking me on the head as I made it to the top. I pulled my way over the edge and rolled onto the ground. Just as I was rolling to a stop I heard footsteps coming. I was hoping it wasn't Treehawk.

"Timmy!" I heard Papaw yell out.

He then said, "Here he is!"

I looked up to see Papaw and Cat heading my way. I didn't have time to acknowledge them. I took hold on the rope and began pulling it out. Suddenly the rope stopped, and then was pulled back. I jerked it as hard as I could and I heard a scream. I knew I had slid the rope through his scraped, scratched, aching raw hands.

I pulled the rope all the way out and threw it to the side. Papaw and Cat had made their way to me, and Papaw hugged me.

"Are you okay?" Papaw asked.

"I'm fine. The two men are down in the cave with no way out," I told them.

Chapter 12
Stuck in this Hellhole

*R*ock yelled out my name, "Tim," when she saw me standing with Papaw and Cat. She ran into my arms and kissed me.

"I've been scared out of my head," she said quietly.

Dad stopped short of me and I heard Cat tell him that the two men were in the underground cave with no way to escape. Dad started to go close to the hole.

"No!" I yelled out. He stopped and turned to me. "One of them has a gun. He could shoot anyone that looks down the hole."

We all took a seat in the shade under a tree. The heat was beating down on all of us. The shade brought a little relief. I told them exactly what had happened and how I had escaped from them. "They are not very smart," I finished.

"Most criminals aren't," Dad said.

"Especially the ones who get caught," Papaw said.

"What are you going to do now?" I asked.

"I'll see if they will give up peacefully. If not, then I guess they will starve to death down there."

We heard the two men arguing. They were shouting at each other as each of them blamed the other.

Dad stood up and walked near the hole without getting close enough to get shot. "This is Sheriff Cane. There is no way out other than the way you went in. You have no way to escape. You can throw your gun up and make this easy, or you can stay down there and starve until we have to carry your sorry, dead bodies out."

"We will never surrender, copper!" I recognized the voice of the man with the sideburns. He sounded like an old time Cagney movie.

"That's up to you."

"The ceiling of the cave is covered with bats," I told Dad.

"One other thing, if you point your flashlight at the ceiling, you'll notice the cave is full of bats."

He gave them enough time to shine the flashlight on the ceiling to see that he was telling the truth.

"If you don't come out now we will seal the opening up for the rest of the day and night. The bats get very hungry and upset if they can't fly out at dark to look for food. I'll give you five minutes to decide. I'm tired of messing with you."

I heard baldy say, "Bats freak me out."

"You would rather go to prison, dummy?"

"We have no way out. We are going to prison either way. I want out!" he shouted up.

We then heard a gunshot. It echoed out of the cave. I could hear the beating of wings and screeching sounds. The bats were going crazy. We then heard screaming and shouting. I figured sideburns had shot his partner, but then I heard his voice.

"Are you out of your mind? Why would you shoot that thing in here?" he yelled.

"You need to calm down."

"Calm down. What part of this do you not understand? We have no way out. We're stuck down here in this hellhole with bats. I want out!" he yelled again.

"No one is coming out until the gun is thrown up here!" Dad yelled down. "You have one minute left!"

Sideburns

"Listen to me," I whispered to Sid. "If we surrender we go to prison. If we stay in here tonight we can search for another way out. We might be able to chip that one opening bigger to where we can squeeze down."

"But we don't know where it goes," his buddy said.

"Fifteen seconds left," the sheriff yelled down.

"Look over there. There's a small light coming from that opening. It's a possibility. If we don't find a way out tonight we can surrender tomorrow. It will be the same."

"Okay. But I don't like it."

"What is your answer?" the sheriff yelled down.

When we didn't answer the light from above went black. They had covered the entrance with something. Fifteen seconds later my flashlight quit working, throwing us into total darkness. I hadn't counted on that.

The men had found a large flat rock that would cover the entrance. It took Dad, Cat and me to carry it over and place it to where it was covering the opening.

"We will see if they've changed their minds in the morning. It's really the only option we have. I'm not sending someone down and risk someone getting killed to get them. They can't go anywhere. Can they?" Dad asked as he looked at me.

I wasn't sure what to say. I didn't want to tell them about the opening to the Indian cave. Plus, I didn't think there was any way

112

they could get through the opening. They didn't have any tools to use to make the opening larger. They would have to make the opening twice its size for them to fit through.

"No," I answered. I saw Papaw looking at me. Papaw knew about the cave and the opening. But he had promised he wouldn't tell anyone else. Cat had untied the rope to carry it.

We turned to leave the men trapped in the cave. We slid down the hillside and walked back to the store. As we came down over the dam I heard Mamaw yell out, "Here they come! They have Timmy!"

The back screen opened and folks began spilling out of the kitchen. I saw most everyone except Mom. I figured she hadn't returned from shopping yet. Susie ran up to hug me. Raven did the same. James Ernest put his arm around my shoulders and said, "I should have stayed at the store with you today. I'm sorry."

Everyone gathered on the porch, and I proceeded to tell them what had happened that morning. Rock would cut in and tell them what she had done to get help. She made the story even more exciting.

The people either gasped or laughed when they heard we had sealed them up in the cave for the night.

"So they're in that cave with all those bats for the whole night?" Coal said. She added, "You might open that hole in the morning and have two vampires fly out at you." Everyone laughed.

"You'd better take a cross and some garlic with you," Uncle Morton added.

Deputy Stutts arrived and then left to find their dark blue pickup truck. He came back to tell us he had found it about a quarter mile up the road toward the quarry. He said they had pulled it off the road and into some weeds.

It was blazing hot outside, and the inside of the store wasn't a lot better. Some folks began leaving for their homes. Some of them had window air conditioners that would cool one room. Mom had talked about buying a couple for the house. I was all for it.

Around two that afternoon Mom returned from the shopping trip. She and Miss Rebecca were surprised to see so many people there. She then stopped short of the porch and asked, "What happened?"

The rest of the day was spent telling and retelling the story to folks that came to the store just to hear about it. We sold a lot of soda pop bottles and ice cream. I think most of the people just wanted to stick their hands into the ice and the coolers. I saw Robert Easterling stick his head inside the pop cooler.

I thought Mom was going to have a fit as she heard about it. "I'm never leaving the store again," she said. We knew that wasn't true.

During supper that evening, Dad told Mom that he was going to spend the night up at the cave entrance to make sure nothing happened.

"What could happen?" Mom protested.

"Treehawk is still out there somewhere. We aren't sure what his relationship is with these two men, if any at all. If he catches wind of what happened he might try to rescue them."

"I could go with you," I offered.

"I should go," James Ernest said.

"Neither of you are going. You both are going to stay here and watch the house. Make sure the doors are locked tonight," Dad said.

I found out later that Papaw had told Dad that they should watch the swimming hole. He wouldn't tell Dad why, but told him there was a good reason. I also found out that Cat went with Dad to the cave. Cat watched the entrance hole, and Dad slept near the swimming hole.

Sid - Baldy

Darkness, all around us was darkness. It was black nothing. I was scared out of my mind. The bats began swooping and screeching about an hour ago. They dove at our heads and we swatted and cussed them with every cuss word I knew. I was beginning to think George wasn't as smart as he thought he was.

He talked me into staying down here. How stupid was that! I swung at another diving bat and actually hit it, which scared me worse. Would I get rabies?

I was hungry. We hadn't eaten since breakfast. All we could afford was an egg McMuffin from McDonalds. I was sitting by myself at the small opening where a small glimpse of light had escaped. But it was now dark. It was our only way out, but our attempt to enlarge it was pointless.

We banged around the edges with a rock, but all that happened was the rock in our hands broke into pieces. The banging we did irritated the bats and they screeched even more. I had felt something squishy on the cave floor as I walked around in the dark. I bent over to touch it. I brought it to my nose and quickly realized I had stuck my hand in bat poop. I was then afraid of what disease I would get from the bat poop with the open scrapes on my hands.

I wanted out of this place. A prison cell would feel like Heaven compared to the Hell I was in at the moment.

George and I had stopped talking to each other. He blamed me for the predicament we were in because I let the kid escape. I blamed him for taking the gun inside the hole, leaving me with nothing. I blamed him for not surrendering when we had a chance. I blamed him for the whole plan of finding a fortune in a cave. He was the big brother and should have looked after me. What a fine mess we now found ourselves in.

I was sick of this place. I was sick of bats. I hated caves. I was tired of crime and wanted to see my mommy.

Tuesday, June 29

I had so much trouble sleeping. I woke up every couple of hours, or maybe it was every few minutes. I was thinking about what had happened during the day. It made me think of the Tattoo Man. My mind would go from that day six years earlier to now.

If it wasn't for the bats home I would be all for filling the cave in with rock and dirt. I felt as if that cave would be the death of me.

I also had learned just before bed that Dad and Cat were spending the night keeping watch on the area. I worried that somehow the two men would escape, although I knew it was impossible. I worried about Treehawk.

If the two men were in cahoots with Treehawk then I knew he would be worried when they didn't show up at the end of the day. Would he be out there in the dark looking for them and find Cat and Dad?

I crept out of bed at five a. m., grabbed my clothes, and quietly left the bedroom. I noticed the front door was unlocked. I knew we had locked it before going to bed. I opened the door and looked out and saw Mom sitting in one of the rockers with her head bowed.

She was asleep, praying or dead. She raised her head and said, "You couldn't sleep either?"

"I tossed around all night," I said. "Why arc you up?"

"I was praying and drinking coffee."

"I guess both help."

"I am so sorry about leaving you alone yesterday. I would die if something had happened to you. I should have known better since we knew those men were in the area and had confronted you before," Mom said.

"It's not your fault, Mom. If someone else had been here it would probably mean that two of us would have been in danger. I'm really glad Rock hadn't gotten here sooner."

"Cat told me when Rock discovered you were not here she ran all the way to his place. He told me she collapsed when she got there. Can you imagine running all that way in that heat? It shows how much she cares for you. I've grown very fond of her."

"I didn't know she had run that whole way, wow," I said.

"The deputies are supposed to be here at daybreak to help bring the two men in, unless they still won't come out," Mom said.

"I figure they will be ready. The batteries in their flashlight won't last forever. They probably didn't grow any fonder of the bats during the night," I said. I laughed at the thought of them running around the cave as the bats swarmed their heads. I told Mom why I was laughing and she joined.

I saw movement in the dark. I jumped a little in my seat. Coty climbed the steps and came over for me to scratch behind his ears. He would nudge my arm or hand when he wanted scratched.

I would take my hand away and he would raise his nose and nudge me again, wanting more. I was happy to oblige.

"I'm really looking forward to our Smoky Mountain trip," I said.

"So am I. It should be a lot of fun," Mom said. Anything would be more fun than what we had been through lately. I knew all of us could use a break.

"Are you taking Janie?"

"Hagar and I talked about it and decided it wouldn't be fair to leave her. We're going to tell her she can ask a friend to go with her."

"As long as it's not Delma and Thelma," I said.

"God, no, I couldn't handle that."

"Who then?"

"She's gotten close to Sally and she's been through a lot also," Mom said.

"That would be nice."

The sky was getting lighter by the minute. It wasn't long until we saw a police car coming toward the store. The two deputies got out of the car and approached us.

"Hello, Betty, Timmy," Deputy Clouse greeted us. Deputy Stutts tipped his hat.

"Hello, deputies," Mom said.

"Have any trouble last night?"

"Not that we know of," Mom answered.

"Sheriff Cane said Timmy would lead us to the cave," Deputy Stutts said.

"Sure," I said.

"We're hoping they give up peacefully," Deputy Clouse added.

The door opened and James Ernest walked out. He said he would stay at the store with Mom and Janic, who was still in bed. I jumped off the porch and the three of us left for the cave. Coty followed us.

When we got to the back of the house I said, "We need the rope. We left it on the back porch last night. Derek went over and picked it up.

When we got to the slanted rock I looked across the water and saw the bobcat sitting on the trail. I pointed her out so the deputies could see her.

I hadn't seen her since school was out. Her babies were seven or eight months old now and not really babies any longer. I looked around the area for them with no luck.

We continued up the stream until we came to the swimming hole where Dad was sitting against a tree. We greeted each other and Dad said nothing had happened during the night. We quickly made our way up the hillside to where the cave opening was. Cat heard us coming and stood.

"I guess we uncover the entrance and see what they have to say. Let's just crack it open to where they can hear me. We don't want to give them a shot at us," Dad said.

The two deputies inched the flat rock until a small opening was exposed.

"Get me out of here!" Sid yelled out as soon as he saw the light.

George was quiet.

"Are both of you surrendering?"

"I am!" Sid yelled again.

"What about the other guy?" Dad yelled down.

"Yes! We both surrender!" George yelled.

"We're going to open the entrance up. Throw the gun up when we're clear," Dad directed.

Cat helped the two deputies lift the rock and move it out of the way. We heard something bang off the cave ceiling. We heard the screeching of the bats again.

"You never could throw," I heard Sid tell George.

"Shut up. You throw worse than Granny."

We then heard it bang off the ceiling again. Apparently Sid picked the gun up and said, "I'll show how to do it."

A few seconds later we heard it bang off the ceiling again and then a shot rang out as it hit the floor. The bats released the ceiling and went into a fit inside the cave. I heard the screaming of the two men.

"You shot me!" we heard George say over the screaming of the bats.

"I didn't shoot you! It went off when it hit the floor!"

At this rate I figured the two men would die before we could get them out.

After the screaming stopped, Dad told them, "We're going to lower the rope so you can climb out. Leave the gun lying on the floor."

"I can't climb the rope. He shot me in the arm!"

"I can't climb out either. My hands are messed up!" Sid yelled.

"This is unbelievable," Dad said to us.

The other men began laughing.

"I know we don't have an extension ladder long enough at the house," Dad said.

"Papaw has one in the barn," I told him.

"Will you go back to the house with Linny and Derek? Call Martin and ask if he'll bring the ladder down. They'll carry it back here," Dad asked.

"Okay." We made our way back to the house and I called Papaw.

Papaw said he would bring the ladder right down. Homer and Uncle Morton were there at the store. I filled everyone in on what had happened. Papaw drove up and we went out to unload the ladder. Mamaw had come to the store with him. I saw Rock and Tucky walking toward the store. I waited for them to arrive.

I then decided I didn't need to go back with the deputies since they now knew the way. When they got to the store I hugged Rock and thanked her for what she had done for me the day before.

"It was nothing. You would have done the same for me," she said. She was right.

The three of us and James Ernest walked up to the lake and sat on the dam waiting for the two men to be led back to the store and off to jail. I told the three of them what all had happened. We couldn't stop laughing as I told them about the two men trying to throw the gun out of the cave.

Sheriff Hagar Cane

We placed the ladder down into the hole. Two extra feet of the ladder rose above the rim.

"One at a time climb up and keep your hands above your head as you climb. If your hands go below your shoulder we'll shoot."

My deputies had their weapons aimed at the men as they climbed. Sid climbed out first. I could tell he couldn't wait to get out of the cave. When he was finally out he collapsed to the ground and thanked God.

George then began to climb. He climbed up the ladder a lot slower than his partner did. It was as if he was walking to the electric chair. We handcuffed the two men. As we took care of the convicts, Cat climbed down the ladder and got the gun and then climbed back out. I looked at the George's wound. It didn't look serious, a flesh wound.

Cat then pulled the ladder out of the cave and we began the walk back to the store. The ladder was carried by Cat and Deputy Stutts. Deputy Clouse carried the rope.

"Boys, take a look at freedom. It will be the last you will see for a while," I told them.

As we got close to the dam the two men saw Tim sitting there with Rock, Tucky and James Ernest.

As they walked past us Rock stood up, "It a good thing my brothers and dad didn't get ahold of you two dirt bags first," she told them.

Tim stood up with a rock in his hand. I had the deputy stop the two men. Tim walked up to the two men and tapped both of the men on the head with quick taps.

"Hey, this is brutality!" George yelled.

"It doesn't feel good, does it?" Tim yelled at them.

"And this is for trying to grab my girlfriend." Tim then hit both of them in the head a lot harder than the earlier taps.

"You can't let him do that to me!" Sid complained.

"Do what?" Cat said.

"I didn't see anything," I said. The deputies nodded their heads in agreement.

George stared at Tim as they started walking again and said, "I'm going to get you and your girlfriend."

"Shut up," I told him.

We led them straight to the back seats of the police cars and locked the doors. They kept asking for something to drink. Betty and the others were standing on the porch watching. We went inside and I treated everyone to an ice cold pop as the two men sat in the hot back seats of the cars.

"I guess we better go before our prisoners melt. Cat, thanks for all your help," I said. I kissed my wife goodbye and we left.

"I can't believe you did that," Rock told me as the men walked off the dam.

"It was payback for all the times they tapped me on the head with their gun. I've still got bumps," I told them. She rubbed my head gently and kissed my head. It did make it feel better.

I was thrilled to see the two men taken away in handcuffs. I believed they were capable of doing anything. I really thought they would kill me in the cave if they had found what they were looking for.

Tucky asked, "Did they ever say what they were looking for?"

"No. But I got the feeling it was small. They were looking in small holes in the walls. They even talked about trying to move a boulder that they thought might be on top of it," I explained.

"Maybe a map," Rock suggested.

"That's what I would guess, or maybe a letter, or a small bag of something," James Ernest said.

"I guess we better go back to the store," I said.

"I think I'll head up to Purty's house and see what he's up to," Tucky said.

"Is it okay if I stay for a while?" Rock asked.

"Of course, I'd like that," I said.

Chapter 13
Car Wash

Sunday, July 4

Sunday mornings were my favorite. I enjoyed getting up and greeting the fishermen who came in early. We therefore knew most of them never went to church. Mom thought we should close the pay lake until noon on Sundays. She felt we were keeping folks from attending church services.

Papaw said that if they weren't fishing here they would be fishing somewhere else or doing something worse. He told Mom that it also wasn't up to us to tell people where they're meant to worship. Papaw said that at least they were fishing at a Christian lake.

I enjoyed going to church and seeing my friends. Hearing James Ernest sing was worth sitting through the sermon. I had always liked Pastor White, but lately I was getting more out of the sermons than I did when I was younger. Maybe I had more sin that needed forgiven than I used to have.

Today was going to be a big day. Most of our community was getting together at Clayton's house for a big pot-luck dinner and Fourth of July celebration. Papaw was watching the store until the dinner and then he was closing the store for the day.

Usually my aunts, uncles and cousins came to visit over the Fourth of July, but this year they had all decided not to make the trip. They told Mom they were all going to come down for Thanksgiving.

Since James Ernest got his truck he had been driving me to church. We would go pick up Rock and Tucky. Today was different. The Key family was going to Pikeville to visit Mrs. Key's mother and father. Rock told me they hardly ever see them.

It felt funny sitting in church without Rock by my side. Instead, Susie was sitting there like old times. Women had decorated the church with red, white and blue streamers around the windows. The church looked festive.

We were early because James Ernest had to prepare something for the service. Susie looked at me and said, "This seems like old times."

I started to say that it was exactly what I had been thinking, but instead I said, "Yeah." I was quite the conversationalist.

"I heard about you escaping from the two men who had taken you to the cave," she said.

"Yeah, I was lucky."

"Has anyone seen Treehawk lately?" she asked.

"No."

"Do you think he's left the area?"

"I don't know."

She turned her head and stared at the pulpit for a moment. She then turned back to me and said, "Is it so hard to carry on a decent conversation with me?"

I didn't know what to say, because it was hard. We used to talk about everything. We used to tell each other 'I love you', we used to talk about getting married. We used to go on picnics, and we loved being with each other. Susie had all but thrown me in the ditch, and now I liked Rock. I was really happy with Rock as my girlfriend. I found it hard to pretend all was fine between us, because it wasn't.

It almost felt like I was cheating on Rock if a talked to Susie. I knew it wasn't, but I was over our breakup, and I didn't want other people to see us talking and thinking we were getting back together, because I didn't want it. I didn't want Susie as my girlfriend again.

So I turned to Susie and said, "It is." She looked at me and then got up and moved to a different pew.

I felt so stupid. Susie was just trying to have a conversation with me and I mucked it up. I couldn't do it. I simply couldn't do it. I didn't know how to talk normally to someone I had once loved. I realized I was only fifteen, and would be sixteen in a couple of weeks, but even at that age it hurt, I had feelings. Maybe if I was older I would have handled it better.

I wondered when a married couple got a divorce if they are able to still be good friends and have normal talks. I didn't know any divorced couples that I could ask. None of my friends had ever broken up with each other. Great scot, I thought, we were going to Susie's house for the celebration. It would be hard to avoid her all day. I missed Rock.

The Tuttle clan walked into the church. Shauna was with Purty, and they came up and sat beside me. At least I wasn't going to be alone. The service was ready to begin. James Ernest opened the service by singing *God Bless America*. We then sang two hymns and then two older women sang a hymn. They weren't very good, but they gave it all they had. They were better than I would have been, I think.

When we got home after the service I told Mom I wasn't feeling well and that I would stay home and watch the store.

"I don't want you to do that," Mom said.

"Really, Mom, I want to stay here and keep the store open. The fishermen are sure to get thirsty and hungry. There are a lot of families up there fishing. Papaw can go to the celebration."

"Okay. If you decide later you want to come up, call us."

"I will."

126

"I'll bring home a plate of food and a couple of desserts," Mom said.

"That would be great."

I changed clothes and went out on the porch and plopped down on the swing. Dad came out and sat down beside me.

"Have you ever heard Cat say he wanted to find a job?" he asked me.

"No."

"What does he do for money?"

"He sells the bows and arrows he makes. I'm not sure about anything else. I guess he kind of lives off the land," I said.

"I need to hire another deputy. It would probably only be part time at first. You think he might be interested?"

"I have no idea, but he might," I answered.

"I could use a good man like him on the force."

"So he's no longer a suspect in the killing?" I asked.

"I never really thought he did it."

"Did Sid or George ever admit to killing the man?"

"No, not yet, anyway. We have no evidence to charge them with the murder."

Mom and Janie walked out. They were carrying dishes for the meal. I watched them as they left. James Ernest had already left for the Washington's to pick up Raven. I was already lonely.

Despite being the Fourth of July I was kept pretty busy with customers. The day wasn't as hot as it had been, but it was still in the high eighties that afternoon and the fishermen were coming down to the store for refreshments. One of the fishermen was Fred Wilson who was a widower. He came into the store and bought a soda and a pickle loaf sandwich.

"How the fishing?" I asked.

"I think I caught one that might win this week's contest," he said.

"How big is it?" I asked.

"I haven't measured it yet, but I think it's around nineteen inches," he said.

"That would be the biggest fish caught since we started the contest."

"If you can get away for a minute and come up to measure it I'll turn it loose. I like eating the smaller ones better," Fred said.

"I'll come up in a little while. Where are you located up there?"

"I'm sitting on the dam," he said.

"That makes it easier."

Later, I put a 'Be right back' sign in the window and ran up to the dam and measured the fish. It was nineteen and a half inches.

"That's a good one, Fred," I told him as he smiled.

He returned the fish to the lake, and I returned to the store. I went to my bedroom to get a book to read. I picked it up off the dresser and then dropped it. I bent down to pick it up and glanced under the dresser. Something caught my eye. I was able to reach it and pull it out. It was my missing arrow. I counted the others to make sure I now had six. I did.

I went out to the porch with an RC Cola and the book and sat in a rocking chair. I began wondering what all was happening at Susie's farm. I figured the kids were playing games. The adults were either playing music or talking about local events and people.

Susie

*T*immy was such a coward. I couldn't believe he didn't come to the celebration. I still considered us friends, and I hoped he did also. I was trying to be friendly at the church. Boys are so stupid.

Everyone asked where Timmy was. Betty had said he was worried about the fishermen needing drinks. I think it had more to do with me than the men around the lake. I was surprised Betty would let him stay at the store by himself. It seemed as though it was asking for more trouble. He and I had been kidnapped. He had been kidnapped. He had been robbed multiple times.

I thought that perhaps I shouldn't even go on the trip to the Smokies.

Around five that evening Timmy's papaw's pickup pulled into the lot. I was with him. I could see the surprised look on Timmy's face.

"Your Mamaw wanted me to bring you some food," Martin said to Timmy as he walked toward him holding a plate. I walked up the steps while carrying two more plates of food.

"Thanks," Timmy said.

"I'm going to go up to the lake and check on the fishermen. It looks like we have a quite a few," Martin said as he looked at all the vehicles in the lot. He walked around the side of the house.

I looked at Timmy while I took a seat and said, "I know you're mad at me. But I don't want it to be awkward between us. Or I can back out of going to the Smokies, if you would want."

Timmy looked at me with surprise. I didn't want to back out of the trip. I was looking forward to the adventure as much as everyone else.

"I don't want you to do that," Timmy said. "We're going to have the time of our lives."

"Then what is wrong?"

"I don't know how to talk to you now. I was so in love with you and now I feel…" Timmy stopped.

"You feel what?"

"I can't really explain. I want to be friends now. But how do I do that without everyone thinking we're getting back together every time they see us talking. It's not fair to Rock," he tried to explain.

"We can't control what other people think. I don't believe Rock gets upset when we talk. She was the one who forced me to climb up on your shoulders. We need to be friends, Timmy. I need you as my friend, even if you aren't my boyfriend. I know that Rock really cares for you, and I don't want to come between the two of you. Maybe you should talk to her about it and see how she feels."

"I guess you're right," he said. "I'll talk to her tomorrow."

Timmy was sitting in the swing and I was sitting in one of the rocking chairs. I got up and went over and sat beside him. I leaned over and gave him a hug.

"We can be friends," I said.

After an awkward moment Timmy said, "We have the car wash this Saturday."

"That should be fun," I said.

Martin returned from the lake and asked me, "Are you ready to go back?"

"I'm ready."

I got up and said, "See you, Timmy."

"Bye."

As I rode back to the farm I couldn't help but remember all the great times Timmy and I spent together over the years. All the times he had been so sweet to me. The times we walked through the fields and woods hand-in-hand. I even thought of the times he had defended me and risked his life for me.

We had really messed it up. Rock was so fortunate to have him.

*B*oredom set in for most of the week. The weather forecast each day was for dry and sunny conditions with the highs near ninety and lows each night in the mid-seventies.

I told Dad about finding the sixth arrow. "Oh, okay, good," he said.

The two men, Sid and George, were in jail. Treehawk hadn't been seen for a couple of weeks. Not many fishermen were venturing out in the heat. It seemed like my friends and I were watching the clock tick slowly waiting for the car wash and then the trip to the Smoky Mountains National Park.

We had made our camping reservations at the Cades Cove campground inside the park. Mom and Dad had found a hotel with adjoining rooms in Townsend which was less than ten miles from the campground. Sally and Janie would have their own room and were maybe more excited than I was, if that was possible.

It was the day of the car wash. The bank supplied a water hose and the water, and we had to supply everything else. Papaw was coming down to the store to help Mom while I was away.

The car wash was starting at nine. James Ernest and I went to pick up some of the gang while Purty was picking up the other members. We left around eight-fifteen. Once everyone was there we unloaded the buckets, soaps, sponges, and rags for drying the cars.

We didn't even have a car to wash, but it didn't stop Junior from spraying anyone within range. No one minded the cooling water. We had put up signs at each entrance to West Liberty advertising our car wash. We were charging one dollar for the wash and dry.

By nine-thirty we had a line of cars. We were washing one car at a time. We had six people washing and five drying. One person manned the hose. We took turns doing each. We were efficient. The six people doing the washing were assigned a certain part of the car or pickup. Each car was averaging around five minutes to wash and about the same to dry.

Most of the girls had worn their swimming suits with shorts. I thought they drew in most of the men who came to get their vehicles washed. James Ernest was collecting the money before we began washing the car. A lot of the folks were giving us tips as they left, which was nice.

Some older boys drove in to get their cars washed. They would flirt with the girls as they watched them bend over to wash their cars. Some of the girls were even asked out on dates. The boys were all turned down to their disappointment.

A few of us guys took off our shirts and were ogled by women who drove in. Most of us were lean and muscular for our age due to the work we did of the farms. Purty didn't take his shirt off. I thought it was strange since he liked being naked so much. I thought since he now had a serious girlfriend in Shauna he was now more embarrassed of being overweight. It didn't seem to bother Shauna at all. She seemed crazy over Purty.

We had one driver who said we could wash his car as long as the colored kids didn't touch his car. James Ernest sent the guy away. He squealed his tires as he sped out of the parking lot.

"What was he upset about?" I asked him.

"He didn't like the color of some of our friends. I told him to get lost," James Ernest told me.

"He can keep his dollar and wash his car himself," I said.

We had a steady line of cars the entire day. We decided to stay as long as cars were in line. Around six that evening we finally had no cars waiting to be washed. We quickly closed up before anyone else pulled in. James Ernest told us we had washed one hundred and fifteen cars. With tips, we made a hundred and forty-one dollars. With this money, plus the auction money, we now had enough money to help anyone who didn't have the expense of the trip, plus money to help everyone else.

My back was hurting. I crawled into the back of the pickup and stretched out on the bed. Rock climbed in and laid next to me.

"Would you like to come back to the store with me and have supper with us?" I asked her.

"Okay," she said.

Papaw and Uncle Morton were sitting on the porch when we returned to the store. The lot was full of vehicles, meaning a lot of fishermen at the lake.

Uncle Morton asked, "Since you all are experts now. How about washing my car before I leave?"

"Are you driving again?" I said.

James Ernest said, "I wouldn't wash another car today for twenty dollars."

"How many cars did you wash?" Papaw asked.

"One hundred and fifteen," Rock answered. "And I got asked out twenty-two times."

"Some of those guys had to be better than Timmy," Uncle Morton teased.

"Who said they were all guys? Besides, there is no one better than my Timmy," Rock said.

"I think you had better hang on to her," Uncle Morton said.

"You're right; I could end up like you – without a woman at all."

"I have all the women I want. They cost money," Uncle Morton claimed.

"It could be that all the women know you too well," I said.

"Martin, I used to like the kid," Uncle Morton harassed. We laughed.

For supper we had fried chicken with all the side dishes. We were hungry after the long day without a break to eat. Uncle Morton stayed and ate with us. After the meal, James Ernest took Uncle Morton home on his way to Raven's house. Rock and I walked up to the lake to check on the fishermen. We then went back to the store.

Mamaw and Papaw were ready to go home so they took Rock home. I sat in one of the rocking chairs and was ready to fall asleep when Mom and Dad came out on the porch to swing.

Mom looked at me and said, "Long day?"

"I'm dead tired."

"I thought you would like to know that Cat accepted the position as my next deputy," Dad told me.

"Really? I didn't think he would."

"He starts on Monday, two or three days a week. I think the main reason he accepted was because he told me he needs a vehicle, but didn't have the money to spend on one. I took him today to look at used pickups. He bought one."

"Deputy Cat, sounds like a cartoon," I laughed.

"I think his nametag will say Cata," Dad said.

We stayed on the porch until darkness fell. I watched all the fishermen leave for the day, and then went to bed early and slept soundly.

Chapter 14
Sixteen & Love

Wednesday, July 21

Sixteen years earlier I was born in a small house in Blair Mills, Kentucky, a couple of miles from the store. I wasn't born in a hospital. There was no doctor there to welcome me with a slap. I was brought into this world without those two things, and I turned out okay. So, today was my sixteenth birthday.

Mom had told me it was hotter than blue blazes the day I was born. This day was no different. We had a small fan in our room sitting on the dresser. Every time I woke up during the night I would wonder what the strange hum was. I would figure it out, fall back to sleep and then wake up again wondering what the strange hum was once again.

Mom had told me I could sleep late, but who could sleep in this heat? I was happy to get up and out of my sweat and move around. The first thing I did was go grab an RC Cola from the cooler. I dipped my head inside. I knew there would be no fishermen today.

Coty had slept in our room, and he followed me out onto the porch. He went to the nearest tree and peed on it. I put out a bowl of water for him. He drank it all and I refilled it. There was not a hint of a breeze in the air.

Daylight was coming and I heard the Tuttle's rooster crow. I was sitting in the porch swing trying to generate a breeze on my own. The chain squeaked as I moved back and forth.

Mom told me we were going to have cake that evening and asked me what kind I wanted. I asked for a white coconut birthday cake. Mamaw promised to make cherry dumplings also. She also said she might make a blackberry jam cake. One day in June, Rock and I had gone out blackberry picking. I think I ate as many as I put in the bucket. But we ended up with a gallon bucket full. It took days for the blackberry stain to wash off my hands.

Perhaps I should wash my hands more often.

It was also Rhonda Blair's sixteenth birthday. We were born on the same day. I wondered what I might get for my birthday. I never had asked for anything and Mom had never asked what I wanted. Maybe the trip to the Smoky Mountains was my gift, which was fine with me. I didn't really need anything.

If they had asked me, I may have asked for a new two man tent or some camping supplies for our trip. Rock and I had talked about getting a tent for just the two of us for the trip. Rock and Tucky's sixteenth birthday was on August the third and we would be on our trip in the Smokies when they turned sixteen. So I needed to find a gift for her to take with me on the trip. I wasn't sure what to get her.

I was sweating while swinging. The humidity was awful. As the sun brightened the sky I saw dark clouds to the southwest. The longer I sat there the darker it grew. The clouds were moving fast and coming our way. It wasn't much longer before I saw rain falling on the nearest hillside.

It was as if someone pulled a blanket over my head. Suddenly it was dark again and the heavy rain pounded on the tin roof of the porch. The large drops of water made the dust in the parking lot puff into the air and then fall to become wet dirt. The screen door opened and Mom came out onto the porch.

"Good morning. Did you do a rain dance?" Mom asked. She came over and sat next to me so I could hear her over the tin roof.

I laughed and said, "Cat must have been dancing this morning."

"I didn't know anyone else was up."

"I had a hard time sleeping in this heat," I explained.

"Hopefully this will cool things off. By the way, happy birthday." She reached over and hugged me.

"Thanks."

"What are your plans for the day?" Mom asked.

"Help here at the store, I guess."

"It's your sixteenth birthday. You should do something special."

"Maybe Rock and I will go skinny dipping," I said.

Mom started to say something. But she looked at me and saw that I was smiling. She slapped my arm. The more I thought about it the more I actually like the idea. It would be a nice birthday gift.

As we sat there the rain began to slow to a steady rain instead of the earlier downpour. James Ernest and Dad came out from the store.

"Happy birthday," they both said.

"Thanks."

"I had an idea," Dad said.

"What's that?"

"I could take you to get your temporary driver's license this morning," he said.

I had been studying the state driving manual for the past month. James Ernest would quiz me at night when we went to bed. I thought I was ready for the test.

"That would be great," I said excitedly.

"We'll go first thing this morning," he said.

"Okay. I need to go and take a shower," I said.

Ten minutes later I was ready, even though it was only seven.

James Ernest said, "I think I would like to go with you guys. We can celebrate at Dairy Queen after you pass the test.'

"That's a great idea," Dad said.

Dad said the testing place in Morehead opened at eight. We got in the cruiser and took off.

"Do I get to drive the cruiser back from Morehead?" I asked on our way.

"I don't think that would be a good idea," Dad said.

"You could be the first kid to learn to drive with a police car," James Ernest said.

"What vehicle will I drive to learn?" I asked.

"Either your mother's car or maybe James Ernest would teach you to drive his stick shift pickup," Dad answered.

"I don't want my clutch ruined by you," James Ernest said.

"I know how to drive a stick shift," I said. "I've driven Papaw's around the farm." I had also driven James Ernest's truck, but didn't want to tell that to my dad, the sheriff.

We made it to the building just as they opened. I was the first in the door. The lady gave me the test and showed me where to sit. "You cannot ask anyone for help. You cannot get up during the test," the lady told me. I felt like I was back in school.

I took the seat at the table and began reading the first question. Most of the questions I knew right away. Some of them I had to think about. A couple of them I guessed. The test took me fifteen minutes to finish. I took the test back up to the lady. She graded it as I stood there.

"You passed," she said, with no emotion. I figured I was just another sixteen year old kid to her - one of hundreds.

"Take a seat and I'll get your temporary license," she said.

I walked over to where Dad and James Ernest sat reading pamphlets about road safety and regulations. They looked up to see my smile.

"She's making my temporary license," I said.

"It's too bad you don't study for all your tests like you did for this one," James Ernest said and grinned.

"There was more at stake this time," I joked, although I meant it. This was probably my most important test I'd ever taken.

My name was called and I went forward to get the license. She handed it to me and said, "Be safe as you drive. My kids are out there on the road." The warning stuck with me.

"To celebrate, should we go to McDonald's for breakfast? I don't believe Dairy Queen is open this early," Dad asked.

"Sounds good to me," I said.

After eating we headed home. As we were nearing Rock's house I asked, "Can you stop at the Key house and let me see if Rock wants to come back to the store with us?"

"Sure," Dad said.

He stopped in front of the house. Rock's older sisters were on the porch.

"Is Rock here?" I asked after rolling down the back window.

Sugar Cook yelled, "Rock, your knight in bibs is here."

Rock opened the door. She looked beautiful.

"You want to go back to the store with us?"

"Yes."

"Grab your swimsuit," I yelled.

139

"Why would you need a swimsuit?" we heard Chero tease.

She went back inside and then ran back out the door. Dad opened his door and told me I was driving. I jumped out and got in behind the wheel. Dad told Rock she would need to sit in the back because he had to be in the front. I put the car in gear and drove away.

"We went to Morehead this morning, and he got his temporary license," James Ernest explained as to why I was driving.

"Happy birthday," Rock said after I took off.

"Thank you."

As I came over the bridge in front of the store I turned on the siren. I saw that Mamaw and Papaw were at the store. As I was parking, they, along with Mom and Janie, came out the front door to see what was happening. When they saw me behind the steering wheel they began smiling. Papaw was applauding.

The rain had long ago stopped and the sun had already dried up the parking lot. It had cooled somewhat. It was a good day to turn sixteen.

After sitting on the porch discussing our trip and the test for a few minutes James Ernest took off for Raven's. Dad went to work. Papaw went home to do some farm work and Mamaw stayed to help at the store. I told Mom, "Rock and I are going swimming."

"We're having your party at seven this evening, so be back by then," Mom told us.

"It's not even noon yet. How long do you think we're going to swim?"

"I never know what you might do," Mom said.

Mamaw added, "Be a good boy."

There were still no fishermen at the lake. We had the whole place to ourselves. I went inside and got my swimming trunks and a blanket. We then headed for the swimming hole. We held hands as we walked around the lake. I had to have been the happiest boy in the world, I thought.

I had turned sixteen. We had perfect weather for swimming. I had my learner's permit, and I had my beautiful girlfriend beside me. How could things be better? As we walked, I turned and stopped. I pulled Rock closer and kissed her.

When we got to the swimming hole I laid the blanket on the flat rock and started taking off my shirt and shoes. Rock had carried her swimsuit. But she threw it onto the blanket and began shedding her clothes. First her shoes came off and then her shorts.

She lifted her top up over her head exposing her breasts. I stood there like a dope watching her strip. The only thing left was her panties and she slid them from her tanned long legs. She smiled at me and then turned and jumped into the pool of water. I watched her as she came up. She motioned for me to join her. I slipped my trunks off and two strides later I was jumping toward her.

I came up out of the water and pulled her to the front of me and she said, "Happy birthday," and then squeezed herself to me and kissed me. It felt good, our bodies close together. We kissed over and over until we were kissed out.

We both were greatly aroused, but we had talked about not having sex, and we talked about it again.

She said, "I know we both want to do it."

"I know."

"But we're going to wait, aren't we."

"That's what we had decided. I think we should stick to our plan, even if it's hard," I said. No pun intended.

I didn't want things to change between us, and I had a feeling that having sex would change things. I think Rock would have if I had asked her to, but I didn't think it was the right thing to do and she agreed. I was happy with the touching and kissing that we did. And there was always the fear of having our own Ken and Barbie twins.

We both had heard kids at school bragging about all the different sexual partners they had done it with. I believed about half of it. They made it seem like a conquest more than something they had done with someone they loved. One of the older boys had notches on his belt showing how many girls he had conquered.

Maybe he was the reason so many girls had to leave school for months at a time. After an hour in the water we got out. I slipped on my trunks and Rock put on her shorts. We then laid on the blanket.

"How did I get so lucky?" I asked.

"Lucky about what?"

"To have a girlfriend like you," I answered.

"Because you and Susie broke up," Rock said.

"I'm glad we did," I said. I meant it. I was happy we had broken up. Rock was such an amazing person. I knew she loved me. I knew she would help me any way she could. She was funny and sexy and cute. I looked into her green eyes and leaned over to kiss her.

"I love you," I said.

She looked at me with surprise. She stared at me. She then asked, "Are you serious, or are you saying that because I'll go skinny dipping with you?"

"I'm serious." I then listed the reasons I loved her.

"I love you, Timmy." She rolled over on top of me and kissed me more passionately than she ever had.

She rolled back off and then began to softly cry. A tear ran down her cheek.

"What's wrong?" I asked.

"Nothing," she said as she sniffed and wiped the tear away.

"Why are you crying?"

"I believe that's the first time anyone has ever told me they loved me," she said with her eyes looking away from me.

"That can't be true. Your parents must have told you they loved you."

"I don't remember them ever saying they loved me. They have eight kids, and they're not the sentimental types. I have never heard the word love come out of their mouths," Rock said sadly.

After a moment she added, "One thing I love about our church is when Pastor White tells us that Jesus died for us and that God loves us. That was the first time I had ever heard that someone loved me – not that God loved everyone, but that He loved me. Timmy, you're the first person to ever say 'I love you' directly to me."

I didn't know what to say. It was so unbelievable. It was so unlikely that a child would grow up in a home without ever being told they were loved. I guessed some folks assume a person knows it without having to be told it.

I would tell my child or wife every day that I loved them. I would remember this to remind me to tell the folks I loved that I love them. We were lying there looking straight up into the big beautiful blue sky. White billowy clouds were lingering behind the storm from this morning.

I looked to the left, up over the rising cliff and saw a cloud drifting by that was shaped exactly like a white dove. I knew God had sent it for us. I pointed to the cloud and said. "There's the sign that we are loved."

Rock looked over at it and said, "That is incredible. It looks exactly like a white dove."

We silently watched it float by. Suddenly I felt naked, even though I had on shorts, like God could see me. But I assumed God could see me before the cloud went overhead.

I was getting hot again. I hopped up and dove into the water. Before I rose from the depths Rock was right beside me. Our heads came out of the water with our lips pressed against one another.

Mamaw

Betty and I were in the kitchen baking pies and a birthday cake for Timmy's party. He didn't know that most of the community was coming to the farm for the party. Rhonda Blair was also coming so they could celebrate together.

The party was a surprise for both of them. Everyone was to be there before seven. We would lock up the store and head that way at seven. Martin was getting everything set up. James Ernest and Raven were helping him.

"I don't think he has an inkling about the party," I told Betty.

"He's too busy skinny dipping with Rock to think about a party," Betty said.

"What? They wouldn't," I said, surprised.

"We've already caught them once." Betty went on to tell me about Hagar finding them at the creek. "That's why I bought her a swimsuit. She said her parents didn't have money for swimsuits."

"Sounds like a good excuse if you ask me," I told Betty.

144

"It does, but I believe her. I think it was the way they were reared. The Washington family was like that. Coal told me her kids went swimming naked all the time because they didn't have suits," Betty said.

"Aren't you worried about it?" I asked.

"Of course we are. Hagar said it was normal for teenagers. He said he had done it, and if truth be told, I did to," Betty said.

"You what?! You're grounded, young lady," I teased.

Betty laughed at the thought.

"I guess since you're telling the truth. I think I remember Martin and me maybe skinny dipping in the creeks a couple of times," I confessed.

"Mom! You're grounded for a week." We both laughed.

"After we caught them we decided we needed to have the talk about sex with the two boys," Betty said.

"And how did that go?" I asked.

"Absolutely awful," Betty said. We both laughed.

"I suppose Timmy's having a good birthday," I said.

"I don't want to think about it. He grew up too fast," Betty said. I agreed, but there was nothing that could be done about it.

We had a great time exploring each other's bodies underwater with our hands. We kissed and caressed until I was worn out. Later, we got out and made our way back to the blanket. It wasn't long before I was asleep as the sun's rays hit my back.

I was in love and sixteen. How could life get any better?

We spent the rest of the afternoon napping, talking, and in and out of the water. It was a great afternoon. I knew we needed to get back to the store and get ready for my birthday dinner. I slipped on my shirt and shoes. Rock put on the swimsuit after

145

wetting it in the water. She didn't want Mom thinking we had been skinny dipping since she bought her the swimsuit. She put her shorts back on over it.

We walked back to the lake. There were a few fishermen sitting around the lake. I saw Louis and Mud taking seats in their usual spots. They waved as we walked by on the other side of the lake. I knew they had just gotten off work.

"Happy birthday!" they both yelled. I waved back.

"I'm going to take a shower," I told Rock. "Do you want to take one?"

"I'd like to go home and get a dress for the dinner before I shower," Rock said.

"Mom will drive you up there," I said, as we walked off the dam.

We walked through the back door and Mom and Mamaw were in the kitchen cooking.

"Hi. Did you two have a fun afternoon?" Mom asked.

"We did," I said.

"Would you mind taking Rock home to get a dress?" I asked.

"I'd like to change for the dinner if it's not too much trouble," Rock said.

Mom went to her purse and got her keys and handed them to me. "You can take my car. Be careful."

"I'm not allowed to drive," I said.

"It's not far, and what's the use in having the sheriff as my husband if we can't bend the rules a little?" Mom said.

I took the keys and we headed for the car. I drove her slowly to her house. She jumped out and said, "I'll be right back."

Sugar Cook and Chero were on the porch. They quickly came to the car when they saw me.

"You're sixteen today," Sugar Cook said as she leaned into the open window exposing her cleavage.

"He looks legal now," Chero said as she rubbed my arm.

"You two are enjoying yourselves, aren't you?" I said.

"We could enjoy you more if you went skinny dipping with us," Sugar Cook teased as she licked her lips.

"Ain't you dating Hiram?" I asked.

"Didn't we already have this conversation once? I can skinny dip with whoever I want," she countered.

Chero ran her hand through my hair.

I heard the front screen door open and heard Mrs. Key yell out, "You girls leave Rock's fellow alone!"

"We're just playing with him, Mom!" Chero yelled back.

"You heard Mom, get your hands off of him," Rock ordered as she ran toward the car. She slid into the seat beside me and looked up at her sisters and said. "He's taken."

I put the car in drive and we took off for the store.

"They have about as much sense as a worm on hot pavement," Rock said as I drove.

Chapter 15
A Blue Pickup Truck

After showering and getting dressed I went out to the front porch. Rock was swinging. She looked beautiful in her flowered sundress. Her dark hair was clean and shining. It hung down past her shoulders. She wore a pair of sandals. She smiled at me as I sat beside her.

Mom had taken Mamaw home while Rock was showering. Janie went with her and stayed there. It was almost six when Dad pulled into the lot. He climbed out of the cruiser and asked, "How's your birthday going?"

"It's been great," I said.

"Good evening, Rock. You look lovely," Dad said.

"Thank you, Mr. Cane."

He went on into the house. Rock said, "I'm never sure what to call your dad. I could call him sheriff, Mr. Cane or Hagar."

"I don't think it matters to him. I used to have the same problem. After a while I began calling him dad. But it was strange at first," I said.

We swung for a little while in silence until I asked, "Are you looking forward to the trip?"

"Are you kidding? It's just about the only thing I think about. It was really nice that we could raise money for the trip because I didn't know how I would pay for it," Rock said.

"I would have paid your way. You definitely were going," I said.

"Kenny had some money saved, and he told me he would help me. I knew that Dad wouldn't give me any. He couldn't afford it," Rock said.

"We don't have to worry about it now," I assured her.

She leaned over and put her head on my shoulder. Mom walked out onto the porch. "We'll be ready to leave soon."

"Thanks for letting me take a shower. You don't know how wonderful that is after bathing in a tub or in the creek," Rock told Mom.

"You're welcome. I know exactly what you mean. It was the same here until we put it in. You can use it as often as you want. You're dress is very pretty, Rock," Mom told her.

Rock's face lit up and she said, "Thank you. I made it."

"You sewed that dress?" Mom asked.

"I did. Mom found the material in an old box under her bed. She gave it to me and told me I probably needed a nice dress for the trip."

"Did you have a pattern?" Mom asked.

"No.'

"That is amazing," Mom said.

I wasn't much interested in sewing so I got up and went to get an RC Cola. "You want a pop," I asked Rock.

"I'd take an Orange Crush." I went inside and found the drinks in the cooler. I opened them and came back out.

"Shouldn't we be leaving?" I asked.

"As soon as Hagar is ready," Mom said. She went inside to check on him.

At seven we all headed for the car. Dad flipped the keys to me, and I drove us up the hill to the farm. I could see the farm

149

from the ridge road. A large valley separated the road from the farmhouse. I saw that there were a large number of vehicles at the farm and I knew what was happening. I decided not to say anything about the surprise. I turned into the lane and drove down the hill to the house. People were standing in the yard yelling, "Surprise! Surprise!"

I looked behind us and saw Rhonda in her parent's car. It was a surprise party for the both of us. Everyone was there, the Tuttles, the Washington family, the two Easterling families, Pastor White and his family, Clayton and his clan, Uncle Morton, and Cat. Even Dana and pretty Idell were there. Dana's sister, Tammy, was there.

Every member of the Wolf Pack and Bear Troop were there. What a party!

Two tables were covered with food and desserts. I saw a blackberry jam cake, a coconut cake, chocolate and lemon pies, home baked cookies and banana pudding. A big pot of cherry dumplings sat at the end of the table. The other table had hamburgers and hotdogs and fried chicken, Cole slaw and mashed potatoes, corn on the cob, fresh green beans and peas, and fresh made rolls.

It was a feast.

Pastor White asked the blessing of the food and everyone began piling up their plates. James Ernest and Raven had placed some blankets on the grass for a place for us to eat. We talked and laughed and told the group what we were looking forward to on our trip. We would be leaving in eleven days.

A few of us wanted to see a bear. Others didn't. Some of us wanted to hike to Mt. LeConte. Others didn't. Some of us wanted to do everything.

"I'm anxious to see how pretty the mountains are. They are supposed to have a blue color," Susie said.

"That's why they're called the Smoky Mountains," Purty told us.

"Thanks, genius," Tucky said.

"Who knew?" Junior teased.

"It's a good thing Purty is going with us," Francis said.

"He'll be our guide," I suggested.

"I can see it now. He'll say 'That is a bear coming at us. We had better run,' or 'That thing in front of us is a big mountain,'" Rhonda said, as we all laughed.

"I'll be happy to point things out to you," he said as he stuffed another roll in his mouth.

Sadie kissed him on his creek and said, "They're all jealous of your brilliance, sweety." We cracked up.

"Time for dessert," Purty announced.

"Another great deduction from our mastermind," I said.

Before cutting into the cakes, Mom had everyone gather around to sing Happy Birthday. They sang to Rhonda first and she blew out the sixteen candles on the coconut cake. After singing to me I blew out the sixteen candles on the jam cake.

We then swarmed the dessert table. I got a piece of jam cake and surrounded it with cherry dumplings. Rock took a slice of lemon pie.

After everyone had more or less finished dessert Mom announced it was time to open gifts. Generally we kids never bought each other birthday gifts due to the lack of money. We only had gifts from adults, mainly our parents.

I noticed that I didn't have a present on the table. Rhonda opened her gift from her parents, which was mainly stuff she needed for our trip. Uncle Morton came forward and reached into his pocket and then rang the dinner bell loudly. I wondered what in the world was happening. He handed me a key.

I looked up at him and he said, "I believe it's a key to this." He pointed toward the barn. Papaw and Cat opened the barn doors and out came the 1956 blue Chevy pickup that Papaw had bought at the auction. It now had a matching blue bed cap on it like the one James Ernest had on his.

James Ernest was driving the pickup, and he drove straight down through the yard and stopped it right in front of me.

"Happy birthday," Mom and Dad said.

"This is mine?!" I yelled out.

"It is," Papaw said.

I didn't know what to say or do. The truck had been washed and waxed. It was the prettiest pickup I had ever seen. James Ernest got out and motioned for me to jump in. I got in and closed the door and Mom stood there taking pictures of me behind the wheel.

Rhonda looked over at her parents and said, "Timmy gets a truck, and I get camping supplies." Everyone laughed.

Delma exclaimed, "No one will be safe on the roads any longer."

"No one was safe around him before. Think of what it will be like now," Thelma chipped in.

"I never thought he would live to see sixteen," Delma added.

"God has shown him a lot of mercy," Thelma said as they walked away shaking their heads.

I found out later that the truck was a gift from my parents and Mamaw and Papaw. They had the engine serviced and everything checked. The mechanic said it was as good as new. The pickup only had 17,000 miles on it. Papaw had been told the truck had been bought new and mostly used around the farm and to town and back. Once the owners were unable to drive, they stored the truck in the barn.

I could not believe how lucky I was. It was the best birthday a boy could have. I didn't deserve these blessings, but I was very thankful for them. I no longer had to ride the bus to school. Bernice, the skunk, would never trip me again while getting on the bus. I got out of the cab and let everyone else take turns behind the wheel. The men popped the hood and looked under it. They circled the truck trying to find something wrong. It was difficult.

It wasn't long before the men went to the porch and began playing instruments. James Ernest sang a couple of songs. They made him sing *I'm so Lonesome I could Cry.* Everyone loved when he sang the song. They asked Coal and Raven to sing a song. Coal then did one by herself.

Darkness had enveloped the farm but the party went on. Pastor White sang a song he had written that was beautiful. The younger kids played hide-and-seek in the dark. I sat with Rock on the edge of the porch listening to the music. I really enjoyed it when our friends sang together.

James Ernest asked Cat if he had any Indian music he could share.

"I'm not a very good singer, but I could do one of our Indian chant songs," he said. "You have to help me. Give me some drumming on the porch floor. I'll show you what I mean."

He got down on his knees and began to imitate a drumming beat on the wooden floor boards. The Wolf Pack began to copy the beat. He started his chant in Shawnee. It continued for the next five minutes. Others joined him in the chant.

When he finished we all applauded him. "What does the song mean?" Pastor White asked.

"It's a song for blessing. We're asking the Great Spirit to provide food for the village, either in crops or meat from hunting," Cat explained.

"Did your tribe do rain dances?" Susie asked.

"We did when our crops were suffering from lack of rain. But most rain dances were done in the southwest where it was so dry," Cat told us.

"I told Mom you were doing one this morning," I said.

"I had nothing to do with the rain this morning," Cat said. We all laughed.

The men then played some old bluegrass tunes. One was *Blue Moon of Kentucky* which was written and performed by the legendary Bill Monroe. I was eating my second bowl of cherry dumplings and a piece of coconut cake. The party began to break up around eleven.

As Mr. Washington was leaving he put his arm around my shoulder and said, "That is a mighty fine pickup, Timmy. Happy birthday."

"Thank you. It was really a surprise," I said. I drove my new truck home. Rock was sitting next to me, and Mom was by the window. Tucky was in the back. I was careful as I drove to Rock's house. When we arrived Mom got out so Rock could exit. Rock gave me a kiss before getting out.

"I had wonderful day with you," she said.

"Me too. Love you," I said.

"Love you, too," she said as she slid out.

Tucky waved goodbye. Mom looked at me and simply said, "Love?"

"Yep," was all I said.

Thursday, July 22

It had been the best day of my life. I loved every minute of it. It was the ultimate birthday. It was past midnight. I was lying in the top bunk while James Ernest read in the bottom bunk.

"I can't believe I got a pickup for my birthday," I said.

"That's the tenth time you've said that. Why don't you go sleep in it and then maybe you'll believe it," James Ernest said. I thought maybe he was tired of hearing me go on about it. He was trying to read *To Kill a Mockingbird.* I wasn't sure why he wanted to read about how to kill a mockingbird. What had mockingbirds ever done to him – mocked him?

I was so wound up I knew it would be forever before I could go to sleep.

"You think I might be able to drive my truck to the Smokies?" I asked.

"You don't have a license."

"I could get it by then," I reasoned.

"I don't know. We're leaving in ten days."

"I told Rock I loved her today," I blurted out. I was all over the place. My brain was jumping from one thing to another to another.

"Why did you do that?" James Ernest asked.

"Why do you think?"

"Does she love you?"

"Yes."

"I'm happy for the two of you."

"Have you ever told Raven you love her?"

"Of course I have."

"She's going to be lost when you leave for college," I said.

"I hope not. She has a lot of friends here. You and Rock could invite her to do things with you," he said.

"We will. Maybe she'd go skinny dipping with us."

"You're a good friend," James Ernest said. Then we both laughed. I wondered if I'd be lost without James Ernest there with me. I suddenly realized that within a month my life would never be the same.

Rock

Lying on the floor between Chero and Adore I struggled to get to sleep. Since dating Timmy I had seen how different our lives were. I had been spending time at the store and eating meals with his family. I loved my family, but we weren't normal.

I'd come to realize that never hearing the word *love* spoken in our house was abnormal. Timmy's family had no problem letting each other know how they felt. I had heard Timmy tell his Mom he loved her. He had also told his grandparents, his sister, and James Ernest he loved them. And now he had told me he loved me.

I knew I loved him, even though I had never told him so. It had never occurred to me to tell him until today. The word was one we never used, like a foreign language we knew nothing about. Love was a four letter word in our family. But now I knew the word was never used as an insult or to hurt someone. It was a word of salvation.

God loved us by giving us His only son. Timmy loved me by giving me his time and kindness and gentleness and protection. I loved him by giving him all that I had to give. I would risk my life for him.

156

The only member of my family I felt close to was Kenny. We were twins. We had the same yearning for something better than the life our parents had forced on us. I was sleeping on the living room floor with five other siblings while all my friends had a bed to sleep in. Our family just existed. I wanted to soar. I wanted to contribute to the world. Timmy had increased that yearning within me.

I saw how he welcomed each minute of his life and tried to use it for fun, or to make someone's day, or to laugh with someone, or help someone, or to love someone. And he loved me. I would love him forever. Even if someday he stopped loving me, I would love him.

Chapter 16
To the Mountains

Saturday, July 31

We were packing the pickup trucks with bags of clothes, tents, sleeping bags and supplies that we were taking with us to the Smoky Mountains. Dad had found foam to place on the floor of the pickup beds. The foam would make it a lot more comfortable for the trip.

There were twelve of us, five members of the Wolf Pack and seven members of the Bear Troop. Six would ride in each pickup. One of the pickups was mine. Dad decided my driving was good enough to take my test. On Friday he took me to Morehead for the test. I passed it with flying colors. I had trouble with the parallel parking but got my license anyway.

James Ernest and I were driving our trucks. It was determined that it was best if Purty left his rusted pickup at home. Rock, Tucky, Sadie, Junior and Francis were riding in my truck with me.

Raven, Rhonda, Susie, Purty and Shauna were riding with James Ernest. Mom and Dad were going to lead the trip with Janie and Sally in their back seat.

We were all gathered at the store as we loaded up the gear. Mom and James Ernest had decided we should wait until after church was over to leave on the trip. Dad told us it would take around five to six hours to drive to the Smokies. We figured longer with food and bathroom breaks.

Dad had gotten three walkie-talkies to take with us so that each vehicle had one. We had a way to communicate. I don't believe I had ever seen such excitement from a group of people. Everyone was talking and laughing.

We figured Purty and Rhonda could spell one of the drivers if we got tired. Being a new driver, I wasn't sure how I would do on such a long trip. We had a large cooler that held lunchmeat and other items that needed to be kept cold.

Everyone that had forty dollars gave it to Susie. She was in charge of the money. She also had the money we had earned from the auction and car wash. Susie would pay for all the gas and our camping fees.

Papaw and Mamaw were going to stay at the store while we were gone. Cat was going to drive Dad's cruiser to work. Since Dad would be gone all week, Cat agreed to work five days to take his spot so the police force wouldn't be left short-handed.

Everything was packed and ready for the trip. We had binoculars, hiking sticks, backpacks, cameras, a camp saw for firewood, lawn chairs, camping cups and plates and pots, tents and rope. It was decided Coty would stay home with my grandparents. We had read that dogs had to stay on a leash in the park for their safety and the safety of others. We knew Coty would hate being on a leash. He had never been on a leash in his life.

We were ready.

Sunday, August 1

I left the store to pick up Rock and Tucky for church. I couldn't believe the day had finally arrived. I was beyond excited.

Rock jumped in and sat beside me. Tucky closed the door and we headed to the church.

When the service was closing Pastor White told the congregation about our trip and then prayed for our safe journeys. I had a feeling deep down that it was a good thing that he prayed for us. Who knew what we might get into?

We all met in the church parking lot after the service was over. The kids kissed and hugged their parents' goodbye and then loaded into the pickups. Papaw was at the store, so Dad and Mom were dropping Mamaw off there.

When we got to the store each of us was told we could pick out a drink and snack for the road. We loaded up and took off for the Smoky Mountains. Rock was sitting beside me with her pretty sundress on. Junior, Francis, Tucky and Sadie all decided to start the trip in the back.

We waved to Mamaw and Papaw as we drove away from the store. I had never been on a big vacation before. When we lived in Ohio our vacations were a weekend trip to Morgan County. None of us had ever been to the Smokies.

As we started down the road Rock hugged my neck and kissed me on the cheek. "This is going to be so much fun," she said. She had her hair pulled back in a ponytail. She turned on the radio and we listened to the top twenty station. *I Got you Babe* by Sonny and Cher was playing. It was the number one song of the week.

We began singing it to each other. Once we made it to the highway I was able to relax a little. It was a little scary since it was my first driving on a highway. Now, I was able to put my right hand on Rock's leg as I drove. She placed her hand on top of mine.

I asked, "What are they doing in the back?"

Rock looked through the back window and said, "Kenny and Sadie are sitting together holding hands. Junior and Francis are lying down. They look to be asleep."

Rock usually called Tucky by his given name. I had to think of who Kenny was since I was so used to him being called Tucky.

I looked over at her and she gave me a quick kiss. I was driving behind Dad with James Ernest behind us. Susie was riding in the front seat with James Ernest and Raven.

"Is everyone okay back there? Over," Dad's voice came over the radio he had given each of us.

I heard James Ernest say, "Everything is okay back here. Over," in his deep voice.

Rock picked up the radio and said, "This is Rock. We are good. Over and out."

Dad came back on and said, "There's a rest stop up ahead in twenty-two miles. Let's pull off and take a break."

Twenty minutes later we pulled off the highway and into the rest stop. Everyone exited and took off for the restrooms.

"Where are we?" Junior asked as we walked to the restroom.

"We're somewhere between Lexington and Berea," I said.

"Isn't that where James Ernest is going for college?" he asked.

"It sure is."

After a ten minute break we loaded up again and took off. We had decided to stop at the next exit that had a McDonalds to eat lunch. We saw a sign for a McDonalds shortly after getting back on the road. Ten miles later we were stopping again.

We were standing inside waiting to place our orders when Rhonda asked, "Where's Susie? Did she go to the bathroom?"

Sadie said, "I just came from there. She wasn't in there."

A worried look came onto Mom's face. "James Ernest, was she in the truck when you left the rest stop?"

"I think so. Rhonda and Susie switched spots. I thought Susie was in the back."

"She wasn't back there with us," Shauna said.

Purty added, "We thought she was in the cab."

"Oh, no," Mom said.

We all got worried looks on our faces.

"I'll go back and get her while you guys eat. I'll take mine to go and eat it on the way," Dad said.

James Ernest looked sick. I knew that he felt he should have checked to make sure everyone was in the truck.

"Everything will be okay. Don't worry," Dad said as he left with his bag of food.

By the time we were finished with our meals I saw Dad pulling into the lot. Susie was with him. She looked toward us and we all began clapping and hollering. She smiled, while the other customers stared at us, trying to figure out why we were causing a commotion.

Mom met her at the door with a hug and asked her what she wanted to eat. Mom ordered it while Susie told us what had happened.

"I had to go back into the restroom. When I came out I saw you guys pulling onto the highway. I figured sooner or later I would be missed, so I went in the office and waited," she told us.

James Ernest said, "I'm so sorry I left you."

"It's okay, really."

"Next time I'll try to leave Purty," James Ernest said.

We all started clapping.

"Hey, you wouldn't have any fun without me," Purty yelled out. We had to agree, it would be a lot less fun.

As we were leaving the restaurant, Rhonda asked Susie, "Don't you need to go to the restroom?" We all laughed. Susie took her food with her to eat on the way. I made sure everyone was loaded.

Francis decided to ride up front with us for a while. She said she was getting a headache in the back.

An hour later we were leaving Kentucky and passing by the I-75 Jellico exit in Tennessee. It was my first time in Tennessee. Little did I know then that I would visit the Smokies almost every year after I was married. We loved the Smoky Mountains.

An hour later we were coming into Knoxville. I knew we were getting close to the Smokies. Later, we took an exit and left the highway and were headed to Townsend. I was tired. I had no idea how tiring driving could be for long stretches. The truck was running great.

Once we were in Townsend, Dad told us he was going to stop at their motel and register. We could take a break and use the bathrooms if we needed. He found the place and pulled into the lot. Dad got the keys to the rooms and we all went to check them out.

We could see the mountains to the south of us as they rose into the sky. The blue haze of the Smokies was something to behold.

We continued a couple of miles when we came to a visitor's center. We pulled in and got out. We went inside and found maps and info and magazines. They had a booklet with the hikes we could take. They had a booklet that listed all the waterfalls and how to get to them. We loaded up on info. A mile further down the road we saw a wooden sign that said *Great Smoky Mountains National Park*.

Dad pulled off the road again. We exited and took pictures of the twelve of us hanging all over the sign. Another car had pulled off the road and Mom asked the man if he would take a picture of us all. He did.

A few miles further we came to a dead end. The sign showed that Cades Cove was seven miles to the right. A rocky stream ran along the twisty road all the way to our campground. I was amazed by the beauty of the mountains. It reminded me of Morgan County but in a grander scale. I loved every inch of it.

We pulled into the campground and stopped at the ranger check-in station. He gave us a map of the campground and where our campsites were. He gave a list of rules. I was beyond excited. To the left of the station were a small general store and the restrooms.

We finally made our way to the campsites. Our two campsites backed up to the forest. We were more secluded than a lot of the other sites. Dad gave James Ernest the phone number to the motel where they were staying in case we needed them. He told us they would check on us every so often. Then they left us. Mom said they were going to drive around the eleven mile Cades Cove loop before heading back to Townsend.

We began unloading everything and setting up the tents. We had two large tents. I had bought a new two man tent and Purty also had one. The campground was filled with large trees, and each site had its own campfire ring and picnic table. I had expected it to be hotter since we were further south, but I was surprised that it was cooler here in the mountains. It felt good.

The girls took off to the restrooms while the Wolf Pack began putting up the tents. We placed the two large tents together in the middle of the two sites. I placed my two man tent away from the boys' tent and Purty placed his on the other side of the girls' tent.

We had the tents up by the time the girls returned.

"What are we going to do now?" Junior asked.

"I read that early mornings and late evenings are the best times to drive around Cades Cove. Let's go check it out," James Ernest suggested.

We discovered that once you leave the entrance to the campground and turn left you begin the one-way loop. At the entrance was a parking area and within was a box that held information about Cades Cove. We grabbed four of the brochures and placed a dollar in the collection box. Behind the parking area we could see horses in the field and stables where you could sign up for a horseback ride in the cove.

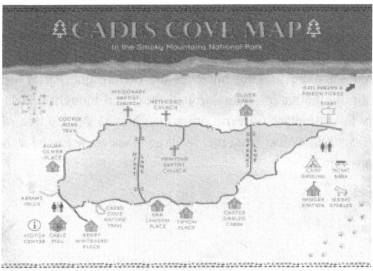

I gave our brochure to Rock so she could read it as we drove through the park. We gave another one to the guys in the back of the truck. The drive through the cove was great. Deer speckled most of the large mown fields. Old log cabins and churches stood down lanes to be explored at our leisure.

It was slow driving since it was a one lane road and folks took their time watching the wildlife in the fields and taking pictures of the beauty that surrounded us. The road traveled around the outskirts of the large cove with blue hazed mountains rising all around it. Every so often there were pull-offs where drivers could park and walk, or take pictures, or just look at the beauty.

Cars came to a standstill. After sitting for a couple of minutes a man walked by and I asked, "Do you know what's going on?"

"There's a bear and two cubs in a clearing up ahead. You may be here a while."

"Thanks."

I could see the excitement in Rock's face. "Tell the others and walk on ahead if you want," I told her.

She gave me a quick kiss and scooted out of the cab. She went to the back and told the others about the bears. They all piled out. Rock stopped and told everyone else in James Ernest's pickup. They got out. I didn't mind being left behind.

I sat there looking out over the picturesque valley of fields with the mountains rising around them and thought that this was my favorite place on earth other than home. A lone tree stood in the field thirty feet from me. A large black crow cawed as he flew onto a limb.

It brought back memories of Bo, my pet crow. I guess, in reality, I was his pet human. He had adopted me and sat on my left shoulder until one day he suddenly disappeared. Perhaps he had flown down here and liked it and stayed. I had worried that he had ended up dead on the side of a busy road somewhere. It was much better to think of him flying around Cades Cove in his last years.

"Caw, caw," the crow cried out. It swept out of the tree and landed just on the other side of the barb wire fence that separated the road from the field. I watched as it hopped along like crows do. His head would turn and look up at me every now then as he searched the ground.

A gray squirrel scampered across the road in front of the truck and under the fence but stopped short when it saw the crow. They stared at one another before the squirrel ran off to the tree the crow had just abandoned.

"Hello, Bo," I said, through my open window. The crow looked up, cocked his head, and flew away. "Caw, caw," was his goodbye. Two deer came out of the tree line on my right and passed in front on my truck and then gracefully leaped over the fence and into the field.

Once they were twenty yards away they began grazing on the grass. The vehicles in front of me began to move. I followed until James Ernest stopped to let his riders climb back inside. I then saw Rock's huge smile as she and the others headed to the truck. She slid in and said, "That was amazing."

I was able to drive once everyone was inside. Thirty yards up ahead she pointed toward what they had been watching. A large black bear was near the bottom of a tree. Her two babies were clinging to the side of the tree. As we passed by the baby bear on the bottom reached up and bit the others butt. They then climbed higher into the branches.

Halfway around the loop we came to a visitor center with restrooms and a store. We parked in the large parking area and got out to look around.

There was an old white two story home with a cantilever barn and a working grist mill.

Typical Cantilever Barn

A small stream ran past the mill feeding water to turn the large paddle wheel. There were also a smokehouse and a blacksmith shop scattered around the mill, as well.

We walked around the farm looking at all the different buildings and tools. A man inside the grist mill explained to us how it worked. It was getting late and we had only gone halfway around the loop so we headed back to the trucks. I thought it would be fun to hike through the middle of the loop. I would suggest it later.

The second half of the loop was just as wonderful and we made it back to the campground as darkness came. Tucky quickly built a fire and we took out some hotdogs from the cooler to cook for supper.

Everyone looked tired from the day of traveling except for Junior. He was a bundle of energy. He asked as we were cooking the dogs over the open fire, "What are the plans for tomorrow?"

"Has anyone had a chance to look at the pamphlets or brochures yet?" James Ernest asked.

"Laurel Falls isn't far from here. It's on the way to Gatlinburg. It's a two mile round trip hike and it's supposed to be the most popular hike in the Smokies," Susie told us.

"I thought it would be fun to hike through Cades Cove," I suggested.

"You mean around the loop?" Rhonda asked.

"No. I mean we could walk through the fields and the trees. Just think of the animals we might come across," I explained.

"That could be fun," Tucky seconded.

"We could come across some bears," Raven said.

"I would protect you if that happened," Purty said.

"The only way you would protect us would be to lie down in front of the bear and let him eat you while we ran," Tucky said

"I would have fond lasting memories of you, my hero," Shauna said. We all burst into laughter. Shauna kissed him on the cheek and he was fine.

"The hike to the falls would be relaxing and give us a day to unwind a little. We could even play in one of the streams," Raven said.

"Okay, how's this? We hike to Laurel Falls in the morning and then go in to Gatlinburg for lunch. Then in the afternoon we relax in the stream. Then on Tuesday we go for a long hike into the mountains," James Ernest said.

"Sounds great," Purty said. We all agreed. We had a plan.

After eating, we sat around the fire for a couple of hours. The campgrounds smelled wonderful. The aroma of campfires filled the air as the temperature dropped to chilly. The fire felt good. We talked about how wonderful the Smokies were and what all we had already seen. Everyone was suddenly tuckered and talked out. We made sure to put all food back into the cooler and stored it back in the truck, per the campground rules.

No one wanted a bear ripping through their tent due to the smell of food. We had to ask Purty several times. Shauna assured us she would make sure he didn't have any food in the tent. He and Shauna were sharing his tent. Rock and I were in my tent. The others split up and went to the girls' tent or the boys' tent.

A few of us made a trip to the restrooms before turning in.

Once Rock and I were inside our tent she snuggled against me and we kissed.

Chapter 17
Don't Call the Sheriff

Monday, August 2

*I*t was the first fartless night in a tent that I could remember. Purty usually ran us out of our tent sometime during the night. It was a welcomed change. I woke up wondering what Shauna's experience had been. Would Purty still have a girlfriend, or had she met his bad side? I wondered.

I stretched my body getting the kinks out from sleeping on the ground. The sleeping bag offered little softness. Rock opened her eyes, looked at me, and smiled. She had the most wonderful smile.

"Are you ready for a big day?" she asked.

"I am, if I can still stand up. My body aches," I told her.

"I was nice and comfy inside my sleeping bag," she said. She unzipped her bag and scooted out of it. She was topless. I looked away. She explained, "The fewer clothes you wear the warmer your sleeping bag gets inside. It's all about your body heat."

I didn't hear anyone else up so I motioned for her to join me. I unzipped my sleeping bag and she slid in beside me. I then zipped it back up. She was right. All of a sudden the inside of my bag got warmer. We made out until we heard the boy's tent next to us unzip and bodies begin to exit.

We both quickly got dressed and joined the others around the fire Tucky had just got lit. It looked to be a beautiful morning. It

171

was too hard to bring enough food for twelve teenagers for six days so we only brought food for supper around the campfire. So our only hope for food was the small store near the restrooms.

Everyone needed the restrooms so we headed that way.

"Where's Purty and Shauna?" Francis asked.

"They must still be in their tent," Sadie said. She turned back and walked over to the tent and began slapping it. She said, "Get up sleepy heads. We're going to the store for food."

There was no answer. "Hey, guys," she said a little louder, but still nothing. She unzipped the tent and looked inside.

She looked back at us and said, "They're not here."

We all headed toward the tent. James Ernest looked inside. He said, "Their shoes are gone. Did anyone hear them last night or this morning?"

No one answered. A few of us shook our heads.

Susie said, "Maybe they got up early and went for a walk."

"Maybe Purty farted and Shauna took him to the woods and killed him," Tucky said.

"That's my guess," I said. We laughed. It didn't seem as though anyone was taking their disappearance too seriously.

"They will show up," Rhonda said.

We continued toward the store. After using the restrooms, brushing our teeth, and the girls fixing their hair, we entered the store. Most of the gang bought a pint of milk and either donuts or snack cakes for breakfast. I got an RC Cola and orange cupcakes. The breakfast made for hiking.

When we came out of the store we gathered and were waiting on the others. Francis pointed and said, "There they are."

We looked across the road and saw them walking toward us holding hands. When they got close Rock asked, "Where were you two?"

Shauna answered, "We woke early and went for a walk. I wanted to see the horses. The stables are up that lane." She pointed toward the lane.

"We were worried about you," Francis told them.

"It sure looks like it. Instead of sending out a search party, you're standing here feeding your faces," Purty teased.

Rhonda and Susie came out of the store and Susie said, "You found the two lost sleep walkers."

Rhonda then said, "This place does not have showers. What are we supposed to do?"

"I guess we bathe in the streams or do sponge baths," Tucky said.

Rock added, "We're used to that at home."

"It's only six days," Junior chimed in.

"Ewwww, yuck, gross," were a few of the replies.

"Are we ready to head to Laurel Falls?" James Ernest asked.

We got back to the campsite and made sure the fire was out and everything was zipped up in the tents, and then we took off. We found out that there were only two main roads in the park. One was the road from Gatlinburg to Cades Cove and the other was the road that took you over the mountains, from Gatlinburg to North Carolina. Both roads met at an intersection near the main visitor center outside of Gatlinburg. There were other side roads such as the one that went to Clingman's Dome, the highest point in the Smokies.

It was a twenty-three mile drive from Cades Cove to Laurel Falls and then another four miles to the Sugarlands Visitor Center. During the drive we passed scenic overlooks, roadside waterfalls, other campgrounds and quiet walkways. The twisty road was fun to drive, but it was hard to look at all the beauty as I drove.

Susie had decided to ride with us and she jumped in the cab beside Rock. She and Rock continually talked about the mountain stream that ran along the road and the splendor of it.

They kept looking for bears in the water with no luck.

When we got to the parking area for the hike we found most spots already taken. There were two parking areas, one on each side of the road. We finally found two spots and parked. We decided we didn't need to take backpacks since it was only a two mile hike and still fairly cool.

Rhonda and Sadie carried their cameras. A few of us took walking sticks. I took the one Uncle Morton had carved for my birthday years earlier. I figured I had brought it; I might as well use it. It could come in handy to fight off bears.

We crossed the road to the trailhead and began the hike. The trail followed a stream that we figured led to the waterfall. We were walking twenty feet or so above the water. The trail rose and fell as we walked. At times, we could wade out into the water if we had wanted.

Catahecassa

Being a deputy on the Morgan County police force took some getting used to. My tribe had taught that we didn't live by white man's rules, and now here I was enforcing them. My tribe lived as though they thought they were still living in the days before the Europeans took over our lands.

I felt the past should stay in the past. I believed I could learn from the past, but I wanted to look to the future. It did no good to hold on to the grudges or anger of our ancestors. I liked my new home and the people I lived among. I took it as a sign of respect when Sheriff Cane asked me if I would be interested to becoming a deputy.

I didn't want to live like my neighbors, but I was happy to help with crops, or other issues that they needed help with. I liked my freedom. I was free to do as I liked. But I also needed money to live. I couldn't live on wildlife alone. I needed money for food. I needed a vehicle for travel to town. Therefore, I accepted the part time position. It was good for me.

Today, I was assigned to traffic control on the outskirts of town. I was parked off the road partially hidden. I learned quickly that we were very lenient as far as the speed limit - to a point. We mostly looked for reckless driving. But going sixty-five in a thirty-five mile per hour zone was deemed reckless.

The car whizzed past me, and I pulled out and began the chase. I caught up by going close to ninety. Once I caught the car I saw that he was going close to seventy. I turned on my siren. He sped up. I radioed the office to let them know I was in pursuit. The chase lasted a couple of minutes on State Route 519. The driver finally pulled over to the side of the road in a secluded spot.

I got out of my vehicle and carefully approached the driver's side window. My hand was on my weapon, but it remained in the holster. I got up to the window and by the time I recognized the driver it was too late. Treehawk raised his gun over the window opening and fired. I was knocked backward by the blast and landed in the road. I could hear a distant siren. The door started to open. My right arm was useless due to the shot's wound. I knew I was a dead man.

Suddenly he closed the door and put the car in gear. Before taking off, he pointed the gun out the window and toward my head. I could hear the siren closing. The shot rang out just after I rolled to my right, barely escaping the bullet that would have killed me. My foot was lying in front of the rear tire. I jerked it out as he hit the gas. The tire nicked my boot.

175

Deputy Stutts stopped short of where I laid on the pavement. He jumped out of the cruiser and ran to my side. The bullet had gone through my right arm, just above my bicep muscle.

Linny placed a tourniquet near my armpit to stop the blood loss. Within minutes Deputy Derek Clouse arrived on the scene. They helped me into the back seat of Linny's patrol car. Clouse said he would pull my cruiser off the road and go get help to take it back to the office. Linny sped off taking me to the Morehead hospital.

"Did you get a good look at the shooter?" Linny asked.

"Yes."

"Did you know him?"

"Treehawk," I answered.

"We thought he had left the area," Linny said.

"If he did, he came back," I said.

"I'll get you in the hospital and then call the sheriff," Deputy Stutts said.

"Don't do that. They're on their honeymoon. I'll be fine," I told him. I didn't want them to return because I got shot in the arm. If he returned I also knew they would make the kids return. I didn't want that happening due to me.

*T*he hike was easy and fun. Junior was fooling around trying to impress us with his gymnastic moves on the trail when he did a back flip too close to the bank and he slid all the way down and into the water. There were hikers coming the opposite way who got to laugh at him along with us.

He was sitting in a pool of water when he looked up and said, "Well, this is embarrassing."

"Now you know what it feels like to be me," Purty said.

176

Junior climbed back up the bank and we continued. It wasn't long before he heard the roar of the waterfalls. We knew we were getting near. We rounded a corner and there were the falls. It fell in layers. The top falls had a fifteen feet or so drop. It flowed a little ways and then dropped another ten feet or so and flowed under a bridge.

Sightseers could view it from the bridge that crossed the stream or follow a trail to the top of the falls. A sign warned hikers to remain on the trail, due to the slippery rocks. Rock and I walked out to the middle of the bridge and let the mist cool us from the hike. I kissed her and then we decided to go to the top.

We all ended up at the top and decided to rest a spell before hiking back down the trail to the trucks. Other hikers enjoyed the view by doing the same as us. There were families with young kids. There were young adults who looked like they might be on their honeymoon. There were older couples probably over seventy that had made the hike.

One of the older couples came over and sat near us on a large flat rock. I said hello and they greeted us back.

"Where are you folks from?" Rock asked them.

"We came from Michigan, an hour north of Detroit. We're on our honeymoon," the lady said.

I must have looked stunned, because the man said, "You look surprised."

"I wasn't expecting that," I said.

"I suppose not. But we're having the time of our life," he said.

"That is so great," Rock told them.

"If I may give you two a bit of advice," he said.

"Please do," Rock said.

"Enjoy your youth. It looks like you guys are. Then enjoy every day of the rest of your life," the old man said.

It wasn't the great key to life I expected, but I said, "Thank you. We plan to."

James Ernest rose from his seat and asked if we were ready to head back. We followed him. He made a quick count to make sure no one was left behind.

We got back to the parking area without any incidents. We headed to Gatlinburg. When we got to the Sugarlands Visitors Center he pulled in. I followed his lead and parked next to him.

Inside we found animal and plant exhibits. We found maps and books and restrooms.

I asked one of the rangers if he could suggest a breakfast place for us.

"There's an all-you-can-eat pancake house in town. Should be the perfect place for a hungry group of teenagers," he said.

"Are there showers anywhere? We're camping at Cades Cove," Rock asked him.

"Just as you enter Gatlinburg there's a laundromat with showers. Turn left at the first road and it's in a small shopping area on the left. The Happy Hiker's outfitting store is next to it. You can't miss it."

"Thanks. That helps a lot." she said.

"Are you guys doing any hiking?" the ranger asked.

"Yes. We're here for the week and plan to hike a lot," I told him.

"Would you like suggestions?"

"Of course. This is our first time here."

"A great hike with a terrific view at the end is the Alum Cave Bluff trail. I also suggest the Chimney Rock trail. It's harder but worth it. Also, be sure to drive the Roaring Fork Motor Trail. But there are hundreds of great trails," he said while handing me a booklet of trails.

"Thank you so much," Rock and I said.

"Have fun and stay safe," the ranger said.

I knew we would have fun, but knowing us, I couldn't promise that we would stay safe.

We pulled into the pancake house parking lot that the ranger suggested. The morning rush had passed, so the waitress was able to push three tables together for the twelve of us. Most of us ordered the pancakes. Francis got a hamburger and fries. Shauna ordered a BLT and fries.

"Let's see who can eat the most pancakes," Purty challenged.

"All of us against you," Junior said.

"That still wouldn't be fair. He'd beat us," Tucky said.

"Control yourself," Shauna told Purty as she placed her hand on his arm. Purty turned and quickly kissed her.

"You're right. I'll just eat a dozen or so," Purty said. We all laughed.

It was great to see Purty so happy. He was truly enamored with Shauna. And for some reason, she seemed to really like him. I was thrilled for him.

Our group ate so many pancakes I wondered how the restaurant made any money off us. Purty stopped with six. I ate four large buttery pancakes with lots of maple syrup poured on. Our waitress was an older lady who could have been our grandmother. She seemed to enjoy our banter and teasing. She told us to come back while we were visiting. We told her we would definitely return.

We had decided to pay for the meals out of our pooled money. Susie paid the bill and left a generous tip for the waitress.

Chapter 18
A Bear

*J*ames Ernest told us that he and Raven had seen a spot that he thought would be good for playing in the creek on our way back this afternoon.

We all wanted to walk around downtown Gatlinburg and look in the shops while we were there. We wanted a relaxing day and this was a great way to relax. We agreed that if we got separated that we would meet at the trucks at two that afternoon. It was almost noon.

Rock's birthday was tomorrow and I never had bought Rock a birthday gift. I decided to wait until she saw something she liked and buy it for her. I had brought a lot of extra money to buy gifts and candy and stuff. We stopped in a candy shop where a man in the huge window was pulling taffy. It was almost mesmerizing watching the machine turn round.

I went inside and bought a large box of vanilla salt water taffy for us all to share. We looked in tee-shirt shops. It seemed as though every other shop sold the same things. We saw the *Ripley's Believe it or Not* building on the main strip. We saw a store that had amazing pictures of animals that a photographer had taken. I thought that would be a fun job to have.

Rock saw a white sleeveless blouse that she really thought was pretty in one shop. She even showed it to Susie. I figured it would be a good birthday gift. We all had great fun walking around town, holding hands and joking with our friends.

In one of the stores I got separated from Rock for a minute and I saw Susie standing nearby. I hurried over and asked, "What size blouse would Rock wear?"

Susie looked at me like I was crazy. I explained, "Tomorrow is her birthday and I want to buy her this blouse she saw and loved. I have no idea how girl's sizes go."

"She would wear a medium. That's very nice of you," Susie said. Then she asked, "What shop was it in?"

"Remember the white blouse she showed you?"

"Oh, yeah. It was really cute. I could go get it for you."

"You don't mind?"

I took out my billfold and handed her twenty dollars. Rock walked up to us as I was handing the money to Susie.

"Isn't this town amazing?" she said. To my amazement Rock didn't ask why I was giving Susie money.

Susie found Rhonda and they left the store. It was almost time to meet back at the trucks. "We need to start heading back," I said.

We walked down the street eating taffy. It was really good.

When we all got back to the trucks I noticed that Susie had a package in her hand. She nodded to me that she had gotten it.

We headed for the mountain stream. I thought it might be a good time to try out the fly rod. When we stopped I mentioned it to James Ernest and he said, "We need a fishing license to fish these streams."

That was the end of that.

Catahecassa

The doctor was stitching me up. He said, "You were a very lucky man. There is no major damage."

He had no idea how lucky I was. The good Lord had to be watching over me. It was the only way to explain why I wasn't lying in a morgue.

I knew that somehow Treehawk had known I was patrolling that road. He deliberately sped through the area so I would pull him over, and he would be able to kill me, gaining his revenge.

This was now twice he had tried. I wouldn't give him another chance. Now, I was coming for him.

Sheriff Cane

We had driven to Pigeon Forge and spent the day letting Janie and Sally ride go-carts and other fun activities. We ate a late lunch and then drove back to our motel. We were going to spend the rest of the afternoon at the pool.

There was a note on our door asking me to come to the office. The girls went inside to change while Betty and I went to the office to see what was wrong. We were instantly worried that something had happened to one of the teenagers.

The desk clerk handed me a message that asked me to call the office in West Liberty. I knew they wouldn't interrupt my honeymoon unless something serious had happened. We hurried back to our room. I picked up the phone and called collect to the office.

My secretary told me about Cat being shot and who had shot him. I told her, "I'll be back tomorrow." Betty shot me a worried look.

"Everyone's okay," I told her.

"No, no, no," my secretary told me. "We didn't even want to call you, but Linny said you would be upset if we didn't let you know. Cat is fine. He begged us not to call you. He'll be really upset if you come back. Promise me you'll stay with your lovely wife and enjoy the week. We'll see you next week."

"Are you sure?"

"Yes, positive."

"Is he in the hospital?"

"He has probably already left. They were patching him up and sending him home to rest," she said.

"Tell him to take the rest of the week off. Okay."

"I will."

"See you next week."

I hung up and Betty wanted to know what had happened. I explained it to her.

"He's okay, though?" Betty asked.

"She said he was fine."

"I understand if you need to return."

"I knew you would. But they made me promise to stay. They didn't even want to call me, but Linny thought I would get upset if they didn't."

"Poor Cat."

"I get a feeling that Cat won't sit around waiting on him to try again," I told Betty.

James Ernest eased into a pull-off near the spot we were going to play in the stream. We got out of the trucks. Some of the girls wanted to change into their swimming suits. They stayed in the back of the trucks to change.

As I placed my feet in the mountain stream I could feel the coolness of the water. It was refreshing after the day of hiking

184

and walking around Gatlinburg. The water ran over rocks causing small ripples. Below a small cascade was a deep pool of water. I submerged myself in the water and let it envelope my body. It cooled and refreshed my body even though it was colder than I was used to.

The girls finally made their way down the bank and joined us in the water. Rock swam to the middle of the pool where I stayed mostly immersed in the water. She began splashing me. I dove under the water and grabbed her around the waist and dunked her. She came up laughing. She put her arms around my neck and kissed me and then pushed my head under the water.

The couples paired up in the water as they flirted and kissed and played. I noticed Susie and Rhonda sitting on a large rock taking in the sun.

Rhonda

Shauna really liked Purty. He had really matured and become a lot more caring for others since he met her. I wondered if Shauna had brought this version of him out, or had it always been there, and I hadn't seen it. He was still goofy at times, but he was also funny and loyal.

He had pursued me for so long, and all I had done was push him away. I now wish I hadn't. I saw how happy he and Shauna were. I knew he would do anything for her. I also know he would have done the same for me if I hadn't rejected him.

I felt like a third wheel in our group. I knew Susie felt the same. It was almost like we were a couple. Our friends didn't mean to make us feel this way. They tried to include us in games and all the activities, but we couldn't help feeling as we did.

Susie had confided in me that she had made a terrible mistake. I still couldn't believe she and Timmy weren't a couple anymore.

We all had thought they would stay together and get married and have a wonderful family. We all talked about the shock of it. Rock was wonderful. She was probably the most striking of all of us. She was nice, and caring and a great friend. She never said anything bad about a person.

She had her charm and hooks in Timmy, and I wasn't sure Susie would ever be able to counteract that. I watched the two of them hold on to each other and kiss. It seemed magical.

James Ernest

*H*ow did I get so lucky to have the friends I did? I looked around the stream and saw the happy faces on them all. We were having the time of our lives.

Two weeks after returning home I would be leaving for college. This part of my life would come to an end. I would miss each and every one of them. Each person had their own uniqueness and personality. We gelled together to form an unbreakable kinship. We were family.

I didn't want to leave them. I wanted to stay with my friends. I wanted to stay with Raven. I loved her dearly. But I knew to accomplish what a wanted in life I had to go to college. I knew going to Morehead State University would give me the education I needed to teach, and I could say home while going there. The school was known for producing teachers. But I didn't have the money to go to there or any college other than Berea. I felt Berea was the perfect choice for me, even though I had to leave home.

Raven's dark wet skin glistened in the sunlight. Her smile brightened the day. She kissed me and said, "I love you, James Ernest."

"I love you."

We spent the rest of the afternoon in the stream. We had finally had enough and decided to go to the campground and relax around the campsite.

We loaded up and began the slow drive back. Timmy told me he was going to go by the motel and check in with Mom and Dad. We gave everyone the choice of who to go with. Francis and Junior decided to go back to the campsite in the back of my truck.

Timmy had Rock, Tucky and Sadie riding with him.

$\mathcal{A}$s I turned right towards Townsend, Rock looked in the back and said, "It looks like Tucky and Sadie are both asleep."

I knew I could use a nap myself. We got to the motel just before six that evening. I saw my parents' car in the parking lot. Rock and I got out trying not to disturb the sleeping beauties.

I knocked on the motel door and thirty seconds later Dad answered.

"This is a surprise," he said.

"We were on our way back to camp and I thought I should check in to tell you we are all fine. Mom came through the adjoining door from Janie's room and gave us a hug. She then asked, "What did you guys do today?"

I told them about our hike to Laurel Falls. Mom said they were going to go there tomorrow. Rock then told them about our trip to Gatlinburg and our afternoon playing in the water.

"What are your plans tomorrow?" Dad asked.

"I believe we're going to take a longer hike into the mountains. The ranger at Sugarlands told us of a couple good hikes. You ought to stop in there when you go to Gatlinburg. It's really nice," I told them.

"I think we're going there tomorrow," Mom said.

Rock asked what they did today. Mom told us. "By the way, we saw something you guys might enjoy doing one day."

"What?" I asked.

"They have tubing on the creek across the road. It looked like fun. We might do it one day. I thought maybe we all could do it one day together. I think Janie and Sally would like to be with you guys at least one day," Mom said.

"That does sound like fun. I'll mention it tonight to everyone," I said.

"We were going to visit you guys tonight. I guess we don't have to now," Dad said.

"You better tell Tim the news," Mom said.

"What news?" I quickly asked.

Dad then told us about Cat getting shot by Treehawk. He made sure we knew he was okay. "The only reason I'm not going back is because they assured me he was okay," Dad told us.

"I can't believe that happened," I said. Rock had tears running down her cheeks.

We discussed it for a while and then I said we needed to get back before Purty ate all the hotdogs. They laughed.

"We'll see you tomorrow night," Mom said.

Before leaving I went and knocked on the adjoining door. Janie opened the door and I said, "Hi, squirt."

"Hi, Timmy," she said and hugged me.

"Are you two having a good time?"

"The best. Hi, Rock," she said.

"I'll see you later."

Rock and I left. When we got back to the campsite we saw that the others were already eating around the fire. I wasn't very hungry, but I fixed myself a hotdog.

"Were they there?" James Ernest asked.

"I have news. Cat was shot this morning," I told them.

"He's okay. He was shot in the arm," Rock said, trying to ease their concerns.

"He stopped a speeder outside of West Liberty and the driver shot him when he walked up to the window," I continued.

"Who was it?" Tucky asked.

"Treehawk."

"It was a setup... an ambush," James Ernest reasoned.

"Apparently," I said.

We spent the next hour eating and talking about Cat. Some of our gang didn't know Cat very well. Some of them didn't know he was now a deputy. Darkness began overtaking us. I saw two skunks coming our way from one of the adjacent campsites.

"Don't panic," I told everyone.

"What?" Rhonda asked.

"They won't bother us if we stay calm," I said. Everyone turned their heads toward the spot I was looking and saw the skunks. They were now right behind Francis and Junior. The skunks were sniffing the ground looking for scraps of food. One of them walked right across Susie's feet. She remained still.

"They are sort of cute," Rock said.

"I didn't know we invited Bernice," Purty said.

"Tucky, what does skunk taste like?" Junior asked jokingly.

"It's not that great. The meat is tough and has a smell," He answered.

We all looked at him to see if he was joking. I had a feeling he wasn't.

"Are you serious?" Sadie asked as she stopped holding his hand.

"Our parents tried it once. No one liked it," Rock told us.

"Did it smell like a skunk's spray?" Francis asked.

"No. It had a funny aroma when it was cooked," Tucky said.

Tucky looked down at the skunks and said, "You could try one of these."

We all laughed. The skunks didn't seem to like the sudden outburst. They ran off to find food elsewhere.

I told the gang about the tubing in Townsend. Everyone liked that idea. We decided to do it later in the week. Before it got too late we decided to visit the restrooms. Some wanted to brush their teeth and wash up. Some just wanted to use the toilets.

Afterwards, Rock and I went for a short walk. The moon was up in the sky, but there was only a quarter of it showing. A road circled through the campsites. We walked the road and watched the other campers. Some were just sitting around their fire. Some were playing games by lantern.

On the opposite side of the campground a small stream ran past. We made our way to the stream and took a seat on one of the large rocks. It was relaxing listening to the gurgle of the water as it flowed past. Rock ran her fingertips up my arm making them tingle. It felt so good and loving. I turned and kissed her. She placed her head on my shoulder.

Fifteen minutes later we got up and headed back to the tents. Some of the gang had gone into their tents. Tucky and Sadie, and James Ernest and Raven were still staring into the flames of the fire.

When we walked up Sadie asked, "Where have you two been?"

"We were sitting next to the stream over there," Rock said and pointed.

"This is really nice," Raven said.

"You mean the fire?" Rock asked.

"I mean everything. The whole trip is great. We could do anything here, and I would love it," she said.

I had to agree. I felt the same way. We finally put the fire out and went into our tents. I undressed and slipped into my bag. The inside of the tent was total darkness. I could hear Rock undressing. She then unzipped my sleeping bag and slipped in next to me. I quickly noticed with my hands that she was totally naked. She kissed me and we enjoyed our time in the tent.

Tuesday, August 3

"Happy birthday," I said when Rock opened her eyes that morning. She hugged me and said, "I'm sixteen."

"Let's get married," was the next thing she said.

"What?"

"I'm just teasing. I saw all the small wedding chapels in town and thought this would be a great place to get married, but not now," she explained.

She had slipped out of my bag once we had gotten sleepy last night and slept in her bag. She got up and quickly dressed. "I've got to go to the restroom."

"Okay. See you later," I said as I closed my eyes.

She unzipped the tent and left. I heard her talking to someone as she walked away. I suddenly needed to pee. I got up and slipped my shorts on. I left the tent and faded into the woods to pee behind a tree. Tucky was up so he and I then walked to the store. He said Sadie had already gone to the restroom.

We stood outside the store waiting for the girls. James Ernest and Raven were walking our way.

"Are we going to hike Alum Cave Bluff today?" I asked.

"Sounds good to me," James Ernest said.

"Are we going back to the pancake house before the hike?" Tucky asked.

"Okay. We probably need a good meal since the hike will take most of the day."

Rock and I decided not to buy anything in the store since we were heading for pancakes. Most of the others agreed. Purty had to buy a cake to tide him over.

Before leaving for Gatlinburg I got Rock's gift from Susie and gathered everyone around. I announced it was Tucky and Rock's sixteenth birthdays and we sang to them. I then handed Rock the bag. I was surprised when she opened the bag and pulled out a wrapped box. Susie must have had them wrap it. She opened the box and saw the blouse.

"This is the blouse I saw in town yesterday. I love it. Thanks, Timmy," she said. She threw her arms around my neck and kissed me in front of everyone.

"Wait, I've got a gift for Kenny," Sadie said. She handed him a small box. He opened it and pulled out a beautiful pocket knife. It had bears carved on the handle. I could tell he really liked it. Everyone then wished both of them a happy birthday and we hopped in the trucks and took off.

In the restaurant that morning I told our same waitress that it was Tucky and Rock's birthday. She put a candle on each of their stacks of pancakes and the whole restaurant had sung to them. They were thrilled.

After stuffing ourselves with the breakfast we headed toward North Carolina. We drove to the parking area for the trail. I had noticed a bulletin board at the beginning of the Laurel Falls trail. There was another one here. The board held general rules for hiking. It had a map showing where we were in the Smokies. It had a guide for animals, plants and trees we might see on the trail.

There was also a warning posted. It said there had been bear activity on the trail and said we should make noise as we walked, especially going around bends, so we wouldn't surprise a bear on the trail.

We all became excited at the prospect of having a first-hand bear encounter. At the trailhead was a sign that read:

Alum Cave Bluff 2.3 miles

Mount LeConte 5 miles

We began the hike. We let Purty and Shauna lead the way. We all knew we could outrun Purty if we needed to. Purty would be our sacrifice to the bear.

There were only a few cars in the parking lot. It was nothing like the Laurel Falls hike as far as the crowd. As we walked the path we would stop anytime we heard a sound. The bear warning placed us on high alert. The first forty minutes of the hike ran along a mountain stream and was uphill, but fairly flat. We came to a large boulder. The path went right through the middle of it. We had to squeeze through a part of it. There were steps inside it. We stopped while pictures were taken.

Once we got through the boulder we heard a pecking sound. I looked up toward the sound and saw a pileated woodpecker on the side of a tree. "Woody!" Junior cried out. We stood and watched it search for insects in the bark of the tree. We continued and came to a sharp hundred and eighty degree turn in the path.

The trail then began to climb the mountain. It was a definitely a harder portion of the hike, but still not real bad. It was a steady incline. Suddenly we heard branches breaking to our right. We stopped in our tracks. The bear came into view as it lumbered into an opening in the trees. It stopped and looked at us. Sadie and Rhonda were both taking pictures. I thought we should ease away.

Then we saw the babies. Three small bears were tailing their mother. I knew this was not good. A mother bear would kill to protect her cubs. The mother looked directly at me. I slowly motioned for everyone to continue the hike. We needed to leave the bears alone. Purty made a sudden move to pick up a stick. The bear growled and rose up on her hind legs.

I thought that it might be a good time for the sacrifice. The bear took two quick steps toward Purty. Purty's eyes almost bugged out of his face. I thought I heard Purty whimper. I finally got everyone to move on. We all were breathing hard as we stopped five minutes later after quickening our pace away from the bear.

We did a quick check to make sure we had everyone.

"That was something. I thought she was going to take Purty out," Tucky said.

"Why would you pick up that stick?" Francis asked.

"I needed something for protection," Purty explained.

"What do think that stick would have done?" I asked.

"I could have poked her in the eyes."

"She could have poked you down her throat after you did that," Junior said.

"That was scary. I think I've seen all the bears I want to see after that," Shauna said.

"Did anyone bring extra clean underwear?" Purty asked.

We all laughed as we began hiking again. A half hour later we came to a point with a great view.

We decided to take a break and look at our surroundings. I saw something out of the corner of my eyes. I looked down to see a small ground squirrel looking up at me. "Ain't you cute," I said.

"Thank you," Rock said.

"I was talking to this little guy," I said. I pointed down.

There were low growing bushes all around the rocks we were sitting on. The squirrel seemed to have come out from under one of them. Then others started noticing other little ground squirrels. James Ernest and Tucky had backpacks on with water and snacks. I knew we had packed some bags of peanuts.

"Can I have a bag of peanuts?" I asked. Tucky took his pack off and found me a bag. I opened it and dropped a nut down to the squirrel. He picked it up with his tiny paws and stood up on two les and started eating it.

"That is the cutest thing I've ever seen," Rock said. I began passing the bag to others after taking out a few for us to give to our little friend. We spent the next ten minutes feeding them. The squirrel even took one from the palm of my hand.

A couple came down the trail and James Ernest asked them how much further Alum Cave was.

"Maybe fifteen to twenty minutes more."

"Thanks," we all said.

We got up and headed that way. Before getting there we saw a outcropping of rocks that ran out from the mountain maybe a hundred yards. The ridge of rocks was only six to ten feet wide and a hundred feet or more above the forest floor. We saw a man sitting at the very end of the ridge.

"We have to do that," Tucky said.

"No way," Sadie said.

"It's too dangerous," Susie said.

I knew it was dangerous and that we shouldn't do it. But I also knew I really wanted to be sitting out on that point. I also knew that if it was just the wolf pack that was here we would already be climbing on it. We decided they were right, so we continued our hike.

There was a spot where the trail was very narrow and a wire rope had been attached to the stone wall so we could hold onto it while passing by. It wasn't long before we came to the large overhanging bluff. The dirt underneath was made up of orange clay and was dry and loose.

I looked out at the view. It was something to behold. Blue cast mountains and peaks as far as I could see. Green pines and oaks and maple trees filled the sides of the mountains and valleys.

The ranger was right. The hike wasn't that difficult, but the view was wonderful. We all took seats on the ground together as we looked out over the great expanse.

"This is my best birthday ever," Rock announced.

The overhanging cliff stretched to at least two hundred feet long or so. It was impressive. We stayed up on the bluff for at least an hour.

After returning to the trucks we talked about what we wanted to do with the rest of the day. Everyone seemed tired after the five mile hike up and down the mountain.

"I'd love to take a shower," Sadie said.

"Me too," Raven echoed.

"The ranger told me where one is in Gatlinburg," I said.

"We don't have soap or towels," Susie said.

"We could find a store and buy some cheap towels and some soap," James Ernest said.

That was what we decided to do. We decided to check the shower place out first and ask where to find what we needed. I led the way since I knew where to go. We entered Gatlinburg and made a left at the first street. There on the left was the laundromat.

Rock and I went inside and asked about showers. The lady said they supplied towels and they had soap and shampoo we could purchase. We were set. We went out and told everyone.

They had four shower stalls. Four of the girls went first. The guys headed for the Happy Hiker store next door.

The store had everything a person would need for hiking and camping in the Smoky Mountains. They sold patches for each of the trails in the park. For fifty cents I got an Alum Cave Bluff patch.

Across the street from the shop was a KFC restaurant. I was tempted to go over and get a piece of chicken, but I refrained.

The four girls were done and the other three girls and Purty went next. I asked James Ernest how he was doing on gas. We decided to stop in Townsend and fill up. The gas was a lot higher in Gatlinburg. It was now our turn to shower. It took us about half the time it took the girls. We headed back toward the campgrounds.

An hour later we were filling up at the station. James Ernest said, "Did you see that little drive up restaurant on the right when we first entered Townsend?"

"Yeah, it looked like a little cottage. It was called burger shack or something like that."

"Let's stop there and eat. It's five o'clock, and I know everyone is hungry."

"Okay," I said.

"I'll meet you there. I'll go and see if Mom and Dad are at the motel and see if they want to eat with us."

"Sounds like a plan."

I got in and took off while Susie was paying for the gas.

Mom, Dad and the girls were there and they agreed to go with us. The shop had three picnic tables sitting on the side on the building under a large oak tree. We ordered one large order for everyone. Burgers and fries for all, plus drinks. Dad said it was his treat. As we waited for the food, we told them about our hike and the bear encounter. Rock told them about the ground squirrels.

Janie and Sally wanted to go and feed them.

"The hike wasn't that bad. There were a few kids their age up there," Shauna said.

"The view was unbelievable," Raven added.

The burgers and fries finally came. It was the best burger I had ever eaten. Everyone thought so. As we were eating, something blue caught my eye. I looked over and saw two bluebirds sitting on the shop's eave. Then two more came and landed. Bluebirds were my favorite. I loved the way the sun lit up the blue feathers on their backs and they have the pretty orange bellies.

I pointed toward them. We all admired their beauty. I would only see bluebirds around our county every once in a while, unless I was at Homer and Ruby's. They had a few that stayed around their house. I believe Homer had put out some bluebird houses on his farm. Maybe I would place some around our store.

Mom and Dad came back to our campground with us. Tucky built a fire and we got out the marshmallows. Janie and Sally had a great time roasting them until the skunks wandered in again. Mom wasn't very happy about it either.

I quickly explained to leave them alone. I thought Mom was going to scream when one of them rubbed up against her leg.

"Just like a cat," Purty told Mom.

"It's nothing like a cat, Todd!" After the skunks left Mom was more at ease. She looked around at the tents, and then asked, "Why are there two small tents?"

I didn't know what to say. I knew Mom wouldn't want to hear that Rock and I were sleeping alone in one of them. I also knew Shauna wouldn't want Mom to know the truth. I looked across the fire at James Ernest. He smiled as Susie said, "We have seven girls in the Bear Troop. Our big tent is too small for all seven of us so we divided up. Two, two and three," she explained.

Susie saved my butt.

"Today is Rock and Tucky's birthday. We should do something to celebrate," I said, changing the subject.

"That's right. We forgot about it," Dad said.

Rock said, "That's okay. Timmy bought me the prettiest blouse for my birthday."

After it got dark Mom and Dad left for the night. Dad asked what we were doing the next day.

"We had talked about hiking through Cades Cove or hiking the Chimney Top trail," James Ernest said. We haven't decided yet.

"Let us know what day you want to go tubing. The girls want to go with you," Mom said.

"Probably Thursday," James Ernest said.

Chapter 19
Problem Skunked

Wednesday, August 4

I woke up the next morning wishing I was in my bed. Not that I wanted to be home, I wanted my bed. Aches were mounting the more I slept on the hard ground.

We had decided to hike up to Rainbow Falls. The ranger had told us to make sure we drove the Roaring Fork Motor Nature Trail. On that drive was the parking area for Rainbow Falls. It is the largest falls in the Smokies and a five and a half mile round trip hike.

It was a nice morning. It was probably going to be our last day in Gatlinburg, so we decided to go to the pancake house again before the hike. I was looking forward to the days adventures.

After visiting the restrooms and the store we headed toward Gatlinburg again. I was a little tired of pancakes so I ordered two pecan waffles and sausage. Some of the others liked my idea and ordered the same. Our same waitress we had every day waited on us again.

"What is the adventure today?" she asked us.

Tucky told her, "Roaring Fork Motor Trail and a hike to Rainbow Falls."

"That sounds like fun. The trail starts right up this road. I wish I could join you," she said, while pointing out the window.

"The more, the merrier," Rock told her.

"If I was sixty years younger I would. But if I was sixty years younger I'd give you girls a run for your money. Your boyfriends would only have eyes for me," she teased as she gave us a sexy pose.

"I do have eyes only for you," Purty told her.

She pretended to blush and waved her hand at him,

"Y'all are so sweet." She left to place our orders.

This was only our third full day here and I already was having the time of my life. I loved everything.

The temperature was supposed to hit eighty in Gatlinburg. I was sure it would be cooler in the mountains. Our waitress, Sandy, began bringing our drinks out.

"Your food will be right up," she said.

Catahecassa

*I*t was time to do something about Treehawk. I had been laid up for the past two days while my arm was healing. I was at the point where I felt some strength returning. At least I could put a shirt on. I had placed warning wires around my camp in case he tried to attack in the night.

I wasn't sure if he knew I had survived his attack or not. I knew he could easily find out I had. Whether he would stick around to finish the chore or leave the area again was something I didn't know. I had the rest of the week off. I would do some investigating now that I had a vehicle.

I called a friend from my tribe and asked her about Treehawk. She said he had left the area after his release. No one knew where he had gone. I asked her to call the station if he showed up.

I was spending the morning going to places he may have stayed. I began with the hotels in Morehead. I wore my police

201

uniform to give the appearance I was on official business, to me it was.

The license number of the vehicle he was driving had been reported stolen. I knew he would be driving something different by now.

*M*y waffles were very good. I was ready for a long hike. We left the restaurant and headed up the road. We saw a large round hotel sitting on a hillside. Just past it the two-lane road turned into one lane. The motor trail was a six mile one-way loop through the mountain. Again, we saw a box that had information material for the drive. We stopped and took a few. Susie dropped a dollar in the box.

There were old homesteads scattered along the road every mile or so. As we climbed the mountain there were spots to pull off and take in the views. We came to the parking area for Grotto Falls, which was less of a hike. We continued until we came to the Rainbow Falls area. We parked. Three of us put on back packs filled with water and snacks. We had a first aid kit in one of the packs.

Purty and Shauna wanted to lead the way. The trail sign read: Rainbow Falls - 2.7 miles. The trail was well maintained and a fairly easy hike for the first mile or so. We followed the water most of the way and even crossed it using bridges or large split logs that served as bridges.

The bulletin board didn't have any warnings for bears. Some of us were disappointed. The second half of the trail became steeper and rockier as we climbed. We stopped often and took pictures along the rocky stream. A large tree's trunk split off in two different directions. We took turns placing our head above where it split as the two girls snapped pictures.

They were already on their third roll of film. I wasn't sure how many they brought with them. My question was answered when Rhonda said, "Before we leave town I need to buy more film."

As we walked, Rhonda posed the question, "We have five couples in our group. How many will end up married?"

Even I knew this was a loaded question.

"Who wants to go first?" she asked.

Sadie said, "I believe three will."

"Which three?" Rhonda then said. That was the question I knew was coming. There was no way to answer it without hurt feelings arising.

"I think we should stop this game," I blurted out.

"This is fun, no one cares," Rhonda said. It was easy for her to say since she didn't have a boyfriend with her.

Sadie answered, "I think Tucky and I, James Ernest and Raven, and Purty and Shauna. Those are the three I think will end up married."

"Who else has an answer?" Rhonda asked.

"Who do you think?" Sadie asked Rhonda.

I tugged on Rock's arm and she stopped. We were the last in line. I didn't want to hear any more of their stupid gossip and thoughts.

We fell back and let them go ahead.

"I think James Ernest and Raven and also Purty and Shauna," Rhonda said. It was the last answer we heard.

"What's wrong? You didn't like the game, did you," Rock said.

"People are going to get their feelings hurt by something like that. Did it surprise you when Sadie named who she did?" I asked her.

"No. The only one I would name would be Raven and James Ernest," she said.

"You weren't offended that she didn't name us," I asked.

"Maybe a little, but I know why none of them would name us," she said.

"Susie," I answered for her.

"Yes. They all think we're just a temporary thing and you'll end up with Susie. I'm surprised she didn't name you and Susie," she said.

"That's why I didn't like the so-called game. I felt like it was meant as a way of telling us we don't belong together," I said.

"What do you think?"

"Rock, I love you. I've told you that. And you love me. Who knows what the future holds? I don't plan on going back to Susie. None of them knows how strong our relationship is. My only plan is you," I said.

She kissed me right there on the path. A young married couple came up behind us as we kissed. He told us, "Get a room."

We laughed, and then I heard them laughing as they walked on ahead of us.

"Thank you for caring about my feelings. You are so sweet," Rock said.

"You too," I said and quickly kissed her again.

"I think Rhonda is now a little jealous of Shauna," I said.

"I think so too,"

We walked the rest of the way to the falls by ourselves. A half hour later we could hear the falls and suddenly it was in front of us.

Purty and Shauna were sitting on a rock looking up at the falls.

"There you two are," Purty said. "We were beginning to think you got lost."

"It's hard to get lost when there's a wide path," I said.

"You were right, Timmy. Couples began getting mad at others because of the game," Shauna said.

"It was a stupid game," I said.

"Are you guys mad?" Purty asked.

"No," Rock said.

I said, "People can think what they want. I don't think everyone wants to know what others think about them. I didn't want to get involved."

I looked at Rock and asked, "You want to go behind the falls."

"Of course. Don't you?"

"You guys coming," I asked.

"No. We're happy here resting," Purty said.

The falls was probably eighty feet high and folks could walk behind it. We read that on sunny afternoons the mist from the falls produced a rainbow, giving the falls its name. We saw Junior and Francis behind the falls. Tucky and Sadie saw us and came over. Tucky asked, "Can we join you guys?"

"Sure," I said. We made our way over and around large rocks to get behind the falls. It was so cool to stand behind the falling water and look out at all the people that had hiked up. We stood there and kissed. I was hoping Rhonda had taken a picture of us.

"You still have any film left? Where's your camera?" I asked.

"Susie has it. I asked her to take a picture of us back here," Sadie said.

We ended up spending about an hour at the falls. We drank water and ate snacks. Some of us waded out into the water at the bottom of the falls. The mist soaked us.

"It's too bad we aren't the only ones here. I'd let you take me skinny dipping," Rock whispered in my ear as we stood in the pool.

"We could do it anyway," I whispered back. We laughed.

"We'd give everyone a good show," she said.

The water felt great after the long hike. We looked back at the falls and there was the rainbow. It was something to see.

We began our walk back down the mountain. We walked hand-in-hand and laughed a lot on our way,

Rock and I were trailing the group again. I wanted to be alone with her. I enjoyed her company, and at times it was hard to find alone time with a group of twelve. As we walked, a young couple caught up with us. I had seen them at the waterfalls.

"You two seem awfully happy. You must be in love," the young lady said.

Rock turned and said, "We are. But so do you two."

"We got married this past Saturday. We're on our honeymoon," the man said.

"Congratulations," we told them.

"I'm Joan, and this handsome hunk is Ted," she told us.

"I'm Rock and this is Timmy," Rock told her.

"Did you say Rock?"

"I did. My parents are on the weird side."

"I like it. You have a unique name," she said.

"Are you two getting married?" Ted asked.

We laughed and I said, "Maybe someday, we are only sixteen."

"You make a cute couple," she said.

"Thanks. Did you get married in one of the small chapels?" Rock asked them.

"We did. Our parents came down for the wedding," she said.

"We are with that large group ahead of us. We're all from the same small community in Kentucky," I said.

"We're from Midway. It's a few miles west of Lexington."

"We're from Morgan County, West Liberty area, south of Morehead," I explained.

We ended up talking to the newlyweds the rest of way down the mountain. We told them about our clubs and that my parents were here on their honeymoon. They told us where they were staying and what all they had done this week. We told them about our campground and about Cades Cove. They said they were going there the next day.

When we got back to the bottom on the trail she said, "If you're ever in Midway look us up." They said their names would be in the phone book. "Our last name is Collins."

I couldn't believe it. I explained the shocked look on my face.

"We could be related," I said. "What are your parent's names?"

He told me and I said I would tell my Mom that evening. I would get in touch with them at their hotel if we were related. We then said our goodbyes.

We continued the trip around the wonderful loop stopping to look at different log cabins and farms.

It was mid-afternoon by the time we got through the loop drive and back into Gatlinburg. We then decided, since we were so close, to drive on to Newfound Gap and go to Clingman's Dome. Newfound Gap was located at the North Carolina-Tennessee border. It was also the spot where President Franklin D. Roosevelt stood to dedicate the Great Smoky Mountains National Park.

We pulled into the parking area at Newfound Gap. There were restrooms there and a great view of the mountains. We were near the highest spot in the Smokies. After a spell, we left and took the right turn to the Clingman's Dome parking area. We had to walk a steep half mile paved path to the observation deck.

We now stood at the highest spot in the Smoky Mountains and we learned it had the second highest elevation east of the Mississippi River. Purty stood on the edge of the deck and yelled, "I'm the king of the world!"

The crowd turned and looked at him and then laughed, as did we. By the time we got back to the trucks we were tuckered out. By the halfway point back to town Rock was asleep. I glanced in the back and saw that everyone else was also asleep. I had to be sure to stay alert and awake. I stuck my head out the window to help me stay awake. The winding road helped in staying alert.

Back in town, while they bought the film I bought a soda hoping it would help keep me awake. I also bought one for Rock. She woke up when I opened to door to get back in. I handed her the soda.

"Can you try and stay awake?"

"What's wrong?"

"I'm having a tough time staying awake," I told her.

"Okay. I'll rub your leg."

"That should do it," I said.

We left town, and I knew I had another forty-five to sixty minute drive ahead of me. We turned on the radio. There weren't many stations to choose from. We found a country station. By the time we got back to the campground I thought I was going to need toothpicks to hold my eyelids open.

I parked the truck, got out, went to our tent, laid down on my sleeping bag, and went to sleep.

When I finally woke up I heard the gang outside. I thought I heard Mom's voice. I went out to join everyone. I found out I had been asleep two hours. Everyone was cooking hotdogs over the fire.

"There's sleeping ugly," Purty greeted. I think it was a greeting.

I said hello to my family and took a seat next to Rock.

"It sounds like you all had a fun day," Mom said while looking at me.

"We did. What did you guys do?"

"We took your advice and hiked up to Alum Cave Bluff," Dad said.

"We got to feed the ground squirrels," Janie said.

"They were cute," Sally said. Sally was sitting next to Shauna with Janie on her other side.

"Did they eat out of your hand?" Rock asked them.

"No. Mom wouldn't let us. She said they might bite us," Janie said sadly.

"Mom could be right."

Janie then asked, "Did they eat out of your hand?"

I thought about it and said, "No. I was afraid they would bite me." She smiled, as did Mom.

I looked at Mom and asked, "Do we have relatives in Midway?"

"I don't think so. Why?"

"We met a newlywed couple today and they live in Midway. His name was Ted Collins. I thought we could be related."

"We have some distant cousins that live in the Lexington area. He could be related, I guess," Mom said.

My hotdog was good and brown and I began eating it.

"I think we've agreed to go tubing tomorrow. Are you coming with us?" James Ernest asked.

"The girls want to. Is that okay?" Mom asked.

"Of course," Raven answered.

"As long as Jane doesn't cry when I tip her over," I said.

209

Janie frowned at me and said, "You may be the one crying."

"Hopefully, no one will be crying," Mom said laughing.

I knew that Mom and Dad probably wanted a day to themselves. It was their honeymoon.

After eating, Mom said it was time for them to leave. Suddenly, we heard a loud roaring coming toward us. Three men on motorcycles were coming around the road interrupting everyone's peace. They parked the bikes in the camp site next to us.

"That's pleasant," Mom said sarcastically.

James Ernest told Mom, "We'll pick up the girls around ten in the morning."

"There is a good breakfast spot in Townsend. We will treat all of you to breakfast," Dad said. He told us where it was, and we agreed to meet them at nine-thirty.

We said our goodbyes and they left.

Later that evening, as we sat around the fire, the three young men made their way toward us. All three looked to be in their early twenties. They didn't look like normal campers. They had ridden in on motorcycles disturbing the campground with the loudness of the bikes and now they were going to disturb us. They had thrown up a circular tent for the three of them.

One of them said, "Howdy," while the other two checked out the girls. Both of their eyes stopped when they saw Rock sitting beside me. She had her arm inside mine with her hands gripping me tight.

"I'm Butch. This is Pedro and Slim. Thought we would come over and be neighborly."

"Where are you guys from?" Purty asked.

Butch ignored Purty as he focused on Rock. He asked, "You're awfully pretty. Where are you from, Honey?"

210

"Not Interested, U.S.A.," Rock answered.

"Never heard of it. Got a mouth on you too. I like that in my women," he said.

James Ernest stood and said, "This is a private party, if you don't mind."

"Don't look like no party to me," Slim said, and then started laughing loudly.

"If you ladies would like to do some real partying you can mosey on over. Have a little drink with us. You never know where the night might lead us," Butch said.

"I think it's time for you three to leave," Tucky said as he stood.

"You can even come," Butch said as he eyed Raven. I could feel Rock's hands shaking. It was either that, or my body.

"We're happy where we are," Raven told him.

"What about you two, there, sitting alone?" Pedro asked Susie and Rhonda.

Butch circled the fire as he eyed Rock and then Susie. As he neared I slowly stood. He took his left arm and pushed me aside, toward the fire. He leaned down toward Rock. I caught myself and did a full body slam into him, sending him sprawling.

He got up off the ground and shook himself off. Tucky and James Ernest were soon beside me.

"It doesn't seem like this was a neighborly visit, so I think it's time for you guys to leave," Tucky said.

Other campers were standing and watching the action now. A couple of men began walking our way.

Butch saw them coming and said. "You girls know where we are if you care to visit. We'll be here a couple more nights. You can spend them with men instead of boys."

They turned and walked back to their campsite. The two other men made their way on in to our camp.

"Are you kids okay?" the older man said.

"I think so," James Ernest said.

"I'm Mike and this is my son, Ed."

"Thanks for checking on us," I said.

"We never have trouble in campgrounds. I'll report them to the rangers in the morning," Mike said.

"Thanks, Mike," I said.

"If you need anything we are right there. I hope you enjoy the rest of your stay," he said.

We all said, "Thanks," as they turned to leave.

Butch and his buddies were sitting around their fire drinking beer and throwing the bottles into the fire. We knew that alcohol was not allowed in the park. The confrontation put a damper on our moods. We decided to turn in for the night. James Ernest and Raven, along with Tucky and Sadie stayed around the fire.

James Ernest

I wanted to stay up and keep an eye on the three men. I didn't trust that they wouldn't still try something. I knew the beer they were drinking would make them stupider and braver.

They kept glancing toward us. Pedro finally yelled out, "Girls, we have something for you. Come and see!" As all the fires went out throughout the campground the three men began to fade with each minute. Pedro rose from his seat and walked over to the fire. I saw him unzip his pants and begin peeing on the flames. His stupid friends joined him.

Slim staggered, and his momentum took him into the fire. He began screaming and dancing as he tried to put out the flames on his pants. We sat there and laughed at their antics. They finally climbed into their tent. I had seen the skunks going from campsite to campsite looking for leftovers that had fallen on the ground. I took a bag of chips out of our food bag and held it open.

A half hour later the skunks made their way to us. Our campfire was one of the last still glowing. I gave each of the skunks a piece of chip. They seemed to like the salty treat. I handed the chips to Tucky.

I got up and walked over to Butch's tent. I heard deep snoring coming from inside. All three of them were passed out. I quietly unzipped the tent. I went back to the fire and took the chips.

"What are you doing?" Raven said.

"I know what he's doing," Tucky whispered. The three of them began to giggle, while trying to hold the laughter inside.

I took a couple of steps with the chips in hand. The skunks followed me, wanting more. I gave them each a small bite. I walked a few more steps. They followed. Within a couple of minutes, the skunks and I were standing just outside the unzipped tent.

I slowly placed a few potato chips inside. The skunks hesitated, but the smell and longing for the chips lured them inside.

I quietly zipped the flap shut. I wished them a good night.

We sat there for another good hour waiting for the moment to arrive. It didn't come. We decided to head to our sleeping bags. I kissed Raven goodnight. Tucky kissed Sadie.

I had trouble going to sleep. I kept imagining what would happen when it all went bad. I figured the skunks must have settled down inside the tent, asleep for the night with the three men.

Chapter 20
Blood Curdling Screams

Catahecassa

My search for where Treehawk was staying turned up nothing. I went to all the hotels and motels in a thirty mile radius. No one had seen him or heard of him. My other thought was that he was camped somewhere, possibly in the Cumberland National Forest, hidden away. In that case, I would never find him.

I would have to wait for him to appear again. Hopefully, it wouldn't be to my demise.

Thursday, August 4

We were awakened by blood curdling screams in the very early morning. I sat up in my sleeping bag listening to the shrieks of horror. It seemed so close I wondered if it was coming from one of our other tents. I unzipped my tent and hopped out. I was standing in my underwear watching the round tent in the neighboring campsite. It looked like two large black bears were wrestling inside.

The dawn was just breaking. It was light enough to see the tent bounce up and down with screams coming from the inside. I actually wondered if the three guys were brawling with a bear.

I heard one of the men yell, "My eyes! My eyes!"

Another guy was screaming, "Help! Please!"

Everyone from our group stood there beside me in various forms of dress. I looked around and saw other campers standing and watching. Mike and Ed ran over and asked, "Do you know what going on?"

James Ernest calmly said, "I believe they found two skunks in their tent when they awoke."

The men began laughing, as did the rest of us.

"I don't think I would go over to help if I was you," Tucky said.

"Wasn't planning on it," Mike said.

Profanity filled the air from the tent.

Suddenly there was a large rip in the side of their tent. Pedro's head popped out and then his hand, which carried a large knife. He was sucking air and scrambling to get out. His eyes were twice as big as last night. Once Pedro was out, the tent sort of collapsed. The two skunks slithered through the opening, looked at all the people standing around laughing and applauding.

They took their bow and headed for the woods in a hurry, apparently not enjoying the men's company any more than we had. Pedro was sitting at the table bent over and crying. Mike and Slim crawled out on their hands and knees to face the laughter. A few minutes later Butch stood up and yelled, "Who did this?!"

No one answered. I heard Slim say, "You must have left the flap open last night. You were wasted."

After a few minutes of coughing and gagging the men stood.

I heard Pedro say. "What about our gear?"

"What good is it now?" Butch said.

They got on their bikes. They revved them up as loud as they could. It was so loud it shook the ground. I could smell them as they left. They rode away never to be seen again.

Junior said, "That's what it's like when Purty farts in our tent." Purty began chasing him around the grounds with no chance of catching him

Tucky said, "I'd have to agree."

I went inside my tent to get dressed. I could even smell the skunk's aroma inside our tent.

At nine, we loaded up and headed out to meet Mom and Dad at the restaurant. The girls wore their swimming suits under their clothes. Rock wore the new blouse I had bought her. She really looked pretty. Her tanned skin glowed even more next to the soft white fabric.

We arrived at the restaurant on time. Mom and Dad were already there. They had two tables that were pulled close together for all sixteen of us, eight at each table. I was hungry and ordered two BLT's and a soda.

"You should have stayed around last night for the excitement," Purty said. I couldn't believe he was going to tell Mom and Dad about what had happened.

"What happened?" Mom asked.

I was sitting at the other table listening. I rolled my eyes as he started telling the story.

"They did what? Hagar, you need to do something!" Mom exclaimed.

"James Ernest already did," Junior said.

Most of us started laughing. I held mine back, unsure what Mom and Dad would say. "What did you do, James Ernest?" Dad asked.

He turned from the other table and began telling about luring the skunks into the tent. Purty took over and told about the men waking up to find them and how the tent rolled around the ground.

216

Purty picked up his table knife and stood while sticking the knife into the air. He showed how the man was coughing and gagging. He more or less acted out the scene for the fascinated customers and waitresses. Even two of the cooks stopped to watch. By the time the story was over, the entire restaurant was roaring with laughter. Apparently everyone loved the ending as much as we did. Purty was applauded.

I was rolling in laughter by then. Shauna loved the performance.

"I guess you did take care of it," Dad said.

"Did they stink real bad?" Janie asked.

"They did," Francis answered.

After breakfast was over we headed for the tubing office. They had different trips we could take. One only took about an hour. Another was two hours and the longest was four to five hours. We chose that one. We had all day and wanted to enjoy the water. They told us what to look for when we got to the end. They said a bus would pick us up and bring us back to the starting point.

Mom told us, "We are going to drive to Clingman's Dome today. We will meet you at the burger restaurant at four." That sounded good.

The tube rental gave us an extra tube that had a bottom in it for our snacks. We put water in a pack and placed it in the tube. I tied the extra tube mine. The girls stripped down to their swimsuits. The guys wore swim trunks or cut offs. Purty decided to take his shirt off. No one said anything.

We set off down the Little River. I would have called it a creek, but it was called the Little River, which seemed appropriate. We quickly found that it was going to be a slow float down the river, perfect for relaxing. I held Rock's hand as we drifted. Janie and Sally were trying to splash everyone by using their hands and feet. I didn't mind the splashing at all; I welcomed it on the warm day, which frustrated the girls.

Somehow Purty managed to flip his tube over. I didn't even think it was possible. We had life vests. Some of us wore them, others didn't. I didn't. I placed mine in the spare tube. When it got too warm, Rock and I would roll off our tubes and float in the water for a while.

We saw ducks on the water and deer along the banks. Birds flew up and down the river looking for flying insects. The sky was blue except for a few billowy white clouds that dotted it. Wildflowers grew on the riverbanks.

We saw a rope tied to the limb of a tree. We stopped so we could take turns swinging out and dropping into the water. Janie said she didn't want to. I knew she was scared. But after watching everyone else have fun she decided to try it.

"When you get all the way out you have to let go. You don't want to land back on the bank. Okay?" I said.

She grabbed the rope high, ran and jumped. I yelled, "Let go!"

She did. She landed in the water and popped right up to the surface. I was there waiting for her. "That was fun," she said. She had a huge smile on her face. She dog paddled back to the bank wanting to do it again. I needed to teach her to swim. She and Sally were acting like they were having the time of their life.

Shauna swam over to where Rock and I were.

She said, "Timmy, can I give you a hug." She looked at Rock and asked if it was okay.

"Sure."

Shauna hugged me right there in the middle of the river.

"If it wasn't for you I'd be dead now, and who knows what Sally would be going through. I owe you so much. We are both so happy. I never dreamed of happiness like this."

"I'm glad I was there for you. But you don't owe me anything. You should thank God for placing me there," I said.

"I do, every night. But you didn't have to help me through it all. You are a great guy." She then kissed me on the cheek and swam away.

"You are a great guy," Rock said, as she kissed me on the lips.

"Who's next?" I yelled out. Rock jumped up on my head and dunked me.

Last fall I had talked Shauna out of jumping off a cliff. I then helped get her away from her Mom and Stepfather, who was raping her. She had no friends and seemed like the saddest person I had ever met. She and her little sister, Sally, now lived with Homer and Ruby and were doing great.

We decided we had better float on down the river. There were a lot of people tubing on the river. We even saw some canoers. When we left the rope swing another group took our spot.

The afternoon was fun and relaxing. We got to the end of the trip at three that afternoon. A bus was waiting to take us back. As we were getting on the bus I noticed that Purty had been sunburned. I didn't say anything. I figured he would find out sooner or later.

Shauna

I wanted to sit with Sally on the way back to the office. I had never spent this much time away from my sister. Purty understood, and he sat with Janie.

"Are you having a good time?" I asked her.

"I'm having a great time. I loved tubing," Sally told me.

219

"How has it been with Janie's parents?"

"They've been so nice. Janie and I have had so much fun having our own room. I really like the Smoky Mountains."

"I'm glad you're having fun. So am I. But I miss you, also. Make sure you thank them for everything. I'm so thankful we got out of that house with Mom and him."

"We never did anything fun with Mom and our stepdad," Sally said.

"I know. This is the way families are supposed to be" I said.

"Will we have to go back to Mom some day?"

"I hope not. But don't worry about something that might not happen. Let's be thankful for every day."

"Okay," Sally said.

"I love you."

"Me too."

Ten minutes later we arrived at the office and we unloaded from the bus.

I quickly opened the truck windows to let the heat escape before we loaded up. Some of the girls had brought clothes to change into. They went to the dressing rooms to change. I slipped on my shirt and shoes and was ready to roll.

I was thinking that after we ate at the hamburger shack it would be fun to drive around the cove again. I would suggest it later. The next day would be our last full day in the Smokies. I had suggested a hike through Cades Cove, but nothing had been said about it since. I wasn't sure what we were going to do.

Whatever the gang wanted to do was fine with me.

The girls came out looking a lot better than when they went in. They had changed and dried their hair. It was amazing how pretty all seven girls were. I figured Morgan County must have good water or something. We were lucky guys.

We loaded up. I counted to make sure we had everyone. Janie and Sally squeezed into the cab with Rock and I. We were off.

We arrived at the shack a little before four. Mom and Dad were already there. They had already ordered hamburgers and fries for everyone. Most of us ordered shakes instead of drinks. I loved strawberry shakes. Rock got the same.

Mom told us that we could come take showers in their rooms any time we wanted. "Maybe tomorrow evening or Saturday morning before we head home," Mom said.

We left them and headed back to the campsite.

Everyone was exhausted when we finally got back. The skunk tent had been removed and was empty. We were lounging around the site when a ranger approached us.

"Good evening," he said.

We returned the greeting and he continued. "We were made aware of the incident that happened last night. I came to apologize to you. They snuck in after check-in hours, which is okay, if you register the next morning. I guess they took off in a hurry this morning," he laughed.

"We hardly ever have campers like that in the campground. We are happy you guys are staying with us. Is there anything else we can do for you?" he asked.

"Thank you, but everything has been great except for last night," James Ernest said.

"That's good to hear."

"I do have a question. We were going to hike through the cove tomorrow. We're assuming that's allowed?" James Ernest asked.

"Yes, it is. You can hike anywhere within the cove, but be careful if you come across a bear. Don't approach them. Some people treat the cove like a zoo, which is crazy. These are wild animals, and we never know how they are going to react."

"So, I'm not allowed to wrestle one?" Purty joked.

The ranger chuckled and said, "You are allowed to, but I wouldn't advise it. There are also wild boars within the area. They can be very dangerous. How long are you here for?"

"We head home Saturday morning," Susie answered.

"Enjoy the rest of your stay. Have a good evening." He tipped his hat and left.

Around seven that evening I told everyone that Rock and I were going to drive around the cove. "Who wants to go with us?"

Everyone seemed either tired or too relaxed to go. Sadie finally spoke up and said, "I'd like to go if Kenny will come."

Tucky looked at her and then gave in, "That would probably be fun."

All four of us got in the cab and took off. It was a perfect evening. The temperature had cooled off to around seventy with a gentle breeze in the air. We entered the cove and decided to stop at the first cabin. It was the John Oliver Cabin. We parked and had to walk two hundred yards through a field to get to it.

The restored beautiful log cabin stood at the edge of the field in a clearing. We posed on the old porch as Sadie took pictures. Rock took a picture of Tucky and Sadie kissing at the door. Deer were grazing in the field. I knew the pioneers had a hard life but they had to have loved the cove. It was paradise.

We walked back to the truck and continued around the loop. The deer speckled many of the fields again that evening. Twilight was coming to the cove. Within an hour it would be dark. We drove to a pull-off that was a little higher up. From that vantage point we were able to look back into the valley and many of the fields. I stopped. We took a couple of the blankets from the back and spread them on the grass.

We sat there and watched the wildlife in the distance.

Several herds of deer could be seen in several pastures. Two groundhogs were nibbling on grass thirty yards from us. Crows hopped around hoping for handouts. No bears were within sight.

The mountains rose up all around the valley. The blue cast mixed with the setting sun brought a magical hue to the cove.

"This is beautiful," Sadie said.

"This moment was worth the worth trip," Rock said.

"The gang doesn't know what they are missing." Tucky later added, "I wonder if the skunks will be back tonight."

I laughed and said, "They may never be back. They're probably traumatized."

"Not as much as Butch, Pedro and Slim," Rock said. We laughed.

Vehicles passed by as we sat there. A few would stop for a minute or so and then continue. I wanted to stay until the sun was below the mountains. We were facing southwest so the sun would set to our right. Cars were not allowed to enter the cove after dark.

"How can anyone who looks at the beauty around us not believe in God? I mean, look at His creation," I said.

"Most atheists look at the bad in the world, like war, or hunger, and say 'If there is a God why would he allow all of this bad to happen?' Sadie replied.

"What is an atheist?" Rock asked. "I've never heard that word."

"It's a person who does not believe there is a God," Sadie answered.

"I assumed everyone believed in some form of God," Rock said.

"I believe ninety percent of the world does," I said. "The thing is God gave us all the good things. Man is the one that causes the bad. We have free will to do what we want. Some people want to cause bad things, like war. You can't blame God for that."

"People like to blame God for all their problems, but then they take credit for all the good things in their life. You can't have it both ways," Tucky said.

As we sat there solving the world's problems the sun was setting fast. I laid back on the blanket and looked up at the darkening sky. Pink and orange adorned the clouds in the horizon.

Rock positioned herself next to me and kissed me. I wrapped my arms around her. I heard kissing sounds from the blanket next to us. Hardly any cars were passing by. We stayed there on the blankets until the cove filled with black. and the only thing we could see was the sliver of moon and the stars in the sky.

It was quiet except for the nature sounds. Out of nowhere Sadie asked, "Have you two had sex yet?"

I said, "What?" I had a hard time believing she had asked what I thought she had asked.

Rock simply answered, "No. Have you guys?"

I couldn't believe that the two girls were talking about this.

"We haven't either," Sadie said. "We've talked about. We want to. But we haven't."

Over the years I had learned to not get involved in girls conversations. This was one I definitely didn't want any part of.

"We've talked about it, also. But we think we should wait. Having a baby wouldn't be a good thing at our age," Rock told her.

"Have you caught any big fish lately, Tucky?" I asked.

"Not lately. Been trying not to have sex," he said.

I burst out laughing, as did the girls. We laid there on the blankets and laughed for five minutes.

Then Sadie said, "You two are so cute together."

Rock said, "Thank you. I think you guys are too."

"I think we had better head back. The others might think we're off having sex," I said.

"Do you guys think James Ernest and Raven have?" Sadie asked.

"No way," I quickly answered.

"Has he told you that?" she asked.

"It might be a surprise to you girls, but we guys don't talk about having sex. I just think I know him well enough to know they will wait until they're married," I said.

"That's what I would like to do," Rock said.

"But you can always fool around," Sadie said.

"Oh, yeah," Rock said. Both girls giggled like girls.

We packed the blankets in the bed of the truck and took off. It was pitch black on the road. About half of the one lane road goes through the trees, with forest on both sides. When I say it was dark, I mean it was spooky dark. Since we were the last vehicle to leave the cove there were no sounds of engines or anything else.

It took around twenty minutes to get to the end of the road. We were back at the campgrounds. I pulled into our spot. The others were still sitting around the fire.

"How was the cove? Did you see any bears?" Purty asked.

"It was wonderful, but no bears," Rock answered.

225

"We're going to hike it tomorrow, aren't we?" Junior asked.

We all turned toward James Ernest and he said, "I think that would be fun. What do you guys think?"

Everyone agreed.

They told us the skunks had not been there that evening. The four of us decided to walk to the restrooms before turning in. Susie and Francis wanted to tag along.

When we got back everyone was in their tents. I was lying in ours thinking about the great week we had spent in the Smokies. Rock and I began quietly talking about it when we abruptly heard Shauna scream out, "Is there a skunk in here?"

It took everyone a minute to realize what was going on. When I finally realized that Purty had finally revealed his bad side to Shauna, I began laughing. As it dawned on others they started laughing also. Laughter filled the three tents.

I could hear the unzipping of Purty's tent and then, "That is rotten. You'd better check your underwear."

Shauna was standing outside the tent waiting for the smell to dissipate.

"I'm sorry. I guess I shouldn't have eaten that can of beans," Purty begged.

"Welcome to 'Camping with Purty'," Junior called out.

We were still laughing when Shauna yelled out, "There's nothing funny about this at all. It smells like I stuck my head down the hole of an outhouse."

I laid there chuckling for the next twenty minutes. I couldn't stop. We all knew what it was like. We all had been waiting for the moment to arrive. It finally had. We were three tents away and I could smell a bit of the aroma in the air.

"I'm so sorry," Purty pleaded again. He was now outside the tent begging forgiveness. It took at least a half hour before

Shauna reentered their tent. If he had eaten a can of baked beans I figured it would be a long night for Shauna.

Chapter 21
Protecting Susie

Friday, August 6

When I awoke I looked over and saw how pretty Rock was lying there in her sleeping bag. I hated to wake her, but I needed to relieve myself. I quietly unzipped my bag and tent and slipped out. Purty was lying next to the fire pit in his sleeping bag. It wasn't the first time he had been kicked out of a tent on a camping trip.

I hurried over to the trees and peed. The morning was fairly cool, so I built a fire to warm up. Purty looked up from his bag and said, "Good morning."

"I'd bet you don't eat a can of beans next time," I told him.

"I was hungry and we were low on food," he explained.

"Would you rather be hungry or in the tent with Shauna?" I said.

I sat down next to him and said, "You really like her."

"I love her. She's great."

I looked at him deciding if I should ask. "Does she ever talk to you about what she went through with her stepdad?"

"Not in detail or anything like that. I think she's tried to put it out of her mind. I don't think I should bring it up."

"That's probably a good idea. You two seem really happy."

"Not at this minute I'm not. Do you think she'll break up with me?" Purty asked, looking pathetic.

"No. If we haven't kicked you out of the Wolf Pack then she'll probably give you another chance, you knucklehead. One bit of advice, don't eat a can of beans when you're with her," I said.

I looked around when I heard something. Rock came out of our tent. She had on light green shorts and the white top I had bought her. She was beautiful. Her hair was messy, which made her look even better. She smiled when she saw me next to Purty.

She said, "Is it safe to come over there?"

Purty said, "Very funny." Rock laughed.

"Walk me to the restroom," Rock said.

I stood up and went into the tent to get my toothbrush. We walked away. Rock kissed me on the cheek as we left.

"I'm looking forward to the day," I said.

"It's going to be fun."

"You're awfully cute today," I told her.

"Thank you."

We met up in the store after using the restrooms. We got drinks and donuts for breakfast. While we were there some of the others walked in. I saw Shauna and Purty walking by holding hands. I knew she had forgiven him.

On the way back to the camp everyone made fun of Purty. Shauna kissed him and said, "All is forgiven. How could I not forgive this cute face?"

"It's not his face you have to forgive," Junior said, making us laugh.

It was around nine when we started the hike through Cades Cove. We had no agenda other than walk around the cove and have fun. We started out by entering the woods between the entrance and exit of the cove. It was a nice day, blue sky and a light breeze in the air.

I took my hiking stick even though we weren't going up mountains. I figured I might want to poke something with it. We all seemed to be filled with vim and vigor. The day floating on the river seemed to have renewed us after hiking mountains the previous two days.

We walked through the trees. The forest floor was open and easy to walk on. Large green ferns were scattered around. After ten minutes or so we came to a pond that you would never know was there by driving the loop. Near the pond was a storage barn which held the parks mowers and other machinery.

We came to an open field where we counted thirteen white-tailed deer feeding. We stood there watching them until we decided to cross the field. The deer kept their eyes on us and moved a little further away. We entered the woods again and I listened to the birds sing in the trees as I walked.

Out of the corner of my eye I saw something move. I motioned for everyone to stop. Everyone looked where I was looking. A moment later a young fox pup peeked around the end of a large fallen log. He peered at us. He cautiously came on out in the clearing and was followed by two other pups. They walked slowly and clumsily, bumping into each other.

Their mother came out of nowhere and gathered them up and they all disappeared behind the log.

"Well, that was cute," Rock said.

"What were those?" Francis asked.

"They were Red Fox pups," I answered.

We continued our trek through the woods. My senses were alive as I took in every sound and movement around me. My anticipation was great for whatever we might come across at any moment. I had seen wildlife many times in Morgan County but that was only every great once in a while. Here I could see so many different animals while on this hike in Cades Cove.

We exited the trees into a field where five more deer were standing. They watched us as we invaded their field. We could see cars on the loop road to our right. The drivers were probably upset that we were now in their pictures. We continued across the field while the deer kept a watchful eye on us.

Suddenly, Francis yelled out, "Yuck, what's that!" We all headed to where Francis and Junior were looking down at the remains of a dead animal. The hide was shredded and discarded around the skeletal remnants.

Finally there was something to poke. I took my walking stick and poked it under the hide of the animal and flipped it over. There was the head, and it had tusks.

"It was a wild boar," James Ernest said.

"Looks like the Key family already got to it," Junior said.

I began laughing while others looked toward Rock and Tucky. When they smiled the others began laughing also.

"It's too bad we don't have wild boars in Morgan County. There would have been a lot of good pork on this fella," Tucky said.

"The vultures, crows, and animals really picked this guy clean," I said.

It was the first time I had seen a wild boar, dead or alive. By looking at the remains it had to have been very big.

"Makes me want to gag," Susie said.

"It is pretty gross," Sadie added.

"Just think how big that thing was," Purty said.

"That would be scary to come across," Raven added what I was thinking.

James Ernest added the fact, "There was an article in the park's paper that said they do a lot of damage to the land and vegetation in the park by rooting up the ground looking for food."

The thought of walking upon these wild animals made our hike a little less fun, but definitely more exciting.

Papaw

*I*t had been a hectic week. The store was busy most of the week with customers and fishermen. The cooler weather was unusual for August and fishermen were taking advantage of it. The weekly contest had been a huge success. Every day the men would argue and boast that they were going to catch the fish of the week. Thus far the longest fish caught was by a young boy who caught a nineteen and three quarter inch catfish this past Sunday evening.

Mud was upset and said it shouldn't count because the boy was off climbing up a hillside when his dad told him it was time to go. Mud said the boy came down the hill and began reeling in his line to go home when he discovered he had a fish on the line. It turned out to be the nineteen inch catfish.

Folks kept coming into the store asking about the Smoky Mountain trip. Betty or Hagar called almost every day to check on things and give us the latest news. It was as if they were living on every update. Folks also wanted info on Cat's shooting and how he was doing. They wanted to know if the shooter had been caught yet. I was trying to keep an outlook for Treehawk since I was one of the only people that knew what he looked like, having met him in town.

I was also going to the farm every day to feed animals and tend the garden. I was looking forward to their return. But I knew they all were having a great time, and I was happy for them, they deserved it.

I looked out the window and saw Treehawk. I grabbed the shotgun from under the counter, which now had real shells in it, and headed for the front door.

We left the remains behind and continued our walk. We followed the edge of the trees which angled further out into the field. We came to a barb wire fence. James Ernest and I spread the wires so everyone else could bend over and get through. We were careful to make sure no one caught their backs on the barbs. The only one that had trouble was Purty. His shirt caught on the barb and he panicked and bent down further and his shirttail then caught on the bottom wire. For a minute I thought we were going to have to leave him tangled in the fence and go on.

"Oh man, my shirt is all ripped up," he complained, after getting through.

"Better your shirt than your hide," Tucky told him.

"You poor thing," Shauna told him while giving him a kiss. It was perfect example of love being blind.

In the new field we saw a herd of cows to our left. This was another field that was hidden to the drivers on the loop. We decided to walk toward them.

"Hold up," I said as we got closer.

"What?" Susie asked.

"Look in the middle of the herd. I think that's a bear in the middle of them," I cautioned. I could see short black legs as I looked under the cows. It surely wasn't a cow or calf.

We slowly moved forward. "You're right. That is a bear," Tucky said.

233

"Is there only one?" Rhonda asked. We all studied the legs as we closed in on them.

By now the cows became weary of twelve strangers walking toward them. They began to move further out into the field as a group. Only one of them remained and wasn't a cow.

The large black bear turned her head toward us and then turned her body to face us. We froze in our steps, except for some who actually backed up in mid step. She stared at us for a while as though trying to decide what her next move would be. I was hoping she was deciding between running away or lying on her back so we could scratch her belly. She decided to do neither one. She took three big steps toward Susie.

I let go of Rock's hand and ran to the front of Susie, shielding her from the bear. The bear looked at us and then looked behind her toward the trees. We looked at the same spot. There stood four bear cubs on their back legs looking over weeds and logs.

We now knew why she was being aggressive instead of running away. James Ernest softly told us to back up slowly. We did.

"We're leaving you alone now. We don't want to disturb your cubs," he told momma bear.

As we backed away, she studied the situation, and when we were finally far enough away she turned and headed toward her babies. We all took a big breath of relief. I returned to Rock and we all walked toward the opposite side of the field away from the bears.

She looked at me and said, "That was awfully brave of you."

I wasn't sure what to say. I did it out of instinct. I hoped I would have done the same for any of the girls in our group. But how did I know if I would have. The other girls had boyfriends except for Susie and Rhonda.

234

Would I have done the same for Rhonda?

Chapter 22
The Return of Treehawk

Papaw

*T*reehawk was jumping the steps as I pushed the screen door open. I had the shotgun on my shoulder ready to raise and shoot as I went out the door. Before I could get the gun up to shoot he grabbed the barrel and ripped the gun from my hands.

I didn't want to scream putting Corie in danger. He took care of that by placing his hand across my mouth and my left arm behind me. It felt as though he was breaking it. I was no match for his strength. He was a large muscular man. I should have shot him through the screen of the door.

He pushed me toward the raised trunk of his vehicle and forced me inside. The next thing I heard was gravel hitting the bottom of the car as he peeled away.

Mamaw

*"M*artin, what would you like for lunch?" I yelled out. When he didn't answer I walked from the kitchen to the store. His non answer wasn't from his loss of hearing. He wasn't there to answer.

He should have said something before leaving the store empty. Maybe he was filling a car with gas. I looked out the window but he wasn't at the gas pumps. He wasn't sitting on the porch whittling. He must have gone up to the lake, I thought. It was hard to keep him from talking to his friends and teasing them.

As I stood in the store trying to decide what to do with myself I heard a vehicle drive into the lot. It was Homer and Ruby. I was glad to have some company. I knew they were missing Shauna and Sally. I was missing my family also. I was happy they were coming home tomorrow. We could console one another.

I yelled out the screen door, "I'll get us some iced tea." I headed for the kitchen.

When I came back into the store Homer was holding a shotgun.

"Where's Martin?" Homer said, with a worried look on his face.

"I think he went up to the lake. Why are you holding a gun?" I asked.

"I found the shotgun lying on the porch. Is yours missing?"

I hurried behind the counter to look for it. I began moving items as I frantically searched for it. It had to be there.

"It's not here," I finally said.

Ruby came and put her arm around me and said, "I'm sure everything is okay. Let's not worry. There is always an explanation."

"I'll go up and check at the lake," Homer told me. I was so worried. Why would Martin leave the shotgun on the porch? It didn't make sense.

Homer was back within ten minutes, which felt like an hour.

"He wasn't up there. They said they hadn't seen him at the lake all day," Homer said.

*W*e hiked until noon. The hike had already been so much fun. We stopped to take a break under a large, lone tree in the middle of a field. We took off our backpacks and handed out drinks and snacks.

"This was a great idea," Sadie said.

"Yeah, usually when we hike we're in the woods or climbing mountains, but this is so different and cool," Raven said.

I suggested, "We've stayed inside the loop. Maybe we should cross the road and hike some of the fields and woods on the outside."

"We might have a better chance of seeing wildlife. Also, we could check out some of the cabins and old churches," James Ernest agreed.

Rock

I admired Timmy's courage to run and protect Susie from the charging bear, but I also wondered what it meant, if anything. If he had to choose between us I wondered which person he would protect. We were having a great time, and I didn't want to put a damper on our fun so I decided to let it go for now.

It was something I thought about a lot. I didn't want to be involved in girl drama. I felt as though I wasn't that type of girl. I wanted Timmy to really love me as much as I loved him. But I knew if he didn't there was nothing more I could do about it. Timmy had told me he loved me and that Susie was in the past, and I choose to believe that.

But I saw the other girls' looks when Timmy left my side and ran to Susie. Were they seeing something I couldn't see, or didn't want to see? I was so happy with Timmy and hated for it to end.

I also knew that he would always have special feelings for Susie, maybe even a love.

Mamaw

I was tying knots in my apron due to wringing it with worry. "His truck is here. Where would he be?"

"Corie, I don't know. The thing that worries me is that I found the shotgun on the porch. He had to have taken it out there, but why would he drop it and leave it there?" Homer reasoned.

"Something is awful wrong," I told them. "Maybe I should call Clayton or the police."

"I wouldn't call the police yet. It could be nothing and he hasn't been gone that long," Homer told me. He was right.

"I'll call Clayton," Ruby said. She headed inside to call.

Roger Smuckatilly drove up to the store bringing the mail. He got out and walked up the steps and said, "You look mighty worried about something, Corie. No need to worry. I think I've got your mail right today."

Roger tried his darnest, but he had such trouble delivering the right mail to the right person. He wasn't suited to be a mailman, but if he wasn't, I didn't know what else he could do.

"Martin has come up missing," Homer told him.

"Missing what, his mail? I've got it right here," Roger said, God bless him.

"No, Roger. Martin is missing. We don't know where he is. He disappeared," Homer tried to explain.

"You think it's them aliens again?" Roger asked. A year or so ago there was a lot of talk of aliens invading the county. The talk had died down since then, until something comes up missing. Then people would begin blaming the aliens for it all over again.

Ruby came out and said, "Clayton is on his way."

"I hate bothering them. I think they're canning beans today," I said.

"My wife, Lily, pickled some cucumbers last week. I love me some good sweet pickles," Roger told us.

"Did you see anything strange on the ridge within the last half hour or so?" Homer asked Roger.

Roger put his hand to his chin and looked toward Heaven as he thought. He then said, "I was putting the mail in Morton's mailbox. I'm not sure why he gets mail. He's as blind as a bat. How does he read it?"

"The strange thing you saw, Roger," Ruby said, impatiently.

"Oh yeah, sure, a car went flying past me. I waved at him but he didn't wave back. Very unfriendly, I think."

"That was it? How is that a strange thing, Roger?" Homer asked.

"The strange thing about it was he didn't wave. Everyone waves. But the stranger thing about it was, you remember when Robert Easterling was upset because he thought Cat didn't wave at him?"

"Yeah, and," Homer pushed.

"Well this driver that didn't wave at me was the other Indian fella, the one who shot Cata."

"Are you sure?"

"Sure as shooting," Roger said.

"Did you see Martin in the car with him?" I asked.

"No. He was by himself. But he was in the hurry to somewhere."

Clayton pulled into the lot. He and Monie hurried out of the pickup and up onto the porch. We explained what we knew and what Roger had seen.

"He's not in the outhouse, is he?" Clayton said.

240

"We have an indoor bathroom now. And it's been almost an hour," I told him.

"Sometimes it takes a spell," Clayton said.

"So you think he brought his shotgun out to the porch and then went to the outhouse?" Homer said.

"It was just a thought," Clayton said.

"I better head on down the road," Roger said. He turned and headed to his car.

"You still have Corie's mail in your hand," Ruby said.

"Oh, yeah. Here you go Corie. I wouldn't worry. I doubt very much if Martin would leave you. You're a good woman," Roger said.

We all watched the poor guy drive away. I looked down at the mail and saw that none of it was addressed to store. I handed one of the letters to Monie, another to Ruby, and the other one was addressed to the Tuttles.

"Would Treehawk have taken Martin? What reason would he have to take him?" Clayton thought out loud.

We all had no idea. But now I was worried even more.

"I'm going to check the outhouse," Clayton said.

*A*fter our break under the tree we all were lying on the grass either napping or looking up into the sky. It was warm, but nice. The sky was a dark blue with white puffy clouds dotting it.

Two large bucks came out of the trees and began grazing on the grass at the edge of the field. One was a twelve pointer, a huge buck. The other was a ten pointer and smaller than the other. Within a month or so they would square off rutting to see which one of them would get to mate with the does. We watched the bucks for the next fifteen minutes. They were stunning. Then they disappeared back into the trees.

241

"I never understand why some days the sky is a darker blue than other days," I said to anyone that was listening.

James Ernest answered, "It depends on where the sun is. It can depend on your altitude. Also what it is contrasted with. If you look up through the limbs and leaves of this tree the sky looks darker against the green."

"Thanks, Mr. Obvious," Purty said.

"I guess we need to get moving," I suggested.

We began rising from the grass.

We walked north until we came to the loop road. We crossed the road and went through an open field. Later, we came to an old homestead. There stood a log cabin, a barn, two log sheds, and other small buildings. We looked around the place while Rhonda and Sadie took pictures.

We then continued our hike through the adjacent woods. I caught a glimpse of something to my right. I stopped and pointed to a doe and two fawns. They had also stopped and were staring at us. The fawns were speckled with white dots. They soon decided to start playing again. We watched them jump and hop and chase each other around the trees.

We laughed at their antics. The mother soon led them away from our view. As we walked we saw areas where we knew the wild boars had torn up the ground in their search for food. It was unbelievable the damage they caused.

We went inside an old Baptist church. We rested inside on the pews. The church wasn't that much different from the one we attended in Oak Hills. Raven asked James Ernest to sing a song for us. He declined at first, but we all insisted. He stood on the stage and began singing *Amazing Grace*. His voice filled the small church and further out into the surrounding hills.

When he finished the song folks began applauding in the doorway. Other visitors had heard him and were beckoned by his voice.

"Sing another, please," the old man in the doorway said.

James Ernest motioned for Raven to join him. The folks came inside and took a seat. Others from the parking lot followed their lead. We were holding a church service.

Raven and James Ernest began singing one the Negro spirituals Coal had taught them. It seemed perfect in this setting. The pain and hope of the song floated from the voice of Raven, as though she had gone through the cotton fields of slavery. Their voices blended to form a gentle sound of God's love. The room continued to fill as the song drew to an end.

They then lifted their voices to sing *How Great Thou Art*.

By the time they finished singing the lot was full of cars and most of the pews were filled with folks from all across the country.

They started to walk off the stage when a man stood and asked if they would please sing one more song. I suggested they sing *I'm so Lonesome I Could Cry*.

James Ernest started the song with his deep rich tone. Raven sang the second verse. I had never heard her sing the song. She had a cry in her voice that was perfect for the song. She then joined James Ernest as they sang the third verse together. The folks gave them a standing ovation when they finished. We joined in. It was fantastic.

One man shouted out, "Best singing I've ever heard. Where do I buy the album?"

Another woman said, "I didn't know the park put on shows in the churches."

"We were passing through just like y'all. We love hearing them sing. We're out hiking," I explained.

"Well, God bless you kids," she said.

"Thank you ma'am," I said.

James Ernest and Raven stood and talked to the crowd for the next ten minutes. I thought they might have to start signing autographs.

Rock said, "That was so great."

I took her in my arms and gave her a big kiss. Most of our group was talking to different folks in and around the church. We walked away toward the graveyard. I loved looking at gravestones for some reason, maybe because they represented a person's life. All these people had lived here in Cades Cove at one point in time and had died here.

I recognized a lot of the last names from the different home names in our pamphlet.

The others finally were able to break away and we continued our hike. We found a new energy while in the church.

Papaw

Treehawk helped me out of the trunk and led me to a campsite he had built. "You need anything before I tie you up?" he asked.

"You don't need to tie me up. I can't go anywhere."

"I guess you're right."

"Where are we?" I asked.

I didn't expect an answer. I was surprised when he said, "We're just off Brown Ridge Road."

I knew the road was in Blair's Mills. I didn't recognize the area. I figured we were near the dead end. It did me no good to know where we were anyway. I needed the police to know where I was.

"What's the plan here, ransom, torture, what?"

"I plan to exchange you for Catahecassa's life."

"I'm not worth that much," I told him.

"I guess we'll both see. You had better pray you are," he said as he started sharpening his large Indian knife."

Chapter 23
Martin will Die

We crossed the road again and headed across the cove to where we were going to turn back toward the campground. It was mid-afternoon by then and we knew it would be close to sundown before we got back, depending on what we ran into.

Once we got into the woods again Purty said, "I need to find a tree."

The Wolf Pack knew what that meant. He needed to poop.

"We'll walk this way and wait for you," James Ernest told him.

Purty

I could barely walk because my stomach was aching so badly. I knew I needed to poop. There was not an outhouse or bathroom within a couple of miles. I went behind a large tree while the others walked a bit further away.

I wasn't sure if I would make it to the tree. I found a large tree and hurriedly dropped my pants and pulled down my underwear and leaned against it. I quickly got into a sitting position against the tree. I slide down a little further until I suddenly felt a sharp pain near my butthole. It stung like the devil.

I couldn't wait any longer and my bowels exploded. Out of my right eye I saw a snake slither away. Oh no, I had been bitten by a snake. I finished going. I was afraid I was going to pass out and fall into the pile I had just created. I looked around me to find something to wipe with.

Once before on a Wolf Pack hiking trip I had accidently wiped with poison ivy leaves. I had never lived it down. There were no leaves around me. I had one of the Cades Cove pamphlets in my back pocket. I took it out and ripped pages from it and wiped. I saw blood on the paper. I almost passed out again. I moved away from the tree and pulled my pants back up.

I began walking toward the area they were waiting for me. With each step I felt drowsier. I yelled out, "Help!"

I watched all eleven of them run toward me as I laid there on the ground.

"What happened?" Tucky asked as they neared.

"A snake bit my butthole," I said as I closed my eyes.

I didn't expect to hear laughter as I drew my last breath and died. But there it was. All eleven of them were laughing their heads off as they looked down on my dying body.

"I'm not sucking the blood out of his butthole," Tucky said. "I don't care if he is my best friend."

Tucky bent down over me and said, "It's been nice knowing you, Buddy."

James Ernest bent over me and asked, "Were you really bit by a snake?"

"I think so. I felt a sharp pain and then saw a snake slide away, and I'm bleeding," Purty said.

"Let's have a look," James Ernest said.

"You want me to pull down my pants in front of everyone?" I said.

"Now is not the time to get modest. Normally you're throwing your clothes off every chance you get," James Ernest said.

That used to be true. But since Shauna became my girlfriend I stopped the nonsense.

"Would you girls please leave?" James Ernest said.

They walked away and I pulled my pants down. I left my underwear on. I rolled onto my belly.

"You do have blood seeping through your underwear." He pulled my skid marked underwear down to where he could look at the death mark. "It seems like I've done this before. The good news is that it is not a snake bite. It looks more like a puncture wound. Did you stoop down on a stick or something?"

"I don't know. I was in a hurry. I did what I had to do," I told James Ernest.

He looked inside his backpack for the medicine kit. He cleaned and squeezed some disinfectant on the wound. He then placed a Band-Aid on it and said, "I think you're good to go."

I slowly got up and pulled my pants back up.

"Thanks, buddy. I know who my true friend is now," I said as I stared at Tucky.

"Hey! Would you have sucked poison from my butt?" Tucky asked.

"No way. That's gross," Purty said.

Junior said, "White people are weird."

Mamaw

As the afternoon dragged on my worry grew greater. We had no idea where Martin was. We had a suspect, but that was all. Robert and Janice came down when they heard. They brought Morton with them. Clayton went to get Cat. Cat was extremely upset. He knew if Treehawk did take Martin it had something to do with him.

Cat told me he would call the station to let the deputies know what had happened. "But they'll call Hagar. I don't want to interfere with their honeymoon," I said.

"Do you realize how upset they'll be if we don't call them?"

"I guess you're right," I gave in.

Monie said, "They're coming home tomorrow anyway, Corie."

"I keep expecting him to walk around the corner of the house and wonder why everyone is here," I said, and started to cry.

"I know. I know," Monie said, as she rubbed my back.

Pastor White drove into the lot. The men explained everything and they prayed.

Hagar

We took the kids to Gatlinburg and played miniature golf and took a trolley to the top of a mountain. We did anything the kids wanted, more or less.

We returned to the hotel around six. A note asking me to come to the front desk was hanging on our door handle. I let Betty and the kids into the room and headed for the office. The clerk handed me a message asking me to call the store. I knew something else was wrong. They wouldn't call unless something bad had happened.

The clerk let me use the office phone. I placed the call and was surprised when Clayton answered.

"What's wrong?" I asked.

"Martin has disappeared."

"What do you mean, disappeared?"

"We have reason to believe Treehawk came to the store and took him. Your deputies are out searching the area," Clayton told me.

"When did it happen?"

"Sometime around noon today. Homer and Ruby came to the store and found the shotgun lying on the porch and Martin was gone. Around that same time Roger Smuckatilly told us he saw Treehawk flying past him going out the ridge."

"We'll gather up our things and leave as soon as possible."

"We hated to interrupt your trip," Clayton said.

"I'm glad you did. We were heading home tomorrow anyway. We should be back by midnight. Corie shouldn't stay alone," I told him.

After hanging up, I told the clerk we would be checking out due to a family emergency. I went back to the room and broke the news to Betty. After crying and asking questions, she began packing things. I told her I would call the campground and hope a ranger was still there.

I called and luckily caught the ranger just as he was walking out the door. I told him what was happening and asked him to give the kids a note. I dictated what to write:

Martin disappeared from the store today. Treehawk is a suspect. We packed up and are heading home. I wasn't sure when you would be back from your hike. You can head home tonight, or stay and come home in the morning when you're not so tired. Early tomorrow is probably the best option.

Sorry to send you bad news. Hopefully all will be fine.

Sheriff Cane

When I got back to the room Betty was already carrying suitcases to the car. The girls were also packed and ready. I checked the rooms for anything they could have overlooked. We headed for home.

*I*t was getting late and we were maybe thirty minutes from the campground when we heard sounds ahead. It sounded like grunting. We rounded a group of trees and there were a cluster of wild boars. I counted five in various sizes. One large one was definitely the head hog. They were tearing up the ground under an oak tree. I figured they were searching for acorns.

It was unreal how much damage they were doing to the ground. We stayed as far away as we could. One of the boars lifted her head and saw us. She grunted loudly and then the other boars stopped what they were doing and looked up. The leader took four steps toward us. We began backing away. I wanted no part of the pigs. I could think of a million better ways to die.

The other boars followed their leader and walked toward us. The more we walked backward the more they came toward us. Then Francis and Purty did what we all wanted to do, they turned and ran. Purty's butt puncture wound didn't seem to be bothering him much at that moment.

Their fleeing caused the boars to chase. We all decided it was time to save ourselves. We were running across the meadow with wild boars on our tails. For some reason two of the boars liked the looks of Purty and were closing on him. His squeals and screams filled the cove. Rock and I were lucky. We weren't in their sights.

The boars had chased us far enough away from their dig I guessed, because they gave up the chase. All five trotted back to the oak tree with their noses held high in victory. Purty was still running and screaming. The rest of us stood and watched his pathetic attempt to climb a tree.

Purty

I hated pigs, especially when they were alive.

Treehawk

*T*he man was nothing more to me than a bargaining chip. I didn't know him. I didn't care to know him. I knew Cata was close with some of the teenagers in the area and I had waited all week to find one of them, preferably the boy that watched the store. But I got tired of waiting, so I had to snatch whoever I could. This man was the one who was there.

Catahecassa and I had been friends for many moons. But then he seemed to lose his sense of being an Indian and what it meant. I was trying to take back what the white man had taken from us. Cata went his own way and broke our friendship. The Indian way is to support your blood brothers and help, not turn on them.

When I got caught trying to take from the white man, Cata testified against me in the white man's court. I was sent away to prison while he became friends with this farm community. I wanted my revenge. He took away part of my life. I planned to take the rest of his life.

"Were you in with the two men that were looking for something in a cave?" the old man asked.

"I was on my way here when I met them in a bar. We began talking and they told me about this map their buddy had come across. The map had a big X marking a treasure that had been buried near your store. The map said a letter was hidden in a nearby cave with the key to the chest. They were looking for that letter and the exact location of the buried treasure. They were white fools."

"Did you place the body in the lake?" the old man asked.

"Yeah."

"How did that happen?"

"You ask a lot questions. I suggest you stop," I told him.

What I didn't tell the old man was that there were three men in the bar with the map. As the two men told me about the map, the third man told them to stop telling me about the map. He called me a filthy dumb Indian. That was all it took for me to kill him. I followed them to the store that first night and when they got to the lake I killed the fool. The other two men ran away like cowards. I threw the body in the lake.

I didn't care about a buried treasure. They just happened to be going to the same place I was. The treasure I was looking for was the scalp off the head of Cata's dead body. Nothing was more important to me. Nothing would stop me.

We met up at the edge of the field. Our group walked to where Purty was sitting at the bottom of the tree. He looked dejected and defeated. Shauna lowered herself to him and took his hands.

"I'm such a coward," he said. "I don't know why you would like me."

"Purty, I love you. You're my knight. We all ran. Those things were scary to all of us," Shauna told him.

"Timmy jumps in front of Susie to save her from a Bear. A pig runs at us and I drop your hand and run like a mouse from a cat. I'm so sorry," he said as he choked back tears.

I wasn't sure what Shauna saw in Purty, but whatever it was, it made her overlook all his shortcomings and antics. It must be true unconditional love.

He stood and we headed to our camp. The sun was creeping closer to the top of the mountains. I was hungry and tired. It had been quite a day.

We stopped at the restrooms before going on to the tents. When we got to the campsite I saw Mike, our neighbor, walking over toward us. He had an envelope in his hand.

"The ranger came by and asked me to give this to Tim," he said.

"Thank you." Everyone was standing around me as I opened the envelope and then the letter. I wondered why in the world I would be getting a letter.

I read it out loud to everyone. I burst into tears when I read that Papaw was missing. Everyone stood there in sadness as I finished the note. Most everyone had tears running down their cheeks. Papaw was loved by everyone. He had done so much for so many people in the community. I had to get home.

"We need to pack up right now," I said.

"Wait, Timmy. Let's think about it for a minute," James Ernest said.

"What is there to think about? We need to get home!" I cried out.

"Everyone is tired. We can eat, get a night's rest and head out at the break of dawn," James Ernest said.

"You can do what you want. I'm leaving now. This is my grandfather, and I need to find him!" Papaw was my hero. He was a father to me. Papaw was the man I hoped to be one day. What was Treehawk doing to him? Would I ever see Papaw alive again? "I have to go home. We all don't have to leave tonight, but I am. I have to."

"I think we all should go," Susie said, as she looked at the others. Everyone nodded their heads in agreement.

"It will take a while to get the tents down. I'll build a quick fire and we can cook some hotdogs real quick," Tucky suggested.

"Why don't we just ask Mike if we can use their fire?" Junior suggested.

"Good thinking," Sadie said.

"Okay. Everyone pack their stuff real quick. Then the girls can cook the hotdogs while the guys take down the tents," James Ernest directed.

Mike was happy to let us use their fire. Within thirty minutes we were packed up and ready to go. Rock had cooked me three hotdogs to eat as I drove. After Mike heard what was going on he told us to be careful on the highway. "You can help more by being alive when you get there than dead on the highway. You have all night to get there," Mike said. He was right.

We thanked him for everything and we took off. Rock was holding my dogs and a drink as we left the Smoky Mountains.

We decided before leaving that we would switch drivers every hour. Rhonda and Purty would take our places while James Ernest and I tried to get some sleep. I wasn't sure how they thought I could sleep. I didn't want to sleep until Papaw was found and safe.

It took an hour to get to the Interstate. We pulled over and switched drivers. Purty and Shauna took over the cab while Rock and I climbed into the back with Tucky and Sadie.

Rhonda and Susie took over for James Ernest and Raven. We switched again at Jellico before entering Kentucky. Rock and I spent the time in the back talking with Sadie and Tucky. There was no sleep to be found.

We filled up with gas and took off again. Rock tried to comfort me. She told me everything was going to be okay. I loved her for trying, but I realized anything could happen. It was nearing midnight. The traffic was light. I passed James Ernest and increased my speed to seventy. The speed limit was fifty-five but I didn't care. James Ernest followed.

"You're going awfully fast," we heard Raven say into the radio.

Rock said, "He realizes that."

"James Ernest would like for you to slow down to sixty-five, please?" Raven said.

I did. I didn't want to make anyone uncomfortable. Maybe I was pushing it a bit much since I had only been driving three weeks.

Saturday, August 7

"How are you doing?" Raven asked an hour later.

"I'm fine. I'm wide awake and alert," I told them.

"So am I, let's keep driving," James Ernest said.

We rolled into Morgan County at two in the morning. I dropped Shauna off at her home and then drove to the Tuttle's house to drop Sadie & Purty off. I asked Rock and Tucky if they wanted to go home or come to the store and spend the night. They wanted to come to the store.

I pulled into the lot just as James Ernest was doing the same. I was surprised to find that Mom and Dad were still up and drinking coffee. They were surprised when we came through the front door.

I gave Mom a hug and asked, "Is there any news?"

"Not yet," Dad said. "They've been down every road in the county but haven't found anything. It makes it harder when we don't know what Treehawk is driving."

"What makes you think Treehawk took Papaw?" I asked.

Dad explained what had happened and what Roger had seen. "That's our only clue. And of course, Roger doesn't have any idea what Treehawk was driving. He did know it was a car."

"So what are we going to do?" James Ernest asked. Rock was standing next to me, holding my hand.

"Nothing until daylight. We figure Treehawk took him for ransom or something. I expect he'll reach us in the morning with his demands," Dad said.

Mom said, "Your mamaw is asleep in our bedroom. Why don't you four go to the farm and get some sleep? We'll call you if we hear anything. You'll want to be fresh for tomorrow."

I started to argue, but James Ernest said that he thought it was a good idea. We took off for Papaw's farm. Rock wanted to stay with me, which is what I wanted also. We took the spare bedroom and Tucky and James Ernest took the master bedroom.

I slipped off my clothes and climbed into bed. Rock did the same. The bed felt so good after the long drive and sleeping in a tent for five nights. Rock snuggled up to me and we kissed for a little while. Then I was asleep.

I thought I would have trouble sleeping, but I was wrong. I slept like a log. I heard noises in the kitchen that morning. I looked over and Rock was gone from the bed. I got up and put on my pants and shirt.

I walked into the kitchen to find Rock brewing coffee. James Ernest was sitting at the table talking to her. "Has anyone called yet?" I asked.

"No. I woke up and heard Rock in here."

Rock opened the fridge and took out eggs. She had bread in the toaster and began whipping eggs to scramble. I needed a bathroom, so I went out the kitchen door to the outhouse. On my way back to the house I went around to the side porch to see if there were any deer in the valley.

I saw a deer with her two fawns. I watched them for a moment and started to enter the side living room door. A note was stuck between the screen door and its jamb. I removed the note and read:

In exchange for Martin, I want Catahecassa. If this demand isn't met you'll never see Martin again. Catahecassa is to come alone at six this evening. He is to ride his horse down Brown Ridge Road until I stop him. If I see anyone else during the day Martin will die.

Chapter 24
The Ambush

I rushed through the door and into the kitchen. I handed the note to James Ernest. Tucky walked out of the bedroom. James Ernest read the note out loud to everyone. He turned and grabbed the phone off the wall and called the store.

Dad answered and James Ernest read the note to him.

He listened and hung up. Rock scooped eggs onto four plates and placed a dish of toast on the table.

"Let's eat while you tell us what he said," Rock said.

James Ernest said, "They want us back at the store."

I buttered a piece of toast and began eating.

I said between bites, "We can't let that happen. We can't let Cat get killed. And we have no idea if he would let Papaw go even if he did get Cat. What do we do?"

"Do you guys know where Brown Ridge Road is?" Tucky asked.

I didn't, but James Ernest said, "It's in Blair Mills. He must be hiding in the trees down there."

"We need a plan," I said.

James Ernest left the table and came back with a pencil and paper. He drew a map of that area. I noticed that Devil's Creek ran past the dead end of Brown Ridge Road.

"We can wade up Devil's Creek and come in the back way to surprise him before Cat gets there," I said.

"Can we get to the creek anywhere closer to there, instead of wading all that way," I asked.

James Ernest thought for a moment and then said, "We can drive to the end of Collins Ridge Road. We won't be far from the creek. Once we get to the creek it will be less than a mile to where we get out. Black Cave Hollow runs between the two roads."

I knew where Collins Ridge Road was. It turned right off State Route 711 just before we get to our church. We had canoed down Devil's Creek one summer, but I hadn't paid much attention to anything other than Susie at that time.

"We had better get to the store," I said.

"If we're going to do this, should we get Junior and Purty?" Tucky asked.

"Purty might be a burden," Rock said.

"He's good with a slingshot," I pointed out.

"We should ask him," James Ernest said.

We left for the store. When we got there we found most everyone else there. The men were on the porch. I handed the note to Dad. He read it and put it in his pocket.

"What's the plan?" I asked.

"I'm going to do what he wants," Cat said.

"No way!" I said loudly.

"This is between him and me. I'm not risking Martin's life over this," Cat said.

"If he kills you, what will keep him from killing Papaw?" I said. I saw Clayton and Homer nod in agreement.

"We came up with a plan," Tucky blurted out.

Dad quickly said, "You boys are not to go anywhere near there. I certainly don't want a massacre. You hear me."

"But we can go in the back way," I said before being cut off.

260

"What did I say? You guys are not going to get involved!" Dad yelled. "Do I have to put you guys in a jail cell?"

"Maybe you should hear their plan," Uncle Morton said.

"I'm not having anyone else risk their life," Sheriff Cane said.

I looked at James Ernest. I expected him to say something, but he remained quiet. He hadn't said a word. I knew our plan could work.

I left the porch and went inside to see Mom. Rock went with me. Mom hugged me and then Rock. I then went to Mamaw and hugged her with everything I had.

"He'll be okay," I whispered to her.

"There's food on the table if you guys are hungry," she said.

"Rock fixed us breakfast," I said.

I did grab a sausage patty and a biscuit and made a sandwich. Rock did the same. We got drinks from the cooler. We went in the living room and sat on the couch.

Rock asked me, "What are you going to do?"

"I'm going to rescue Papaw. I won't let him get hurt," I told her.

James Ernest and Tucky came inside.

"Where did you get the sandwich?" Tucky asked.

"Kitchen table, help yourself," I said. They were back in a minute. James Ernest went to get both of them a drink.

When he came back in he got us in a huddle and said, "Let's keep a low profile. Don't say anything else about our plan. We'll sneak away when we get a chance. I'll call Purty and see if he wants to help. If he does I'll have him pick Junior up and meet us."

"I can stay and help with the store," Rock said.

"That would be great," I told her.

I heard Henry Washington's voice on the porch. Raven walked in and joined us.

I walked out on the porch and listened to the men.

"We can't risk driving down the road due to his instructions," Dad told the men.

Henry said, "What happens if someone else drives down the road? People do live on that road."

"We thought about that. My office has called everyone that lives in the area and ordered them not to drive down the lane. He has to be near the end of the lane. He wouldn't be on someone's farm. We'll close off the road once Cat begins his ride down the road. We don't want Treehawk escaping."

I wanted to say that Treehawk wouldn't be that stupid. He probably had an escape plan, either through the woods or down to the creek.

Cat had the same thought, "He won't try to drive out if he kills me. He'll know you'll have blockades."

I couldn't believe Dad wouldn't listen to our plan. We could lead the deputies up the creek if he didn't want us involved.

Dad and Cat planned to meet at five. All of the men left by noon. Dad was going to the office, but before leaving he warned us, "I don't want you guys leaving this store until this is over."

2 p.m., Saturday afternoon

Papaw

The heat was bad. I was thirsty. Treehawk would bring me a drink every so often, but never enough. I didn't know exactly what his plan was. I did know he wanted to exchange me for Cat. But I didn't think that would happen. I tried talking to him, but today he was in no talking mood. He seemed to be all business.

This morning he went through an Indian ritual. I took from it that it was to give him strength against his enemies. He sharpened his knife and checked his bow and arrows. I hadn't seen a gun. I couldn't believe he didn't have a gun or a rifle.

He was now sitting on a log and applying war markings on his face. He put stripes on each cheek and a long line above his eyebrows. I was tied to a tree.

James Ernest

*P*urty wanted to help. I had called Junior and he was in. So I asked Purty to pick up Junior and meet us at the end of Collins Ridge Road at two-thirty. Mom and Mamaw were the only women in the house. The other women were coming to the store at five to form a prayer group.

Rock and Raven were still there. The plan was for Rock to get them into the kitchen so Timmy, Tucky and I could sneak out with our rifles and leave. I drove my truck. I hated disobeying a direct order, but Timmy would not stay and do nothing, and I felt the same.

Luckily, Mom and Mamaw went to the kitchen to prepare some food for when the women came. Rock went to make sure they stayed there until we were gone. We left out the front door and hurried into the truck. I started the truck and pulled out of the lot slowly.

I headed up the hill toward our destination. Within ten minutes we spotted Purty's truck at the end of the road. Timmy and I both had knives in our pockets in case we needed them. I had asked Purty to bring his slingshot and a rifle for Tucky.

I pulled off the road. There was a lane across the road that led to a barn. We got out and greeted Purty and Junior. I quickly told them our plan and the sheriff's plan.

"What did the sheriff think of your plan?" Purty asked.

"He doesn't know it. He told us not to leave the house and not to get involved," I said.

"So our plan is to do exactly the opposite?" Junior said.

"Exactly," James Ernest said.

"This is my Papaw. I have to do what I can to save him and Cat," Timmy said. They agreed with him.

It was hot and muggy as we headed for the creek. The water would feel good.

We saw a path going south toward the creek and decided to take it.

Rock

Raven and I were in the store waiting on any customers that came in. Raven or I would pump gas when it was needed. Betty and Corie were still in the kitchen.

I heard Betty call out, "If you all want any lunch you'll have to make yourselves sandwiches."

I said, "Okay." They hadn't yet discovered that the guys had left. I hated the thought of when they found out.

Betty called out again, "Timmy, come here."

Oh, no. Now was the time. I walked into the kitchen with Raven right behind me.

I said, "He's not here."

Betty and Corie both looked up at me with sudden concern on their faces.

"Tell me they didn't," Betty said.

"What are they doing?" Corie asked.

"They had a plan to rescue Martin," I said.

"Where are they?" Betty asked.

I didn't know for sure. I had heard them discussing the plan but I never knew the particulars of it. Raven then said, "You know how much Timmy and James Ernest love Martin. They couldn't wait here and do nothing."

"Hagar told them directly to stay here and not get involved. They could be putting Dad in more danger! How could you two let them do this?" Betty shouted.

Betty pushed past us and ran to the phone. She dialed the police station and asked to speak to Hagar.

"You girls did nothing wrong. Betty is just worried. She now has her father and sons in danger. It's a lot," Corie told us.

Betty

*H*ow much more could I take? I waited as Hagar was called to the phone. "Hello, Betty. What is it?" Hagar answered.

"The boys left the store. Rock told me the boys have a plan to rescue Dad. What are we going to do?"

"I told them not to leave the store." I could hear Hagar take a deep breath. "Do the girls know what their plan is?"

"No, they said they didn't."

"They could be covering for them. I'll be there as soon as I can. Did they take the trucks or walk?"

I quickly looked out the window and answered. "They took James Ernest's truck."

"See you in a bit. Don't worry. The boys can take care of themselves." He hung up.

I walked into the living room and collapsed on the couch and cried. Rock sat down beside me and placed her arms around my neck. I found myself crying into her shoulder. I wasn't strong. I knew I wasn't. Mom was the rock in the family. Despite Dad being kidnapped and held for exchange, Mom was there cooking and helping. She wasn't crying and sobbing. Why couldn't I be more like her?

I heard the front door open and then saw Rebecca coming toward me. She sat on the other side of me and placed her hand on my arm. Mom explained to her and Pastor White what was happening.

I looked up at our pastor and asked, "Please pray."

He did and it was what I needed. I would find my strength in Christ. I knew I didn't have it inside me. But I had Jesus inside me. He would get me through this time. God would give me the ability to face whatever came. Clarity washed over me. I realized the boys had faced many challenges over the years and had found success. They had an inane ability to do the right thing and I had to trust they were doing it again.

When Hagar walked through the door a few minutes later I told him, "We need to trust the boys. They always do the right thing."

Were we doing the right thing? I now doubted the wisdom of our plan. Looking at it on paper is one thing, but carrying it out was another. What if we did the wrong thing and Papaw or one of us got killed? Perhaps Dad was right in telling us to stay home and let them do their job. But I continued with the plan.

We made it to the creek. Stepping into the water refreshed me and gave me a new perspective. Of course we were doing the right thing. I couldn't let Treehawk kill Papaw or Cat. We waded up the creek. James Ernest had told us to keep quiet because we didn't know exactly how close to the creek Treehawk was camped.

The creek banks were made up of sharp sandstone and overhanging trees. I watched the water as Jesus bugs skated across the water out of our way. Bull frogs jumped from the banks into the cooling water. Turtles slid off logs and under the water's surface.

Birds tweeted and sang as we moved up the creek. Each step had to be carefully made so to not slip and fall into the water. Our rifles were held outward or above our heads so not to get wet. A deep gorge emptied into the creek to our left. James Ernest whispered that it was the Black Cave Hollow.

"Our exit won't be much further. Keep an eye out for a trail coming down to the creek," James Ernest whispered.

The landscape was changing from the stone creek banks to muddy leaf filled banks. Large trees filled the forest around us. Ten minutes later I spotted what I thought looked like a trail. We made our way over to it and decided it was what we were looking for. We exited the creek. We helped each other up the slippery bank.

James Ernest led us away from the path and we sat on a patch of moss. "We need to be sure this is the right spot. I need to find the campsite. If we aren't sure where they are we may waste too much time finding it later and get there too late."

James Ernest was right. With his ability to sneak quietly through the forest he was the one who had to go find the camp. We knew that. "I'll be back." He looked at his watch. "It's four-thirty. We have plenty of time, but I need to go."

James Ernest silently left us.

Catahecassa

I sat on the deck of my treehouse waiting for the moment to come. I had spent many minutes in prayer asking God to protect my friends and especially Martin. I even asked God to protect me if it was His will. I was okay with death and my afterlife in

Heaven. Of course I wanted to live. Of course I still wanted to marry and raise a family. And I would fight to keep those dreams alive.

My bow and arrows were ready. My knife was sharpened and its sheath was mounted to my waist. I was dressing in my Native pants and moccasins. My horse, Friend, was ready to go.

It was time to end this. Too many of my friends had been put in danger by the feud between me and Treehawk. One of us would not like the ending, and I did not plan on it being me.

Sheriff Cane

Five o'clock had come. It was time to head to Brown Ridge Road. I kissed Betty goodbye as more and more families arrived at the store. Loraine Tuttle arrived as I was leaving. She started to speak to me and I hurried past her saying, "I have to go, Loraine."

It didn't stop her from continuing to talk. I left in a hurry. I slowed when I saw Cat riding out on his horse. For a moment I thought I was watching a western of TV. Bonanza was coming to life before me. I stopped and waited for him to reach me. I wished him luck. I drove slowly as he trotted Friend behind the cruiser.

Clayton and Monie and the girls were standing at the end of their lane waving and wishing Cat their best. Homer and Ruby and their girls were doing the same. Janice and Robert held a sign that read: Our prayers are with you.

Uncle Morton stood on his porch and waved. I had tears as I saw the support and love the community had for Cat.

We got to the road and turned right. Brown Ridge Road was a loop that came back out on 711. But at the southernmost point of the loop the road also continued toward the creek. This was where my deputies waited for us.

James Ernest

*L*ess than a quarter mile into my search I came to the end of the road. I stayed off the road and went through the trees on the east side of the road. The west side was a large field of corn. I soundlessly made my way up the lane as I looked for the camp.

It wasn't long before I saw a shiny metal ahead of me. I knew it belonged to a vehicle. I made my way deeper into the trees and circled the area. A large hawk screeched from his view point as he watched me. I could be silent, but not invisible. I saw movement. A large man dressed in Indian clothing was pacing inside the camp. I wanted to get eyes on Papaw.

I slowly, quietly moved forward trying to keep my body behind tree trunks. There he was. Martin was tied to a tree. He was watching Treehawk pace.

I heard Martin say, "You don't have to do this. You could leave right now and live your life. Nothing good will come out of this."

"Shut up, old man," Treehawk calmly said.

I had my rifle with me. I could easily take a shot and end this. But if I missed what would happen? I debated for a few seconds whether to take a shot or not. The debate ended when Treehawk walked out of camp and up the road. I looked at my watch and saw that it was five-forty five.

I wanted to untie Martin but I also needed to go get the gang. I decided Martin was safe where he was until we get back. I began running through the woods.

I made it back to the others and motioned for them to follow me. As we hurried I told them, "I found the camp. Martin is okay. Treehawk left the camp to set up an ambush. We need to hurry. When we get to the camp Purty can untie Martin while we search for where Treehawk is."

When we got close to the camp I held up my hand signaling for them to stop. I searched the camp with my eyes to make sure Treehawk hadn't returned. We then ran into camp. Purty quickly began untying the rope around Martin.

I told him, "You need to go hide until this is over."

"I could help," Martin said.

"You're weak and tired. We have this."

Timmy ran over and gave his papaw a hug. We took off.

I led the way looking for signs of Treehawk.

Cat

I jumped onto the back of Friend and began my ride down the road. Hagar and the deputies wished me luck. I kept my eyes busy searching each side of the road. I knew he would find a hiding spot where he could steady himself to shoot. I had never seen him use a rifle so I expected an arrow. He was never a great bow user. He had missed me twice at the treehouse. But I knew he would want to kill me the Indian way.

The true Indian way would be to face me, but he was also a coward. I had my bow over my shoulder and my arrows at my waist. My knife was sheathed on my right side.

There were fields on both sides of me. A house sat on the left side of the road. I saw folks looking out their windows at the mounted Indian riding down the road. Further down, another house was on the right. A young boy stood beside the house and pointed toward me.

Hagar had told me the road was only a mile and a half long. I rounded a corner and saw what I thought was the end of the road.

On the right was a large corn field. On the left was a stand of trees. This was where it would happen. I knew he wouldn't attempt a long shot. I drew nearer and nearer to the trees.

Suddenly from the cornfield a totally nude black boy ran between me and the stand of trees.

I watched as Junior streaked out of the cornfield weaving and hopping across the road between Cat and Treehawk. He was yelling gibberish like a crazy person. Treehawk had been pulling the string of his bow back when we motioned for Junior to distract Treehawk. We didn't know Treehawk would get the full treatment. It worked as Treehawk lowered the bow.

Purty pulled back his slingshot and let it go. The marble smacked Treehawk on his back. He yelled out in agony. He reached for his back at the sudden pain he felt. I saw Cat look at the location of the scream and he rode straight toward it.

As Treehawk saw Cat coming he raised his bow again. As he did Purty pulled back for another shot. The marble slammed into the back of Treehawk's head just before the arrow shot off in the wrong direction. Treehawk dropped his bow and grabbed his head with both hands. He looked up to see Cat flying through the air toward him.

Cat had thrown his bow away as he rode. He now crashed into Treehawk, and the two Indians began to wrestle on the ground. I was frozen at my vantage point. I wasn't sure what to do. Should I rush forward to help Cat? I had my rifle aimed at Treehawk. None of us wanted to kill a person if we didn't have to. The rifles were more for protection.

Treehawk managed to throw Cat off of him. He stood up as Cat rose from the ground. They circled while staring at each other. Treehawk reached to his side and pulled out his long knife.

Cat did the same. They came closer together and Treehawk moved forward and swiped the knife at Cat's stomach. I saw blood drip from the wound.

The two men threw themselves at one another and grabbed each other's armed hand. Treehawk had size on Cat. He seemed to be stronger. Cat was forced backward against a tree. Treehawk's knife was getting closer and closer to Cat's neck. I saw Cat's knifed hand come free.

He drew his hand back and then forward just as another marble hit Treehawk in his ear. The knife went up into Treehawk's gut. Treehawk dropped his knife and slowly drifted toward the ground, blood pouring from his body.

James Ernest fired two shots into the air. We all ran to where Cat was bent over on the ground. His cut was worse than I had thought. Tucky took off his shirt and placed it on the bleeding wound. Cat lay back on the ground. Papaw came running up when he heard the gunshots. We heard sirens coming down the road.

I was standing next to James Ernest. Tucky was bent over Cat applying pressure to the cut. Purty stood there with his slingshot. Junior stood there naked as a jaybird next to Papaw.

And that's the way Dad and the two deputies found us when they ran up. We stood there and watched as Treehawk took his last breath. No one shed a tear.

Chapter 25
Jackrabbit

$\mathcal{T}$he sheriff radioed the station and asked for help. Deputy Stutts took Cat straight to the hospital for his knife wound. An ambulance came to get the body of Treehawk. Deputy Clouse took James Ernest to get his pickup. While we waited, Junior put his clothes on, Tucky and I gathered up the bows and arrows and knives.

Purty went to get Friend, who was grazing in a nearby field. I wasn't sure how we were going to get the horse back to Cat's place. Tucky said he would ride him back, and if that didn't work. He would walk him back. None of us had ever ridden bareback.

"It can't be that hard if I go slowly," Tucky said.

While we waited, I told Dad what we had done. I told him how Purty was a hero. Dad gave me a confused look. We explained how we had sent Junior as a distraction. Junior had come up with his own idea to be naked. It definitely was a diversion.

Dad didn't say anything. I knew he was upset that we had disobeyed him. I never said I was sorry, because it would have been a lie. I would never be sorry for helping Papaw and Cat.

The ambulance finally showed up and took the body.

James Ernest came back with his pickup. Deputy Clouse was sent to gather up Treehawk's supplies at the camp. They were going to come back later for the car.

We helped Tucky up on Friend. He took off slowly. We all followed behind to make sure nothing happened. Soon he picked up speed and seemed to be getting the hang of it. Dad had suggested that we place the horse in Homer's cow field until Cat returns. It was a lot closer. Tucky made it there without falling off. We turned Friend lose and Tucky jumped into the back of the pickup.

We all then headed for the store. The porch was crowded with neighbors and friends who had waited to hear word of how things went. The ambulance drove past the store and Dad and James Ernest pulled into the lot. I could see people holding their breath until I heard Henry say, "I see Martin in the front seat."

Loud hollering and applause filled the porch. Mamaw and Mom came running down the steps to the cruiser. Mamaw threw her arms around Papaw and kissed his face over and over.

We climbed out of the pickup to applause until Clayton asked, "Where is Cat?"

"He's fine. He got cut and had to be taken to the hospital for some stitches. He'll be fine," Dad told everyone.

"What about Treehawk?"

"He wasn't as fortunate. He's dead," Dad announced. The crowd drew quiet once they realized the danger of the quest.

I was hot and thirsty. As though she read my thoughts, Rock brought me an RC Cola. Other girls brought drinks for the other guys. After taking a big drink, Rock gave me a big kiss in front of everyone. Loraine stood on the porch talking a mile a minute. No one was listening to her.

After everyone settled, we began telling about the battle. I made sure they all knew what a hero Purty was. I told how each marble slammed into Treehawk's body. Everyone burst into laughter as I told about Junior running naked between Treehawk and Cat.

"Weren't you scared of getting shot?" Robert asked him.

I answered, "He's faster than a jackrabbit. There's no way anyone could hit him, especially with an arrow."

"That sounded like one of Purty's stunts," Susie said.

Junior said, "He taught me that." We laughed.

Morton cried out, "I'd like to know what went through Treehawk's mind when he saw a naked black boy running in front of him."

"He probably thought he was going out of his mind," Monie said.

"So Sheriff, how much trouble are the boys in?" Clayton asked.

That was the big question. I wondered that myself.

"I knew the boys would get involved somehow. I tried and failed to stop them. That question will have to be answered by each of their parents. As far as Tim, he's not in trouble. The boys had a good plan."

Everyone applauded again.

It was almost dark by the time folks went home. I drove Rock and Tucky home. Tucky hopped out, but Rock stayed behind for a few minutes.

"I was so scared while you were gone," she said as she squeezed my hand.

"The scariest part was watching the knife fight between Cat and Treehawk," I said. "I had never seen anything like that."

She leaned toward me. I met her in the middle as our lips touched. "I love you," she said, as she slid across the seat to get out.

"I love you. See you tomorrow?"

"Sure."

When I got back to the store James Ernest was in the shower. I was too tired to think about a shower. I could barely climb into the top bunk. I said my prayer. The door opened and James Ernest came in.

"Another successful mission," he said.

"Hopefully, it was our last mission. Some day we may not be so lucky," I said.

"I almost pulled my trigger today during the fight," James Ernest said.

"So did I. I had Treehawk within my rifle's sights. But I couldn't do it," I said.

"Me neither. I don't think Cat would have wanted it to end that way," he said.

"I was afraid of shooting Cat. I'm glad Purty got Treehawk with the slingshot. We'll have to ask Cat that question," I said.

"I was surprised they kept him over night at the hospital," James Ernest said.

"The cut must have been deeper than we thought," I reasoned.

"I'm going to sleep. We have church tomorrow."

I closed my eyes and drifted off to the chirping of the crickets outside my window.

Sunday, August 8

*D*ad stayed home to watch the store because Papaw was tired and Mom wanted Papaw to rest after his ordeal. I told Dad I would stay home if he wanted to go to church with Mom. But he told me to go. I had slept late and by the cars and trucks in the parking lot I knew we had a lot of fishermen that morning.

I took a quick shower, got dressed and left to pick up Rock and Tucky. Rock came out in her pretty flowered dress. She said Tucky wasn't feeling up to going. We headed to church. When I pulled into the church lot I saw Mamaw and Papaw standing in front of the church talking to folks.

We walked up and I said, "I thought you were resting this morning."

He rubbed the top of my head and said, "I thought I should come and thank the Lord for looking after me."

"I do that all the time," I said.

"I bet you do," Papaw said as he smiled.

Rock and I walked in and took our seats. I was so happy that Papaw was safe and sound inside the church with me. I couldn't think of anything I wanted more.

That evening Mom closed the store and our family went to thefarm to visit with Mamaw and Papaw. We sat out on the side porch. A nice breeze blew through the eight large oak trees. Mamaw had baked a coconut pie. I was eating a large slice.

Papaw began telling us about his conversation with Treehawk. In all the excitement the evening before, he wasn't able to tell the story. He told us that Treehawk admitted to killing the man in the lake, but he hadn't said why.

Papaw then told us about the letter with a key that the two men had been searching the caves for. He looked at me and James Ernest and said, "So guys, I guess the Wolf Pack has a new quest. Find the letter and key and then find the buried treasure."

"Why would he tell you all of this?" Mom asked Papaw.

"He didn't have anything to lose. I think his plan was to kill Cat and then maybe me. He told me he was never interested in the treasure. He said his only mission was revenge."

"Revenge has been the downfall of many men," Dad said.

"What will become of his body?" Mamaw asked.

"I'll try and contact his tribe to see if they want his remains shipped to them," Dad said.

"I want to go see Cat tomorrow at the hospital," I said.

"You might be able to go see him and bring him home," Dad said.

Papaw switched subjects and said, "James Ernest, you're leaving for college soon, aren't you?"

"I have two weeks before I leave. Freshmen are supposed to be there by the twenty-third."

"We're sure going to miss you," Mamaw said.

"Thank you, but I'll be back all the time. I'll come home on some weekends, and holidays, and during the summer."

"Whoa, I thought I was getting rid of you," I teased.

"The bottom bunk is still mine," James Ernest said.

Monday, August 9

Mamaw and Papaw came to watch the store early. Mom was going shopping with Miss Rebecca on their Monday excursion. James Ernest was making baskets today. I was going to Morehead to see Cat. I was hoping Rock would go with me.

I left around ten and drove to the Key house. Adore, Chero and Sugar Cook were sitting on the porch when I pulled up. They ran out to my truck window.

"Where are you two off to today?" Adore asked.

Before I could answer Sugar Cook said, "Aren't you tired of Rock yet? C'mon, let me be your girlfriend."

"I think you would be trouble," I said.

The three of them laughed. "You're right, we would be. But you would love it," Adore said.

Sugar Cook ran around to the passenger door and opened it. She jumped and scooted close to me. She ran her left hand through my hair while rubbing my inner thigh with her right hand.

"I think you'd better get out before Rock sees you," I said as I moved her hand off my leg.

Rock came running through the front door. She opened the door and grabbed Sugar Cook by her hair and dragged her from the truck.

"Ow! You don't have to be so mean, Rock!" Sugar Cook yelled.

"You don't have to handle my boyfriend. You have that creep, Hiram," Rock said.

"Sisters are supposed to share," Sugar Cook said.

I turned to Rock and asked, "Can you go to Morehead with me?"

"Let's go."

"What is Tucky doing?"

"He took Luck fishing in the creek."

I stepped on the gas and we were off. On the way to Morehead I told Rock everything Papaw had told us the day before.

"That solves all the mysteries," Rock said.

"I guess it does."

"Do you think you could find the letter and key?"

"I doubt it. I might look someday," I said. I thought finding the letter would be like finding a needle in a hay field. I wasn't going to make a full out effort to find it. I remembered the last treasure we dug up in the cabin. It turned out to be nothing more than a few old coins. For all I knew it could be the same treasure. We had found the chest in a cave with the letter inside which led us to the cabin. I told Rock what I was thinking.

"That was the same year we moved here," Rock said.

"It was. Tucky actually was with us when we found the chest."

"I remember that now," she said.

We entered Morehead, and I turned toward the hospital.

We parked in the visitors' lot and went inside. I asked where Cat's room was located. The nurse told us and then said, "Visitor hours don't start until one this afternoon."

"Is there some way we could call him?" I asked.

"Sorry," she said.

I wasn't going to let that keep me from seeing Cat. We turned to leave. The phone rang and she looked down at her notes while on the phone. I grabbed Rock's arm and spun her around and we snuck past the receptionist.

She had told us he was in room 302. We took the stairs to the third floor. A doctor walked past us. He was studying his notes. We found the area that had room 302. There was a nurse's station between us and the rooms. We waited for an opportunity to sneak by. A lady arrived with a cake and all the nurses turned to get a slice. We hurried by without being seen.

As we neared Cat's room an overweight nurse came out of Cat's room. She looked at us and said, "Visitors aren't allowed up here until one."

Rock said, "We brought in a cake. The other nurses are cutting into it."

"Oh, no," she said. She wheezed past us to get her slice.

"Good thinking," I said.

We whipped into Cat's room and closed the door. Cat was sitting up in his bed reading a magazine. He looked up and smiled. "Did you come to rescue me?"

"Maybe," I said. "How are you doing?"

"I'm fine. How is Treehawk?"

I was surprised. I thought he knew he had killed Treehawk. They had whisked Cat up and taken him straight to the hospital. I guess he never heard that Treehawk had died.

"He died at the scene," I said.

"It easily could have been me. It's hard to believe that we once were good friends. Is Martin okay?"

"Papaw is fine. He and Mamaw are watching the store this morning. We were going to take you home if you can leave."

"The doctor was just here and said I could leave as soon as the paperwork is done. How did you guys get in here?"

Rock answered, "We snuck in like an Indian."

Cat laughed and then grabbed his stomach, "Don't make me laugh."

We sat there and talked about the rescue and the fight for the next hour. He asked about Junior running around naked.

"That was a diversion for your sake and ours." We all laughed again.

"You guys are really something. What happened to Friend?"

"Tucky rode him to Homer's farm and we released him in the field with his cows," I explained.

"He's probably enjoying the company," Cat said.

The large nurse finally arrived and had a confused look on her face when she saw us, "How did you two get in here?"

"We came to take him home," I was hoping that would do.

"Oh, okay. All you have to do is sign your release papers and you are good to go. Here are your directions and a prescription for pain medicine."

He signed the papers and said, "Thank you, Joyce. You've been very nice."

She then brought in a wheelchair for him to ride to the exit. Cat changed from the hospital gown to his Indian wear. We got a lot of looks as we left the hospital. The women seemed to enjoy the show.

"Let's go to the Dairy Queen for lunch," I suggested.

"Only if we get it to go. I've been stared at enough for one day," Cat said. We went through the drive thru and headed back to Morgan County.

While we drove he asked about our trip to the Smoky Mountains. We told him pretty much everything that had happened.

We stopped at the store before taking him home. He wanted to see Papaw.

"I am so sorry you had to go through what you did," Cat said.

"I came out of it a lot better than you did. Nothing was your fault," Papaw told him.

We drove Cat home a few minutes later. I asked if we could help him with anything. He said he was fine. I told him I would check on him later. "Hey, what about the prescription?"

"I don't need it," Cat said.

Rock and I spent the rest of the day watching the store so Mamaw and Papaw could go home.

Chapter 26

Gone to College

Sunday, August 22

*I*t was past midnight. The bullfrogs were loud through my window tonight. James Ernest said, "I'm going to miss that sound."

He was silent for a moment and then continued, "I'm going to miss the community. I'm going to miss the church. I'm really going to miss Raven. Most of all, I'm going to miss you, Timmy."

I had been dreading this day all summer. I had no idea how I would get by with him gone to college.

"I'm happy for you, but I'm sad you're going," I said.

"I feel the same way. I love it here so much that I hate to go. But I know I have to go to be able to do what I want with my life," he explained.

"You're already the smartest person I know. You don't need college," I said.

"Your recommendation won't get me a job teaching," he said.

"Are you sure? I could talk to Mr. Davis." James Ernest laughed at me.

"We'll have the rest of our lives to live here in Morgan County. College will be over before we know it," he said.

"I don't believe you," I told him.

James Ernest had known he wanted to be a teacher almost as long as I knew him, or at least as long as he had been talking again. I knew he would be a great teacher.

We finally fell asleep. I dreamed that everything in my life fell apart once he left. I flunked out of high school. Rock broke up with me because I was a dummy. The Wolf Pack kicked me out of the club and made Coty the leader of the Pack. Mom swapped me for Purty. I was made to eat potato waffles and listen to Loraine all day – everyday.

I woke up whispering, "Please don't go. Please don't leave me." I soon realized it was a dream and went back to sleep an hour later.

James Ernest shook me awake and said, "You need to get up for church. We've woke you up three times already. Get up numbskull."

I managed to slip out of bed and get dressed. I went to the bathroom and brushed my teeth and ran a comb through my mop of hair. I grabbed an RC Cola and a banana flip and headed out the door. I drove to the Key house to pick up Rock and Tucky.

Before the preacher came forward to preach James Ernest sang two hymns. Pastor White preached a sermon on going for your dreams and making sure those dreams line up with what God would smile down on. I was sure the entire service was for James Ernest's benefit. At the end of the service Pastor White had James Ernest come forward and he prayed for him

He then announced that there would be an open house at the store all afternoon for folks to come by and see James Ernest off. Why didn't I know anything about it?

When I got back to the store I found the kitchen table full of food and desserts. How did that happen?

The Washington family arrived first. Raven gave James Ernest a gift. All afternoon the store was full of folks wishing him their best and giving him envelopes with money for school. I felt awful. I hadn't gotten my brother a gift. I had been feeling sorry for myself and forgotten about James Ernest.

Cat showed up and brought a leather book bag that he had made from deerskin. It was really neat. I could see how much James Ernest loved it.

Folks were playing music and singing on the porch. Kids were running around the store playing tag and other games. People were there that I didn't even know. Hiram and Sugar Cook showed up with Adore and Chero, and another of the Boys from Blaze. I wasn't sure why they were there.

James Ernest

Thankful and loved was the way I felt. I couldn't believe the outpouring of love at the church and at the store. As I opened card after card that people handed me I found $5 or $10 or $20 tucked inside. Uncle Morton gave me $50.

I believed every person I had ever known since moving to Morgan County stopped by to wish me luck and say they'd miss me. Even Hiram told me he would miss me.

I felt awful leaving Timmy. All week he walked around in a saddened state. I'd ask him what was wrong and he would smile and say, 'Nothing.' I also knew he wasn't mad that I was leaving, but that he would miss me. But I thought I would miss him even more. Timmy saved my life with his friendship. I learned from his goodness and his wide-eyed optimism. He was so willing to help people. I could make a list of people he had helped that would be longer than a grocery list.

Just last week he couldn't stand the thought of doing nothing when Cat and his papaw were in danger. Maybe we were better as a team.

I also hated leaving the Washington family. Raven was my life love. How I wished she was going with me.

Around five o'clock I knew I needed to leave. My truck was already packed. I wanted to get to the college before dark so I could find my way to my room. I announced that I needed to go. The folks that were still there gathered on the porch. Mom and Dad hugged me. Martin and Corie did the same. I hugged the Washington family and Raven gave me a big kiss as everyone oohed and aahed.

Timmy stood by the truck. I wrapped my arms around him. I didn't want to let go. Finally Timmy said, "Let go, weirdo." Everyone laughed. I got in the truck and pulled out of the lot. As I drove away I placed my arm out the window and waved. I looked in the mirror and saw tears dropping down the faces of Raven and Timmy. Then I noticed the tears on my face.

*P*eople began leaving as soon as James Ernest did. Rock stayed and we took a walk up to the lake. It was empty of fishermen. We walked around the lake and settled on the slanted rock. I laid back on the rock and she did same. We stayed like that without talking for a while.

I was watching the white clouds float by. School would be starting again in two weeks. I wasn't very excited about it.

"Let's go for a swim," Rock whispered in my ear. How could I say no to that? We got up and headed for the swimming hole. When we got there we began stripping off our clothes. I took her hand and we ran and jumped in together.

During the next hour I never thought of James Ernest, school, Treehawk or any other thing that had brought me sadness. I joyed in the arms of Rock.

Chapter 27
I'm the Leader Now

Sunday, August 29

*T*ucky and I decided we needed to have a Wolf Pack meeting. We decided to have it at the swimming hole. We met at the store at six and left for the meeting. There were only the four of us now that James Ernest had left for college, five if we counted Coty.

When we got to the hole, we swam for a while to cool off. We then opened the meeting. The whole thing didn't feel the same without James Ernest. We did a half-hearted Wolf Pack chant. Coty joined us half-heartedly. Even he knew it wasn't the same.

"First thing we need to do is elect a new Leader of the Pack," Purty said.

"I think the first thing we should do is decide if we even want to continue the Wolf Pack," I said. The others looked at me like I had swallowed a bullfrog.

"I do," Junior said.

"I do," Tucky said.

"Me too," Purty agreed. "Don't you?" That was the question I had been debating with myself. I loved the Wolf Pack. All the adventures and fun things we had done were truly amazing, but I couldn't imagine the club without James Ernest. Apparently the others didn't feel the same.

"Yes," I found myself saying.

"Then it's settled. I nominate Timmy as our new Leader of the Pack," Tucky said.

"I second the motion," Junior said.

"I third the motion," Purty said.

Coty barked. I wasn't sure what it meant.

I wasn't even sure the club should continue and now they were voting for me to lead it.

My next thought was, "Should we consider asking some other guys to join the club since we only have four now."

"James Ernest will still be a member in the summer, and that's when we do most of our club things," Junior reminded us.

"Who would we ask?" Tucky said.

"Purty, there's your brother Billy. How old is he now?" I asked.

"He'll be twelve soon," Purty said.

"I was turning eleven when we started the club. Who else?" I asked.

"Daniel Sugarman," Purty said.

"No," we all said at the same time. There was nothing really wrong with Daniel except he was kind of a mother's boy and his mother wouldn't let him do half the stuff we did, and we knew it.

"There's Bobby Lee," Junior suggested.

"He's only nine," I said.

"I think that's all we have to choose from," Purty said.

"Would Billy want to join?" I asked. I really didn't know Billy very well. He kept to himself most of the time.

"I can ask him, but I doubt it. He hates the outdoors," Purty said.

"That could be a hindrance," Tucky stated the obvious.

"I guess we stay like we are then," I said.

"I'm happy with that," Junior said.

"So, what's our next adventure?" Purty asked.

"Go to school," I said.

"Booooo," they all chided me.

"I do know of one thing we could do," I said softly, like I didn't want anyone else to hear. They all leaned forward.

"I have a clue to where a clue is that could tell us where a buried treasure is," I announced.

"What?" Junior asked.

"Say that again," Tucky said.

"Guys, he said buried treasure!" Purty yelled out.

"I have a clue to where a clue is that could tell us where a buried treasure is," I said again.

I told them the whole story of Sid and George and Treehawk. I told how they were told a clue is inside a cave somewhere in the area. "That clue comes with a key that unlocks the buried treasure that is shown on the map, I think," I explained.

"Where would be search?" Purty asked.

"In the caves around here, stupid face," I said.

"And they said the clue should be in a cave around here?" Tucky asked.

"That's why they kidnapped me and made me show them the hole cave," I explained.

"But they didn't find the clue in there," Purty said.

"They may have missed it," I said.

"Are there other caves around here?" Junior asked.

"We know of a few. The cave above Devil's creek," I started.

"I don't want to go in that one again. We almost died in there," Purty said.

"But that cave isn't around here," Junior chimed in.

"We don't know exactly where they meant when they said the clue was around here. Around here could mean the lake, or the area, or the county," I said.

"Or the state, or America, or the world," Junior said.

"Yeah," I said, a little defeated.

"What other caves?" Junior asked.

I answered, "There is also the cave where we found Bigfoot. Also the cave James Ernest was caged by Bigfoot. There's the cave between the waterfall on Susie's property where we found the chest and skeletons. And this weekend I heard of Black Cave Hollow in Blair Mills. There must be a cave in that holler."

"So what do we do, search them all?" Purty asked.

"It would give us something to do this fall and winter. It might be fun. We could ask the Bear Troop to go on some of the searches," I said.

"I like the idea. I like going in caves," Tucky said.

"I like the idea of getting Shauna in a dark cave," Purty said.

"Hey, good idea. It would be fun taking Sadie into a dark cave," Tucky said.

Purty said, "That's my sister."

"Yeah, and Shauna is Sally's sister. What's your point?"

"None. I was just reminding you," Purty said. We laughed.

"Do we have a plan?" I asked.

Everyone nodded. So I said, "All in favor raise your hand." Four hands went up."

We closed the meeting with a more heartfelt Wolf Pack chant than we had opened the meeting with.

As we were walking back around the lake I said, "I think the meeting was a success."

"Purty didn't fart once," Junior said.

Purty raised his leg and farted. Tucky pushed him into the lake.

That night James Ernest called from college. We talked for five minutes. He told me his classes had started. He said he was waiting tables at the Daniel Boone Inn in Berea. He said he already loved the school.

I told him about being elected the leader of the Pack and that we were going to look for the treasure.

It was so good to hear his deep voice again.

I finished the evening by watching *The Twilight Zone, Candid Camera,* and *What's My Line.*

I went to bed. Said goodnight to the empty bed below me and slept soundly.

Chapter 28
School

Tuesday, September 7, 1965

It was the stupid first day of school!

The End

Made in the USA
Middletown, DE
24 July 2023

35664606R00166